The Night Sender

The Night Sender

Christina Tsirkas

CT CREATIVE PRESS

The Night Sender
Christina Tsirkas

CT CREATIVE PRESS

This book is a work of fiction. Any similarities to real people, places, or events are entirely coincidental.

First Edition, December 2020
Copyright © 2020 by Christina Tsirkas

EBook: ISBN 978-1-7360109-0-7
Paperback: ISBN 978-1-7360109-7-6
Hardcover: ISBN 978-1-7360109-6-9

For my late grandmother, Ivy deLutio,
a fellow writer & kindred spirit.

If you have chosen to be the deliverer of pain in one lifetime, in your next, you shall be forced to be a deliverer of pleasure. And another's pleasure will deliver pain unto you. For that is the cycle of life, the way of ensuring balance and harmony. Create pain for others, and eventually, you will suffer that pain yourself.

1

"Honestly, Rose, isn't that shade of red a bit garish for an elegant affair?"

Rose's mother turned her disgruntled nose up at the vision of her stunning, yet somewhat suggestively clad daughter.

Rose stood on an elevated wooden platform before the giant wrought iron-rimmed mirror in her room. She wore a beautiful blood red corseted dress that clung tightly to her hourglass frame. The edges of the corset were lined with delicate black lace that flowed down the length of her skirts, creating a sheer black shroud over the bottom half of the garment, which curved outward and fell below her ankles.

"Don't be such a drag, mother. It's my eighteenth birthday celebration. I believe I deserve to look a little more sophisticated, especially considering it's my big night."

"Sophisticated, is that what you call it? With that scarlet red and black lace detailing, you look more a harlot than a lady of the court."

Rose rolled her eyes.

"And I suggest you rein in your enthusiasm about tonight. It's a right of passage that you must go through as a lady of the court, but by no means is it a celebratory affair."

"So you've said about one hundred times now, mother."

Her mother looked at Rose through stern, frustrated eyes.

"It's for your own good. I don't understand you, young lady. A proper young woman would be nervous."

There was that emphasis on proper again. Without thinking, Rose rolled her eyes once again, sending a wave of fury through her mother.

"Foolish girl, we'll see how you are after you've had the pain."

Her mother's tone was sharp, and Rose sensed a tinge of pain in it. But before she could say anything, her mother stalked out of the room, slamming the door behind her, which Rose couldn't help but think was not something a proper lady would do. Her lips curled into a smirk. Maybe her mother did have more fire in her than Rose gave her credit for, she surmised.

Still, sometimes Rose couldn't understand how she was the daughter of Anne Elizabeth Woodburn. Rose's passion and appetite for life were voracious, whereas her mother's hunger seemed meager at best. Over the years, there were plenty of occasions where her behavior convinced Rose that the woman was afflicted with passion intolerance.

Anne was a tall, yet slight woman with a timid nature. She had long, red hair muted with patches of gray that was always pulled back in a tight bun, and pale blue eyes that had lost their sparkle. Anne cared about being a proper lady and somewhat despised passion for the same reason Rose loved it; for its unpredictable nature. Its fervor possessed the power to move people and often gave them the courage to take risks. It beckoned them to venture into uncharted territory, sometimes experiencing things that weren't necessarily considered "proper." Rose often wondered how two people who share the same lifeblood could be such opposites.

She returned her attention to the mirror and began applying a bold red lipstick, almost the identical shade of her dress. Her soft brown waves hung loosely below her shoulders, stopping right at the top of her ample bosom. She smiled to herself. She was ready. She just had to make it through her birthday gathering first, which she was dreading.

It wasn't actually Rose's birthday yet. Her birthday wasn't officially until midnight. According to Dover tradition, all of the ladies of the court celebrated the arrival of their eighteenth year a day early, for, at the stroke of midnight, they went through a right of passage only the women of Dover faced.

At midnight, she would receive a visit from one of the formidable night senders. Only the ladies of the court knew about these creatures, half-man, half-demon, with enormous black wings that allowed them to fly unseen through the night like bats. The physical descriptions were strictly rumors, as court law prohibited the girls from seeing their night sender. They were forced to wear blindfolds from the moment they went to bed. Most of the girls thought of the blindfolds as a mercy, but to Rose, they were a nuisance. She was sure that at some point within the last few decades, at least one woman had to have stolen a glance at them. At midnight, these creatures would swoop in through their bedroom windows and, according to the court, turn them into women.

Their mothers first told them about the night senders when they were sixteen years old. All of the other girls spent the past two years living in fear of their impending nighttime visitor, but not Rose. Rose had been intrigued by the idea and curious about what the experience entailed. None of the mothers would reveal details of what occurred during the visit, only that it was painful and that they would not enjoy it.

Eleven other girls in the court were the same age as Rose, none of whom she counted as friends. And unfortunately, they were the only guests allowed at her birthday celebration since it was their transition year.

Three of the girls already had their visits and were married off to noblemen hand-selected by their parents shortly after. Rose was sure that Savannah, Genevieve, and Vivianna, would regale everyone with their experiences at the party. Better yet, they would likely try to frighten Rose before her big night.

There was a soft knock on the door before her mother popped her head into the room.

"Rose, your guests are here."

Rose took a deep breath and then followed her mother to the formal lounge, which she had adorned with beautiful red, white, and yellow roses for her daughter's birthday.

All of the other court ladies were already seated on two couches that surrounded a long, opulently decorated oval table. In the center of the table were the imported chocolates that Rose loved to devour, colorful pastries, and teacups full of piping hot peach tea. Rose greeted everyone politely and then begrudgingly took a seat on a cobalt armchair across from the two sofas.

Rose's mother was the first to speak. "Ladies, thank you so much for coming to celebrate Rose's most special birthday. I know that this year is a difficult turning point for you all, and that is why it's so imperative you have each other for support."

Rose scoffed. Like these girls knew anything about how to support other women, she mused. All they did was gossip, pick, and judge.

Rose's mother shot her a sharp glare and then continued.

"You're all going through the same difficult experience together, and so I hope it helps strengthen your friendships with one other. There exists no stronger bond than the one you form with your female counterparts. With that, I will leave you all to the celebration."

All eleven ladies of the court clapped lightly, smiling politely in unison at Rose's mother. Rose rolled her eyes. For someone touting the importance of female companionship, Rose could not recall Anne having any close relationships with the court ladies of her generation. She looked up and was met with dagger eyes from her mother. Still, she knew Anne was too focused on being a gracious host to publicly reprimand her.

As soon as Rose's mother left the room, Savannah stood, her frilly violet skirt spreading an additional foot on either side of her, swallowing her thin frame. Atop her russet curls was a gold, emerald encrusted tiara, a gift from her mother at her coming of age party. Every time she wore that regal piece, she held her nose even higher in the air.

"Rose, you must be absolutely terrified of what's to come later tonight."

Savannah's shrill voice always managed to irk Rose. It had a distinct sharpness to it that grated on her ears and her nerves.

"Not really, Savannah," Rose answered coolly.

The gaggle of girls let out a surprised murmur. Rose could only assume it was in regard to her "audacity" to disagree with their leader.

"Well, you should be." It was more a shriek than a statement.

With that theatrical tone, Savannah launched straight into her story, precisely as Rose had predicted. She watched as all eyes fixated on Savannah. Vivianna was the only one to glance elsewhere from time to time, her cat-like eyes moving from person to person, observing.

Rose hadn't realized how stunning Vivianna had become. Her green eyes were striking, the most notable feature of her petite face. She wore a simple olive chiffon gown, a shade lighter than her irises, which complimented her rich, brown skin. Vivianna smiled slyly and turned her gaze towards Rose, who quickly averted her stare.

A screeching vociferation brought Rose's attention back to Savannah's monologue.

"That night, after you all left my party, was the worst night of my entire life. After my mother affixed the mask behind my ears, she left me in my room to wait alone, in angst. I sat on the bed in my white nightgown clutching the locket she gave me. I held it so tightly that my hand started turning white. I was blindfolded the entire time. I mean, I couldn't see a thing. I was already petrified, but then when I heard the creaking of the window opening, my whole body started shivering. I tell you I didn't dare take my blindfold off. When the creaking stopped, there was complete silence in the room. I listened carefully, but couldn't hear a sound. Beads of sweat dripped down the side of my head and into my ear. Then all of a sudden, there was this great weight on top of me, pinning me to the bed."

Savannah balled her fists, shuddering, a look of despair across her face. The court girls gawked at her, some trembling as if this were the first time they were hearing the story.

"It felt like a whole elephant was sitting on top of my rib cage, crushing me. Then came the pain. Sharp fangs sank into my neck, ripping through my flesh. My body thrust as hard as possible, but I couldn't move an inch with the creature pinning me so tightly. That wasn't even the worst of it. Suddenly, an awful, searing pain crept from where this monster bit me all the way down my body. I was writhing in agony." Savannah paused, her eyes closed.

Rose turned her face into her shoulder, exasperated. Her ears were in agony from listening to Savannah for such an extended period. She wished she would finish this unbearable rendition of her story.

"It was like nothing I've ever felt before. It was so terrible I can still feel it." Savannah put her hand on her neck like she was trying to stop a wound from bleeding, only there was no blood, and from what Rose could see, no scars on her snowy skin. "I lay there stiff and not moving, praying so hard that it would just get off me. Finally, I felt its weight lift, but I couldn't will my body to move. I was positively terror-stricken that it might still be in the room. The blindfold was sopping wet from my tears. Still, I waited for hours before taking it off. And as soon as I got up in the morning, I headed straight into the bathtub to get that horrible, filthy feeling off me. The maid scrubbed me down until my skin was raw. I'm telling you, ladies, I'm so sorry you have to go through this." She placed her free hand over her eyes dramatically.

"How do you know your hand turned white?" Rose asked the question with calculated innocence. It was now her turn to give Savannah a headache.

"Excuse me?" Savannah's hand fell from her eyes to her bony hip, her dark eyes scowling at Rose.

"You said you were blindfolded the entire time and couldn't see anything. So then how do you know what color your skin turned while you were holding onto your locket for dear life?"

"I know how it feels when the blood flow is cut off from my hand." Her tone was reproachful.

"So you felt your hand turn white, but didn't actually witness it change color?" Rose teetered between maintaining her composure and allowing the devilish grin that accompanied any exercise in torturing Savannah.

"I suppose you could say that," she stuttered through gritted teeth. "For those of us who took our education seriously, it's quite clear that when blood flow is obstructed, the skin in that area appears paler. Not that I would expect a simpleton like you to understand the concept." Savannah's air of superiority had returned, her pitch rising an octave in the process.

Rose grinned. She wasn't through with her yet.

"How bad were your bite marks?" Rose asked matter-of-factly.

Savannah glowered at Rose, flushing angrily.

"That's enough from you, Rose!" Amelia stood, positioning herself next to Savannah.

"Fret not, Amelia. I am more than capable of managing Rose Woodburn on my own." Savannah motioned dismissively for Amelia to sit back down. Reluctantly, she obeyed.

"You said you felt sharp fangs sinking deep into your neck. But I don't see any scars on your neck," Rose prodded.

Savannah quickly covered the area with her hand.

"Well, obviously they're gone now. I turned eighteen four whole months ago. God, Rose, of all the things to ask me after I tell you that horrifying story. Have you no sense of decency?" Savannah turned away as if she had been struck.

Amelia jumped up from the sofa once more and wrapped her arms around Savannah. "Shame on you, Rose. How dare you be so cavalier with someone who's been through such a traumatic experience?" Amelia spoke in a derogatory manner.

The other girls murmured in sympathetic agreement, although Rose noticed a mischievous glean in Vivianna's eyes. Rose didn't say anything else, but she was sure that deep bite marks would have left a scar that lasted for more than four months. Savannah's neck was perfectly smooth; it didn't have a scratch on it.

Genevieve was the next to tell her horrific night sender story. Thankfully she wasn't as dramatic as Savannah. However, her account of the nighttime visit was still nearly identical, from the white nightgown to the bite, the pain, and the ensuing fear that the creature was still in the room. Genevieve had been so petrified she refused to remove her blindfold until she felt the warmth of the sun on her face in the morning. But like Savannah, Genevieve's neck didn't have any marks on it either, and her visit occurred only twelve weeks ago. Surely there should still be a scar, Rose thought.

Vivianna was the last to tell her story, despite being the most recent to receive a visit. She sat on the couch with her hands folded in her lap as she spoke, her voice monotone.

"Shortly after my party finished, my mother escorted me to my room. As she undid the corset of my dress, she reminded me that it would be a formidable night devoid of any gratification."

Rose listened intently, hoping that her account would be different, but again, it was eerily similar to those of the other two clones. However, there was something about Vivianna that convinced Rose she was lying, or better yet, acting. Vivianna maintained perfect posture and eye contact the entire time. She never stuttered, stumbled, raised, or lowered her voice. To Rose, it seemed more a practiced recitation of lines than sharing a personal story. Still, she listened carefully, searching for any subtle differences.

"The creature climbed on top of me, pinning my limbs to the bed. Though I struggled, it was useless. My strength was no match for the night sender. He bit my neck, and I felt a strange sensation course throughout my entire body, culminating between my legs." Vivianna paused, catching Rose's eye for less than a second.

Rose's ears perked up. There was no mention of pain in that last statement.

"Don't hold back, Vivianna. Tell us how awful the pain you felt was," Savannah whispered dramatically.

Vivianna tilted her head towards the floor, her long, silky black strands covering, or rather, shielding half of her face.

"It was awful," she managed.

The other girls offered sighs of support, but Rose was unconvinced. She deconstructed Vivianna's behavior in her mind. From the moment she opened her mouth, Vivianna recited her story without missing a beat. Yet, when she reached the climactic bite, she made no mention of the supposedly excruciating pain, nor did she have any marks on her neck. Also, Vivianna's entire delivery was emotionless, which Rose suspected was deliberate. By masking her emotions, she provided no intimation of her disposition towards the visit. Vivianna had also maintained eye

8

contact with her audience until her final utterance, one only added in response to Savannah, which Rose reckoned could imply its untruth.

Since they were children, Vivianna had always intrigued Rose, for she also seemed different from the other girls. Rose thought back to the day in the barn six months ago, when she walked in on Vivianna reading her copy of an erotic book. Only the day before, Savannah caught Rose reading it on the wooden bench outside the barn. She snatched the book and, gripping the edge with only her thumb and index finger, paraded it in front of the other girls.

"Look at the filth Rose Woodburn defiles our noble name with, ladies," Savannah squealed. "This book wreaks of sex and lust and indecency. It's grotesque! Only a quean would waste her time on this rubbish." The girls cheered, egging her on. "Let us show Rose where this book really belongs."

Savannah then threw the book into a pile of fresh manure and led her cheering procession out of the barn. For the next three months, all of the ladies of the court called her Scarlet Rose.

Once they left, she retrieved the book and wiped the dung off with a rag. She refused to let Savannah deter her from reading what she wanted. Rose hid her copy in the privacy of the barn hayloft, which is undoubtedly where Vivianna fished it out. When Rose confronted her, Vivianna simply placed the book back behind a bale of hay and crept out of the barn. Rose expected to be chastised by the group the following day, but not a word was said, leaving Rose perplexed.

Vivianna had cheered along with the group following Savannah's speech and even called her Scarlet Rose a few times. Yet, given Savannah's silence on the matter, it seemed she never disclosed that Rose was still reading the novel.

THE REST OF THE EVENING dissolved into mindless chitchat, but Rose wasn't paying any attention. Lost in her thoughts, she pondered what the rest of the night would hold. Despite their horrific accounts, Rose wasn't scared. She was enthralled by her nighttime visitor.

Rose selected a truffle from the table, her mouth already watering at the sight of its velvety milk shell. Amelia shifted uncomfortably on the couch, her plump frame bumping against the girls on either side. Rose simpered. She knew precisely what Amelia was thinking.

When the other ladies of the court ate a truffle, a most divine tasting one from afar, they ate it neatly. They would delicately place the piece of chocolate to their lips and take small, neat bites. Once they finished, they would pat their lips with a napkin even though there was normally no residue around their mouths. They ate the chocolate in such a disgustingly controlled fashion. It always drove Rose insane. Here was this incredibly creamy, smooth, ambrosial, tasty dessert that had arrived from hundreds of leagues away. It was not meant for polite picking. She couldn't fathom their restraint.

Ignoring Amelia's glare, Rose brought the creamy truffle to her lips, her tongue enveloping the sapid sweet. As the rich flavor spread to her taste buds, her eyes rolled back in her head, and a guttural moan was released from her brown-lined mouth.

"Really, Rose, at your transition to womanhood party?" Even Savannah's strident voice could not disturb her bliss.

When her eyes returned forward, all of the girls were sitting upright, their shoulders rigid. They stared at her aghast as if she had just fornicated in front of them. The room grew silent, the air thick with tension. Normally Savannah would reprimand her, mitigating that tension, but this time she only leered at her along with the others. Eleven pairs of reproving eyes bore into her. Rose didn't know what to do. She couldn't understand their apparent discomfort with pleasure, which was why she chose not to make any assumptions about her nighttime visitor. Perhaps their idea of fear and pain would prove to be her idea of excitement.

With a wicked smile on her face, Savannah whispered something to the girls next to her, who sneered at Rose, nodding their heads. Savannah stood, and Rose felt an uneasy knot in the pit of her stomach. She did not want anything to jeopardize her night.

"Why, Savannah, do tell us about that gorgeous crown you're wearing!" Vivianna's voice sounded uncharacteristically loud amidst the solemn silence.

Savannah paused. Her eyes shifted between Vivianna and the archway leading out of the salon.

"I've never seen anything like it," Vivianna enthused. "Isn't it magnificent, girls?"

"Of course, it is." Amelia chimed in immediately, and authoritatively. "Only Savannah is worthy of such a grand piece." Amelia rose and adjusted the crown, making sure it was perfectly centered. Savannah forced a smile as she batted Amelia's hand away and then smoothed her hair.

"Well, now, there's an appropriate subject for a gathering of this sort." Savannah proceeded to expand on the story they had already heard, exaggerating the cut and carat of the jewels. As innocuous chatter returned to the room, Rose gazed at Vivianna with awe. She had somehow diffused the situation without stirring up an altercation, the way Rose routinely did.

FINALLY, AT HALF-PAST TEN, the party concluded. Rose stood next to her mother as each of the girls took a turn politely thanking them for the evening. When it was Savannah's turn, she approached with a fake smile plastered on her face.

Gripping Rose's shoulders tightly, she shrilled sharply in her ear, "I hope you get what you deserve, you aberrant bitch."

Rose returned her fake smile. "Believe me, so do I."

And she did. Only it was quite clear that they had different ideas about what Rose did and did not deserve.

Vivianna was the last in line. She graciously thanked Rose's mother and then, turning to face only Rose, winked. Rose gaped after her, unsure what Vivianna meant by the gesture.

Finally, the procession ended. Once everyone had left, Rose hid a handful of truffles beneath her dress and practically skipped back to her room to prepare for her midnight visitor.

2

Rose stood on the wrought iron balcony attached to her bedroom, looking out over the city of Dover. She wasn't even sure it counted as a city considering how small it was. Only ten thousand people lived in Dover, and it was the members of the court, or rather, the noblemen, who controlled everything and everyone.

The farther Rose glanced, the more uniform the city looked. The cottages were the same shape and styling, each painted in different pastel colors. A blend of light blues, greens, pinks, yellows, and grays all the same distance from each other. Individually they may have been pretty, but together they were boring. Each unit was too similar to the next one. The only structure that was significantly different was the enormous stone castle in which she lived. Divided into separate homes, each with its private grounds, the humongous whitish-gray castle was home to all of the court families. There were no walls separating the castle from the rest of the city, though the common folk knew never to enter.

Rose extended her gaze past the houses and outside the city limits to the open fields. It was at least one hundred and fifty miles to the next city, leaving Dover isolated in the countryside. She often stood on the balcony, imagining herself riding off into those fields in search of something beyond what she already knew.

Part of the "quaintness" of Dover, which Rose considered its most insufferable quality, was that nothing ever changed. Dover had been doing things the same way for more than three centuries now and seemed to consider the concept of change a threat to the city itself. That notion got Rose thinking.

As far as she was aware, the night senders had not been around since Dover's formation. Dover had existed for three hundred and forty-four years, but stories of the night senders only dated back about a hundred years. They were also the only facet of Dover society about which the noblemen were never to know. The ladies of the court so strictly mandated this rule that even a little wretch like Savannah obeyed it. Now, Rose wanted to know why.

The sound of the bell tower tolling brought Rose out of her contemplation. Dover had a giant clock tower located in the central point of the city. It tolled on the hour and the half-hour. The single toll indicated it was eleven-thirty, which meant it was time for Rose to finish preparing for her nighttime visitor. Despite the warnings of fear from all the other girls in court, Rose's cheeks flushed with the heat of excitement at the idea of this unknown visitor entering her bedroom under cover of night. She went back into her room, closing the French doors behind her, but leaving them unlocked.

Rose decided to wear her midnight blue silk nightdress, the one, according to her mother, she should be saving for her wedding night. Yet, for some reason, tonight felt more special to her than the idea of her wedding night. Tonight was about her body and changing her relationship with it; it had nothing to do with anyone else. And to her, self-exploration was of much higher value than marriage to some "suitable" man, especially the way the members of the court callously arranged it.

She ran her fingers over the smooth silk fabric. The blue reminded her of the ocean's deepest depths, the ones that run so deep it would always be impossible for humans to explore every inch of them. The dark sapphire waters would forever hold their mysteries of the abyss, and that's exactly how she felt about herself. In the depths of her being, she held secrets that the court would simply never understand, and ones she vowed they would never uncover. She slipped the gown over her head, indulging in the luxurious way it glided over her skin.

Rose's reverie was interrupted by the abrupt opening of her bedroom door. Her mother must have been angry with her about the party because she usually had the decency to knock first.

Anne stalked in holding a white silk sleeping mask with a delicate layer of cream lace over it. Rose rolled her eyes. Of course, her mother would find some way to get white on her tonight since she had vehemently refused to wear a white nightgown the way the other girls always did. If they wanted to look like sacrificial virgins, that was their choice, but Rose wanted to wear something that made her feel feminine and alluring.

When her mother's eyes landed on Rose's midnight blue nightdress, they narrowed to tiny slits in a pointed glare. Oftentimes, Rose thought her mother glared at her more than she actually looked at her.

"Your best nightgown, really now, Rose?"

"For my most important night, mother."

Anne sighed loudly. Rose smiled in triumph, knowing her mother wouldn't sink to the level of physically removing the dress from her.

"I see you're still far too excited for a night from which you cannot derive any pleasure."

"So you say." Rose shrugged.

"Child, must you always be so difficult?"

Rose sighed. "Not difficult, mother, just different."

Her mother didn't say anything. Instead, she approached Rose and placed the white sleeping mask over her eyes. She fashioned it securely around the back of Rose's head. Despite the silkiness of the fabric, it wasn't sliding at all.

"Rose, you are not at any point to remove this mask tonight, do you understand me?" There was a fierce edge to her voice that Rose didn't wholly understand.

"Yes, mother," she responded calmly, trying to soothe the edge out of Anne's voice.

"All right then, it's time for me to leave you now. Please don't do anything foolish, Rose." Anne's voice was pleading. Unsure what to make of the unexpected change in her tone, Rose remained silent.

Her mother helped position her beneath the covers and blew out the candle by her bedside. She kissed her daughter gently on the forehead and then left, quietly shutting the door behind her.

Rose's bedroom was dark, except for the soft light emanating from the fire still crackling on the other side of the room. The hearth was adjacent to the elegant French doors through which, at any moment, her visitor was bound to enter. The thought stirred a flutter of anticipation within her.

Rose started to replay the conversation with Anne in her head. Her mother articulated something that hadn't completely registered when she first said it but was now dawning on her. Anne warned Rose that she was not to derive any pleasure from tonight. But that didn't mean that Rose couldn't derive any pleasure from the experience, just that she wasn't supposed to, at least by court standards. It seemed to Rose that Anne's words implied she did have some control over the experience. Perhaps she could choose whether to allow herself to feel pleasure or succumb to fear and feel only pain.

Rose's lips curved back into the devious smile of a woman indulging in her first foreign chocolate. It didn't matter what her mother said or thought. As long as she had a choice, Rose would choose to allow as much pleasure as her body was capable of experiencing. She also decided that whatever happened tonight was between her and her visitor. It had nothing to do with the court.

Rose laid in bed, trying not to think. Her heart was beating fast, her stomach knotted. She was far too excited to sleep and knew that at any moment, the clock tower would toll, and she would hear the French doors creak open. With her eyes closed beneath the mask, she focused on the crackling sounds of the fire. She listened intently to the logs shifting in the fireplace, as pieces of them turned to ash and crumbled to the stone floor below, though it did nothing to calm her nerves.

Soon, the clock unleashed its first toll. It was midnight. Rose was now officially eighteen years old, and as soon as the twelfth toll struck, she would find out exactly what that entailed.

3

The French doors eased open soundlessly. A cold gust of wind blew inside, extinguishing what remained of the dwindling fire. The room was now shrouded in darkness. Beneath the silk mask, Rose's eyes were wide, alert, and brimming with curiosity. The cool air felt electrifying against her warm skin and signaled that her moment had finally arrived. Though she could not see him, she sensed his presence in the room. Questions flooded her mind, but Rose dared not utter a word.

The night sender crept in through the French doors and shifted carefully through the room. Despite his massive size, he barely made a sound. When he reached the foot of Rose's bed, his movements abruptly stopped. He stood in a state of shock at the unusual creature before him.

He surveyed her, absorbing her mood with his heightened awareness. She was unlike any of the other girls he had ever visited. The other girls were always lying in bed stiff as corpses in their white dresses, with cold, clammy skin that was visibly shaking. But there was no fear emanating from Rose. Her body was flush with heat, and he could sense that she wasn't dreading his visit; she was anxiously awaiting it.

Her reaction had him in a state of befuddlement. Part of him speculated that this night would be far more entertaining than one of his regular visits. Still, another part cautioned that it could be difficult for him. Not knowing what to expect, he decided to proceed the way he customarily would.

The night sender leapt onto the bed, landing gently on top of Rose, his weight balanced on either side of him. Her heartbeat spiked, but she didn't move. He lowered himself down so that his chest was pressing ever so slightly against hers. He felt her beating heart against his skin, her body warm and alive beneath him.

He extended his tongue and caressed the right side of her neck with it. Rose's body arched with the tingling pleasure that danced along her skin. The night sender felt her warm breasts rise firmly against his chest and fought the urge to take them in his mouth, an impulse that was foreign to him. Typically at this point in a visit, a girl would be repulsed and wriggling relentlessly to get away from him. But beneath him now, this beautiful creature remained blithesome. He allowed his tongue to linger on her neck longer than he ordinarily would.

Rose's body sank slowly back down to the bed. The night sender leaned forward, his warm breath heavenly against her skin, and bit her neck. His fangs sank into her like the quick stab of a needle, and then Rose was gone.

Her mind became lost in a sea of ecstasy as warm sensations coursed through her entire body, starting from her neck and reaching to the very tips of her toes. They ran back and forth, not missing any part of her, even tender portions never before kissed. It felt as though gentle lips were brushing and sucking on her skin. They encircled her nipples, leaving them firm, and enlivening parts of her body that were unknown.

Eventually, the sensations turned, migrating in force in the same direction. They picked up speed and gathered together in a giant wave of pleasure, which was about to break in the deep cavern between her legs. Her body was flush with heat, her blood circulating faster. She was panting in anticipation of the climax she could feel coming.

As the full strength of the wave finally broke inside her pleasure center, Rose felt a sharp contraction and then a deep release. She let out a guttural moan as her whole body went limp.

The night sender laid over her, frozen. His head throbbed with pain, unlike any he had ever experienced. Never before had he seen a lady of the court reach orgasm during his visit.

Rose's head rolled across her pillow. Her whole body felt more awake than it ever had as if in the past seventeen years of her life, she had never been fully alive. She thought of all those delectable truffles that brought her so much pleasure and how they may as well have been ash in her mouth compared to what she felt just now. This night could not possibly be the end.

"More," Rose moaned. "More, please."

The night sender stared down at her in horror.

Rose's left hand moved towards her silk mask. She had to see the creature that had just delivered this immense pleasure unto her. She tried to pull it off, but the fabric wouldn't budge. Feeling along the back of her head, she realized her mother had not tied the mask on but had stitched the fabric together to keep Rose from removing it. She knew her daughter too well.

The night sender sat up abruptly. Feeling his weight lifting off of her, Rose instinctively wrapped her free hand around his arm. His skin was warm and surprisingly soft to the touch, like that of a woman. But beneath it, her hand gripped ridges of solid muscle. The contrasting sensations were remarkably alluring.

Startled, the night sender pulled away quickly and was by the French doors in an instant.

"Wait, don't leave," Rose wailed desperately while still pulling at the silk fabric. "This can't be just one night. You must come back tomorrow. Please, I beg of you." The tinge of desperation in her voice was evident.

The night sender stood by the balcony, paralyzed. He didn't know what to do. Never in his eighteen years of service had he encountered a woman like Rose. Their realm forbade them from ever making more than one visit to any woman. Usually, the women were so petrified of him, or rather, the idea of him, that they couldn't wait for the night to be over. And now, here was this beautiful, sensual woman begging for him to return. He couldn't bear to say no and knew he couldn't risk returning, so instead, he said nothing and catapulted over the balcony railing.

Still ripping furiously at her mask, Rose finally tore through the silk and threw the shredded bolt of fabric onto the floor. As soon as her eyes regained their focus, she realized she was too late. The room was empty. Her night sender was gone. She abruptly got out of bed and sped towards the balcony. Gripping the iron firmly, she leaned over the sides every which way, but it was no use. He had vanished, and she had no idea if he would ever be back again.

The bittersweet disappointment of experiencing the greatest pleasure she had ever known, and not knowing if she'd ever know it again crushed her spirit that night. The rosy glow of her skin stood in stark contrast to her eyes, which were searing with bewilderment. Her body was ripe and wanton as her sense of womanhood was beginning to awaken.

4

The night sender flew quickly over Dover, anxious to return to his realm to make sense of what happened that night. He soared well beyond Dover's limits and into the surrounding forest in minutes, keeping low to the trees to find his mark. As soon as he saw the crooked Willow tree, he dove down from the sky and into the valley below.

In the center of the valley, a narrow river flowed, cascading over a steep waterfall. He flew around the back of the waterfall and into the deep rock formation behind it. The night sender landed on both legs and descended into the dark cavern that was home to his kind.

The cavern ran at least forty feet below ground, growing colder and damper at every level. The night sender glided effortlessly along the uneven, rock-laden path that he knew so well until he reached their lair.

The narrow pathway unfolded into a wide, open area covered in stalactites. There were torches attached to different parts of the walls, lighting the cave with a subtle orange and red glow. Different caves and paths carved out through the rocks lead in numerous directions, creating an intricate underground labyrinth. None of the paths were lit; only the main entryway and the great hall. Unless one was familiar with the cavern, it would be almost impossible for him to find his way in the darkness.

After a visit, the night sender checked-in and then went back out to enjoy the rest of the night, flying through the woods under cover of darkness. But tonight he needed answers. He needed to know what happened in Rose's bedroom, why she was so different from the other girls, and, more importantly, why his head was still throbbing in pain. There was only one creature he trusted who might have an explanation for him, and that was Avidan.

A night sender for 107 years now, if this type of phenomenon ever happened before, odds were Avidan witnessed it firsthand. But before he could speak with him, he had to see Felonious.

The night sender adeptly navigated through the dark caves until he reached the great hall. The great hall was the most open part of the cavern and served as the primary meeting space where the night senders would congregate to address all matters of importance.

It was a large, round room with ceilings that reached thirty feet high. Sharp-edged stalactites hung from above like precariously placed spikes that could kill on impact were they to fall. The night senders had adorned them with candles that emanated a dim glow. In the center of the room, behind a large rock with a round, flattened surface, stood Felonious, looking up expectantly. He was waiting for him.

"Roosha! How was your evening?"

"Fine, Felonious. And yours?"

"Simply wonderful."

Felonious looked down at the symbols on the flat sheet of rock in front of him. As his eyes registered the information he was looking for, he lifted his head to address Roosha.

"So, I see you were assigned Rose Woodburn. I take it your visit went well?"

That was an understatement, Roosha thought to himself.

"Yes, business as usual," he lied.

Roosha knew not to entrust Felonious with any further information. He was a known snitch.

"Excellent." Felonious clapped his hands together and then marked off the encounter on the carved rock in front of him.

Roosha nodded and then left the great hall in search of Avidan.

5

Rose had finally fallen asleep and was now in the throes of a dream. She could not see anything. The room was pitch black. Her sense of sight was entirely lost to her, heightening her other four senses.

She could feel smooth silk against the skin of her wrists and ankles. The silk was taut, firmly securing each of her limbs to the bedpost closest to it. Her body lay comfortably stretched into a giant X shape across her bed.

She listened carefully, trying to make out what, if anyone, was in the room. She heard faint breathing beside her and knew it had to be the night sender. He stood to the right side of her bed, looking down at her. Without her sight, she could not make out his shape or size but felt his enigmatic presence in the room. Despite her restraints, she wasn't alarmed. Instead, Rose's mouth watered with arousal. Whatever he was going to do to her, she desperately wanted it.

Rose inhaled deeply, taking in his scent. He smelled of the forest, fresh bark, and musk. It was a natural, masculine smell that warmed her body with desire.

She heard him move and knew he had positioned himself closer to her because his scent grew more potent. The fragrance wafted up her nose, arousing a sense of animalistic lust. Suddenly, she felt a gentle warmth radiating from above her. There was nothing physically touching her skin, but still, the energy somehow stimulated her body. It felt as if someone were holding embers from the fire only inches above, embers that ignited her tactile sensitivities.

He moved his hands slowly, making sure they hovered over every part of her. The heat enlivened her body and spirit. She felt like a block of ice purposefully being melted down to reveal the raging fire deep within herself. As his hands moved above the very center of her X shaped body, her sensual core came alive like a volcano erupting for the first time. Rhythmic contractions and bursts of molten juices overwhelmed her. She was on fire, or better yet, she was the fire. The intense blue flame burned with pleasure, not pain. And as the inferno spread through her, she arched and writhed in her sleep.

6

Avidan sat outside the cave on the edge of the river.

"Greetings, friend," called Roosha.

"Roosha, my boy! How are you?"

Roosha sat beside him on the riverbank.

"In need of your counsel, I'm afraid."

"Oh?" Avidan looked at him inquisitively.

"Your private counsel." Roosha gave Avidan an urgent, serious glance.

Avidan nodded solemnly. "In that case, let us fly."

They leapt into the air, soaring side by side. Avidan led them further through the forest to a steep hill, miles from the realm of the night senders. They crested the hilltop without a sound.

"Speak freely, Roosha."

Roosha considered where to begin.

"Tonight something happened, something that still has me dumbfounded. I received my assignment as usual and went to visit one of the court girls." He decided Avidan didn't need to know which one. Strangely, he felt protective of Rose. "She was unique... different than any of the girls I've encountered in the past. She wasn't apprehensive at all; she was ready. I felt her anticipation from the moment I entered the room. I thought perhaps at some point, her intrigue would give way to fear, but the opposite occurred. The closer I got to the bite, the more she enjoyed the experience. And now, my head is in the worst pain I've ever felt before." He wanted to elaborate but was still too flummoxed to summon the words.

Avidan smiled at him.

"Roosha, there's something you need to understand. It's taught to every night sender when they first begin their service. From what I've seen, no one ever seems to really learn it until they've experienced it for themselves."

Roosha looked at him, confused. He was reasonably sure he had understood everything they taught him when he was initiated, many years ago.

"Remember the words that govern our realm, the ones etched into the stone in the great hall?"

Roosha nodded. He knew them by heart.

If you have chosen to be a deliverer of pain in one lifetime, in your next, you shall be forced to be a deliverer of pleasure. And another's pleasure will deliver pain unto you. For that is the cycle of life, the way of ensuring balance and harmony. Create pain for others, and eventually, you will suffer that pain yourself.

"We were designed to give pleasure to women. Every part of us has special otherworldly abilities that awaken a woman's sensuality. Our tongues, hands, lips, even our fangs all have special sensors that emit erotic sensations."

Roosha listened intently as Avidan explained.

"Now, unfortunately, most of the women at court are taught by their insipid mothers to fear pleasure. They become rigid, diffident girls instead of full-blooded women. It's a terrible shame. But because of their conditioning, they normally don't experience much, if any, pleasure from their encounter with us. For as powerful as our abilities may be, the mind is still stronger. If a woman is convinced she will not enjoy the experience, then even we cannot overpower her thoughts. But it would seem that the girl you visited tonight is a rarity among the court girls."

"She is a rarity. I knew it when I first flew in her window. Her body wasn't rigid at all; it was warm and exuded excitement. As I said, it's like she was waiting for me to come, not dreading my visit."

Avidan looked thoughtful, as Roosha explained.

"So finally, a girl has decided to enjoy her sensuality. She'll be quite a remarkable woman that one. And that's the exact reason that you're feeling so much pain. The more pleasure the woman feels, the more pain we experience. I'm afraid it's all a part of our punishment, my friend."

Roosha thought about Avidan's statement, remembering the words on the wall.

"And another's pleasure will deliver pain unto you," Roosha contemplated. "So, the pain is delivered in proportion to the pleasure."

"Precisely."

Even though he now knew that Rose would cause him more pain, he still wanted to go back to her. With Avidan's confirmation that she was such a rarity, he felt an overwhelming urge to deliver as much pleasure as possible.

"Avidan, has a night sender ever gone back to visit a girl more than once?"

Avidan's eyes went from shock to fury in an instant. He grabbed Roosha roughly by the shoulder and pulled him in so close that their faces were only inches apart.

"Dare not utter those words aloud, boy! Cease that train of thought immediately before you put yourself in grave danger."

Roosha was alarmed. Avidan was always calm and centered. For him to become this incensed by Roosha's question, there must be something, some crucial piece of information of which Roosha was unaware.

"What happened before?" Roosha barely whispered.

Avidan's fury subsided. He released his grip on Roosha's shoulder. When he spoke, there was an overwhelming sadness in his voice.

"It didn't end well. I will say no more on the subject. Keep the thought entirely OUT of your mind."

With that, Avidan leapt from the edge of the hill and flew off into the night. Roosha remained, staring up at the sky pondering.

The problem for Roosha was that the thought of going back to Rose didn't stem from his mind. If it were only rooted in his mind, it would be much easier to heed Avidan's severe warning. But it was in his heart that he felt the desire to return to Rose and help her discover more of her own womanhood. And while his mind clearly understood the edge in Avidan's words, his heart still ached at the idea of denying Rose the pleasure he was made to deliver. But at the same time, Roosha didn't know how, or if he'd be able to handle the pain that would inevitably be inflicted upon him.

7

Rose awoke in a blissful state. Her body felt tender and warm, and somehow more open beneath the sheets. She stretched out her limbs, spreading herself across the bed, which felt odd after being bound in her dream. A flush of heat spread within her tender pleasure center. She could get used to this feeling, she thought to herself.

As she contemplated her previous night's visit, her hand automatically flew to her neck. Her fingers gently probed the area for any sign of bite marks, and a chance to prove Savannah wrong. But there was nothing there. Rose checked both sides of her neck. Her skin felt as smooth as it always did. She couldn't understand how that was possible.

Rose got out of bed and inspected her body in front of the wrought iron mirror. Her bare neck was in pristine condition, with not even a scratch. No one would believe that a creature had just recently sunk its fangs into her, as she hadn't believed Savannah. She shuddered at what that wretch would say to her when she saw Rose without marks on her neck and vowed to wear a scarf for the next week.

As she stared deeper into her reflection, there was something Rose noticed that did look different to her, her expression. It was softer and more feminine. Her brown eyes still had their sparkling intensity, but they were calmer somehow. And her skin had a subtle radiance to it.

She let the blue silk nightgown slide off her shoulders and down to her hips. Rose ran her hands across her chest. Her nipples were still hard from last night, or perhaps from her dream. She cupped her hands around her breasts and squeezed gently, indulging in how sensitive they now were.

Rose released her left breast and slowly slid her fingers down the center of her cleavage to the top of her navel. The tips felt like a delicate feather against her skin. She traced her fingers further down and was about to press her hand beneath her nightgown when the bedroom door abruptly opened.

Rose jumped and scampered to pull the nightgown back up.

But when she looked up, staring down at her during one of her most intimate moments was none other than Anne Elizabeth Woodburn.

Rose's mother turned away from her, her expression unreadable. Rose hastily refastened the straps, making sure to cover her exposed chest. Her cheeks grew redder as utter mortification set in, an awful contrast to how divine she had felt a moment ago. Two more seconds and her mother would have caught her with her hand beneath her gown, fondling herself. The red of her cheeks turned a deeper crimson from the frustration of not having a lock on her door.

Rose crawled back into bed, wanting to hide as much of her body as possible. Once she was beneath the sheets, Rose's mother sat on the edge of the bed and lightly kissed her cheek.

"Good morning, Rose."

"Good morning, mother," Rose offered meekly.

"How was your night?" Anne asked timidly. Her body was tense, her hands clenched together in her lap. Rose sensed from her apparent discomfort that she didn't want an honest answer to that question; that it was asked more out of duty than anything else.

With the mention of her night, Rose let her mind drift back to the level of ecstasy she reached, and to her ensuing dream.

"Just fine, mother." Rose felt her usual smugness returning as she placed her hands behind her head and relaxed back into the pillows.

Anne looked wary. She stood up and walked silently towards the balcony doors, her eyes towards the floor. Rose could sense some preoccupation in her mother's mind, which usually didn't bode well. But she was too distracted by her reverie to contemplate what it could be. With her eyes closed, Rose's mind drifted, reliving the previous night's events. She began with the anticipation she felt when the crisp air blew in through her window, signaling her visitor's arrival. Her intrigue piqued when the weight of its body was swiftly upon her. Rose's hands were drawn to her neck as she felt the intensity of the bite and overwhelming physical gratification that ensued. She recalled how much she had wanted to see the wondrous creature who delivered her to rapture.

Her eyes snapped open. The mask flashed across her mind like smoke alerting one to a fire. Her mother was probably wondering where the mask was. Rose combed through the covers frantically but didn't see it. She hated that the mask was as white as the sheets, making it that much harder to find.

As she scrambled beneath the linens, Rose heard her mother clear her throat. She looked up, knowing she was in trouble.

Anne stood next to Rose's bed, the shredded silk dangling from her index finger. Her expression had changed from wary to outraged. Her voice was icy as she spoke.

"I see my favorite silk mask didn't survive one night with you."

Rose smiled to herself. She couldn't help thinking that it probably would have survived any other night with her. As she thought of her special night, a sense of defiance grew within her.

"Well, mother, when you affix something to someone's head with stitches, you don't leave them much choice but to rip it off, now do you?"

"Of course not dear," Rose's mother chided. "Heaven forbid you actually obey your own mother's word explicitly prohibiting you from removing this mask."

Rose could almost feel the heat emanating from her mother's furious eyes.

"Exactly, mother. If it makes you feel any better, your stitching was superb. I had a difficult time ripping through the silk."

Her mother's hand started shaking. The shredded lace was vibrating in front of her face now. She sensed that Anne was vacillating between maintaining her ladylike persona and unleashing the wrath within her.

"You see too much humor in areas where you should see an opportunity to show some respect."

"Perhaps if given more of an explanation, or logical basis for these inane behaviors you expect from me, I would show greater respect."

Anne gave her a warning look.

"You are but a girl of eighteen, what do you know?"

That line infuriated Rose. If she was still some silly girl, why had the ladies of the court created this nonsensical ritual by which the girls transitioned into womanhood? What was womanhood to them anyway, she wondered. Was it only about the changing of her body, or worse, getting them ready for marriage? And what was the point of "transforming" into a woman if she was still entrusted with the same limited information she received as a girl?

"According to court authority, I am now a woman of eighteen, and I would know a lot more if this whole ordeal weren't so shrouded in mystery!"

Rose was exasperated. Her cheeks flushed, and anger welled up inside of her. It appeared her mother was attempting to ruin a night Rose regarded as one of her best thus far. She didn't understand why no one was allowed to derive any pleasure from their visit. To her, it was a ludicrous notion. And she resented that her mother wouldn't tell her why.

"Rose, sometimes you are better off not knowing."

"Why can't I be the one to decide that?"

"Because like it or not, not everything in this world is your decision," Anne was shouting at her now. "You've been a woman for less than a day, and suddenly you know everything? Let me tell you something, Rose, there's a lot more to being a woman than getting one nighttime visit."

Anne's voice was cracking. She was having trouble maintaining composure and started angling towards the door.

"Mother, wait." Rose's tone was frustrated but not angry. She could see that her mother was visibly upset. And for a woman like Anne to lose her composure in front of her daughter, Rose knew she was in pain. She wanted to learn the source of it.

"Please, tell me what's upsetting you so."

Anne paused at the door with her back towards Rose.

"Get dressed now, Rose, or you'll be late for high tea." Anne took a deep breath and exited the room without another word.

Rose plopped back down into her pillows. She had forgotten it was Sunday. Every Sunday, the girls of the court met for early afternoon tea in the salon below the library. Rose already had her fill of mindless chitchat at her birthday party. She dreaded having to sit through tea with the girls again, knowing she would be the subject of interrogation, especially by the insufferable Savannah. And after her exchange with Anne, she was both irritated and low on patience.

Rose hated that her mother ruined her morning and was frustrated with how much information Anne withheld. It seemed the only thing she was willing to tell Rose was what she should and should not do, or worse, was forbidden from doing. Rose found it equally maddening that her mother preferred to suffer in silence rather than trust or have a meaningful conversation with her daughter.

She tried to immerse herself once again in the previous night's euphoria, but this time when she thought about her visit, a sadness came over her as she wondered if she would ever have a night like that again.

8

Still feeling defiant, Rose decided she would not be attending high tea. She endured her birthday celebration with that dreadful group of girls, which was enough of a sacrifice. Then, just this morning, she was mortified in front of her mother and had to face Anne's asperity. This afternoon she would be doing what she wanted, not what society expected of her.

Rose stalked past the salon's entrance, where the girls were seated at a long rectangular table and headed straight into the library. If her mother wanted to deny her the information she needed, Rose vowed to find it herself.

She stood at the entrance to the library, gaping at the rows and rows of books surrounding her. For a small city, Dover had amassed an impressive collection of works. Every section her eyes happened upon made her mission seem more fruitless. She wondered how she was supposed to locate any information on the night senders amongst these thousands of books. Unwilling to be deterred, she decided to start in the section that contained volumes on Dover's history.

Rose ran her finger along the spines of the books, combing through their titles. She searched for a title that would suggest it had any information in it relevant to the night senders. But none of the descriptions fit. Biographies on different noblemen, books on Dover's trade system, its agriculture, the castle, and the city's history all lined the shelves in great numbers. None of the titles indicated that they would contain anything remotely relevant to the night senders.

Finally, she found one book entitled *The Ladies of Dover* and pulled it off the shelf. It had to be about the women of the court. She flipped through the pages, scanning the chapter titles, but did not uncover any promising leads. The content seemed downright frivolous to her. There was an entire chapter dedicated to the importance of high tea and its role in maintaining a bond of sisterhood with fellow court members. Rose rolled her eyes. If high tea was of such high importance, she considered just how low Dover's expectations of its elevated women were.

Rose flipped through the rest of the chapters, but there was nothing useful in the book. She put it back on the shelf next to another title, *The Nobleman's Way*. That's when logic hit her like a brick square in the face. Rose wondered how she could have been so stupid. Of course, the library wouldn't contain any information on the night senders! Both men and women had access to the library, and the number one rule impressed upon all the women in court was that the night senders were to remain secret.

Rose felt a shimmer of hope within her. She knew now that she was searching in the wrong place, which explained the lack of available information. If she could now figure out where to look, she might be able to find what she needed.

She knew the library had a basement, though it was off-limits to visitors. The parlor below the library took up only about half the depth of the actual building, leaving plenty of room for some type of storage area. She considered that it would be the perfect place for a private collection of works containing secrets of which Dover's citizens were to remain unaware. But how could she ascertain whether that was the case, she wondered.

Rose walked towards the massive mahogany desk in the back of the library. Its size was intimidating, along with the intricately carved lion devouring a lamb at its base. Behind the thick wood sat a small, slender woman who Rose recognized by the gray streak in her otherwise raven mane. It was Vivianna's mother. She must be the librarian, Rose thought.

"Hello, Mrs. Weston, how are you today?"

The woman looked up from her desk.

"Why, Rose Woodburn, what a pleasure to see you. Vivianna always speaks very highly of you."

"She does?" Rose blurted.

"Why yes, dear," Mrs. Weston smiled politely at her.

Rose quickly closed her open mouth. She hadn't meant to spout out those words so abruptly. But she was surprised, not just by Mrs. Weston's statement, but by the sincerity in her voice. Rose was unaware that Vivianna had any regard for her, let alone high regard.

"Is there something I can help you with?" Mrs. Weston prompted.

"Ah, yes. At least I think so." Rose wasn't quite sure how to ask for what she needed. She certainly didn't want the other girls of the court getting wind of what she was doing. She knew she had to be very careful with her words.

"I was wondering if there is perhaps a … a special section in the library … or a private area … reserved for ladies of the court?" Rose stammered.

"A special section?" Mrs. Weston raised an eyebrow.

"Um, yes … one that contains books that would only be necessary for the ladies of the court." Rose saw the puzzled look on Mrs. Weston's face and grew nervous.

"Why, Rose, I'm afraid I'm not quite sure what you are asking of me." Her tone was pointed despite the woman's seemingly innocent expression.

Rather than arouse any further suspicion, Rose offered the first plausible explanation that came to mind.

"You see, Mrs. Weston, now that I've turned eighteen and am a woman of the court, I've decided I need to take my role more seriously. I was hoping to find some books that would help me better understand what is expected of me so that I can meet those standards impeccably."

Mrs. Weston smiled encouragingly, and in that brief second, Rose's hopes shot to the sky. Was it possible that Vivianna's mother understood the underlying reason for Rose's request? Though it was foolhardy, she clung to the unlikely hope.

"Why that's lovely, dear! It's nice to see a young woman regarding her position so highly. There's a wonderful book you'd love called *The Ladies of Dover*. It's right in the history of Dover section. Let me show you the way."

ROSE WALKED OUT OF THE LIBRARY with her hopes dashed, and a book she swore she would never read. As she stepped onto the cobblestone lane to head home, her peers emerged from the salon. Rose adjusted her yellow scarf, wondering if this day could get any worse.

"Why, Rose, dear! We missed you at high tea." Savannah's voice was dripping with phony, accusatory sweetness.

"Oh, Savannah, I'm sure there was far too much gossip afoot for you to have missed little old me." Rose was in no mood for Savannah's antics.

"But of course, we all missed you, my dear. We were concerned that last night was just so painful you couldn't even bring yourself to join us for tea."

That comment infuriated Rose. The last thing she wanted to talk about with Savannah, or any of them for that matter, was last night. She was already angry and refused to lose her composure around these wretches.

"I'd rather not discuss my night. It's far too soon for me." Rose feigned distress, placing her palm against her forehead.

"It's quite all right, dear. Not all of us can handle that level of pain. It takes a real lady." Savannah's head tilted to the side as she read the title of the book in Rose's hand. "I hope from your library selection you've finally decided to try and become one. Enough with that erotic nonsense. All that sexual profanity will only make you a whore, and a whore isn't fit to be a lady of the court."

Savannah's eyes shifted upwards to the scarf around her neck. Rose knew that would be her next line of attack. The blood boiled beneath her cheeks. She refused to give Savannah the satisfaction; she would strike first. Rose was about to retort when a wasp landed on the side of Savannah's neck. A devious feeling overcame her.

"Savannah, quick! You've got a giant mosquito on the left side of your neck!"

Savannah's eyes grew wide, and her hand instinctively slapped at the side of her neck, crushing the wasp against her skin.

"Ouch!" Savannah leapt off her feet in pain.

Rose smirked.

"Oh, I am sorry. It must have been a wasp, not a mosquito. I suppose this time, you will have a mark on your neck."

Savannah's whole face turned bright red.

"You will regret that, Rose Woodburn, believe me, you will!" Her ear-piercing octave made Rose cringe.

Savannah placed her hand over the sting and stalked off, yelling back to the other lemmings.

"Let's go, ladies."

One by one, each of the court girls glared at Rose and followed Savannah down the street. Vivianna was the last to fall in line, lingering farther than usual behind the others. She stopped to survey the book title and then met Rose's eyes.

"Shame about the library. Information can be so limited; that is unless you know where to look."

She winked at Rose and then rejoined the procession of court girls.

9

That night, as Rose was getting ready for bed, she couldn't stop thinking about Vivianna. Her mother seemed so genuine in the library when she told Rose that Vivianna spoke very highly of her. But Rose did not understand why Vivianna would mention her at all, let alone in a positive light. The two of them weren't close. Their childhood friendship faded many years ago when Vivianna succumbed to Savannah's self-imposed authority over the girls. As far as she was aware, Vivianna thought as little of her as the rest of the herd.

Rose contemplated the incident outside the library, replaying the events in her mind. Vivianna deliberately stopped to address her privately, careful not to alert the other girls. She noted the book Rose was holding and then offered a cryptic comment about the library and knowing where to find information. Rose pondered whether Vivianna had any inclination as to the classified information Rose was seeking. She didn't see how that was possible. She never had a conversation with Vivianna about the night senders, and carrying one book out of the library surely could not be construed as incriminating.

The unnecessary speculation was making her dizzy. Rose chided herself for wasting so much time on the subject. She never gave much, if any, consideration to Vivianna before, outside of recognizing that she had potential but seemed to prefer blending in with the group. Though now, Rose wasn't so sure about that. Perhaps there was more to Vivianna than she had noticed. She decided she wanted to find out.

But it would be impossible to talk to Vivianna around the rest of the court girls. All of them were such lousy gossipers. Anything they heard, they repeated to anyone they came in contact with, even if it was taken entirely out of context. The rumor mill didn't concern itself with accuracy.

The sound of the clock tower seized Rose's attention. She heard one toll, indicating it was now half-past eleven. Exactly this time last night, she was waiting in anticipation of her visitor. Tonight she was feeling somewhat differently.

Rose was desperately hoping that somehow he would come back, even though she knew the girls only ever received one visit. But her sense of desire was at odds with the logic thrust upon her by her mind.

Rose endeavored to recreate the previous night as if going through the same motions would cause her night sender to magically reappear. Again she wore her fancy blue nightdress and lit a fire in the fireplace that was already starting to burn out. She had retrieved the shredded silk mask and mended it in the afternoon with a needle and thread. In rebellion against the white, she used a red silk ribbon to stitch it back together and would wear it again that night.

She walked out onto the terrace, and peered into the vast expanse of darkness for any sign that her night sender was nearby. Rose glanced down towards the rooftops and streets of Dover, but they were empty. The city was quiet and more beautiful at night. The faint light from the yellow-hued street-lamps made it seem as though fireflies were dancing along the cobblestone paths.

She looked up to the sky but saw nothing other than the sliver of moon between the clouds. She mused that a starless atmosphere was fitting with her joyless night.

Finally, Rose went back into her bedroom, closing the terrace doors behind her. She left them unlocked, hoping against all odds that her nighttime visitor would return.

10

As soon as he saw her room go dark, Roosha landed softly on the balcony. He wasn't sure why he was there. He knew he shouldn't be. He spent the entire day fighting an internal battle, going over Avidan's words in his mind at least a hundred times. But when darkness set in, his wings guided him to Rose's balcony once again. It was wrong, and it was dangerous, but still, he was there.

He peered inside the window and saw her lying in bed beneath the white sheets, the same mask over her eyes. He wanted to go in and take a closer look at her, but the silken fabric made it impossible to tell if she was asleep, and he dared not enter while she was awake. Roosha promised himself that he would only observe. By no means was he to have any interaction with her.

A strong gust of wind from behind him blew the doors slightly ajar. Roosha wasn't surprised that they were unlocked. Part of him was pleased they were. He took it as a sign that she did want him to return to her, and her desire stirred unfamiliar feelings inside of him.

The greater part of him remained paralyzed in fear over what to do. He knew the unlocked doors should not elicit any reaction in him, yet they did. They beckoned to him, willing him towards her. Roosha's hands clenched the railing firmly. Inherently he knew it was in his best interest to remain on the balcony. Still, he found himself peering through the narrow opening between the two doors wanting to be closer to this woman who called to him like a siren.

41

She was somehow more beautiful than she had been the previous night. He wasn't sure if it was her newfound womanhood, or whether he had not genuinely seen her the night before. More likely, it was the latter. For years he made it a practice to complete the visits quickly and discreetly, never lingering. Not once had a court girl captured his attention enough to alter his course of action, until now. As she lay there still, Roosha absorbed Rose's smooth, alabaster skin, a delicate contrast against her deep blue dress. He wanted to run his hands across her supple surface to see if it was as soft as it looked from afar.

Despite his urges, Roosha remained on the balcony perched like a gargoyle statue, his eyes fixated on Rose.

Her body began moving gently from side to side, swaying beneath the sheets. Roosha figured she must be in the throes of a dream. Her cheeks flushed the same delicate shade of pink as her full lips. He took in the sensual curve of her mouth, wanting to make her moan the same way she had the night before. As if his words dictated reality, Rose's back arched up, her delicate lips parted, and she released a primal sound from deep within in the same pleasurable way.

Without diverting his attention from Rose, Roosha instinctively moved his hand to open the balcony doors.

The moment he realized what he was doing, he abruptly stopped himself and leapt from the balcony into the night sky. He flew fast and hard, putting as much distance between him and her room as possible. Roosha was shocked by his inability to remain in complete control of himself around her. The sound of her moan caused his mind to disconnect from his body, allowing his male instincts to grasp a firm hold over him. He knew if he were unable to regain control, they would drive him down a treacherous path.

With a foreign pain inside of him not derived from another's pleasure, he flew home that night, vowing to himself that he would never return.

11

When Rose awoke, all she could see was a thick, white haze. She blinked several times, thinking she was still half asleep, but each time she opened her eyes to a wall of white. Panic began to set in, as she worried the immensity of her enjoyment of physical pleasure was impacting her vision. Rose swatted at her face and felt a layer of silk instead of skin. Then she remembered she had worn the mask to bed. She yanked the silk off her face and sat up, allowing her breathing to return to normal.

"Another peaceful morning," she muttered.

Her eyes glanced towards the balcony doors. They appeared to be open, but it was hard to tell from across the room. She slid out of bed and walked over to inspect. She was sure the doors had fully shut last night, and now they were ajar, with only about two inches between them.

That minuscule measurement was enough to plant a seed of hope within Rose. Had the night sender returned, she wondered. Was it her bringer of pleasure who had opened the doors during the night? Curious, she stepped onto the balcony to search for any trace of this creature, not knowing what to look for.

Unfortunately, there was nothing to be found. The balcony looked the same as it always did, its planters overflowing with ivy undisturbed. Rose leaned over the black railing, but Dover and her home were both the picture of ordinary. Still, Rose had a lingering feeling in her. Even though she had no evidence of his presence, intuitively, she could have sworn her night sender was there last night.

But as the minutes passed, her reasonable side chimed in, arguing that the wind could easily have blown the doors open, seeing, as they were unlocked. The realist in her chipped away at her intuition, making her second-guess herself.

TWO FULL WEEKS went by without any visit from the night sender.

Every night, Rose prepared for bed in the same ritualistic fashion. She wore her sapphire nightdress, adorned her face with the silk mask, and left the balcony doors unlocked. After five days of frustration, she flung the doors wide open, hoping it would convey a welcome message. But each morning, disappointment weighed heavy, as nothing was ever out of place, nor was there any sign that someone had entered her room. And worse, she had not experienced any physical gratification.

Her body was anxious. Since that night, she had had constant dreams in which she was being pleasured by the creature. Each morning, she was met with a warm, burning sensation between her legs that never seemed to cease. It was a fired arousal that she desperately wanted to satisfy; only she had no idea how.

In all of her courtly lessons over the years, from etiquette to ballroom dancing, to botany, Rose couldn't recall a single one discussing anything related to sexual urges or desires. The only time they had bothered to touch upon a subject even close to that was when the girls started getting their monthly cycle, and the lesson had been very brief. The teacher explained that their "lady business" was an integral part of their ability to bear children for the noblemen. She instructed the girls to wear a rag and wash it daily. They were not to speak of their bleeding to anyone, as if their monthly visitor was taboo, a source of shame and embarrassment over their bodies. She refused to entertain any other questions on the topic, leaving the girls relatively uninformed.

When Rose was fourteen years old, she suffered from horrible cramps with no knowledge of how to ease the pain. She dared not broach the subject with anyone after her instructor's admonition that it was imprudent. Thankfully, her mother noticed her discomfort and drew her a hot bath, which helped.

Rose wished she could talk to her mother in the hope that she would help her now like she had then. She wanted to ask Anne about her urges but doubted Anne could possibly understand how strong they were. Her mother had already made it clear there would be no discussion of the night senders. And Rose couldn't imagine sitting across the table from Anne describing the physical arousal she was feeling, and asking for advice on how to satisfy herself. Certainly, that wouldn't be construed as "proper" and might merit some type of punishment in her mother's eyes.

Unable to confide in her mother, unarmed with any knowledge of her own, and with no one to teach her how to pleasure herself, Rose began to feel mounting frustration. She wondered if the purpose of the night senders was to inadvertently force the court girls into marriage. She reasoned that the night senders must instill the court girls with this insatiable desire so that they were left desperately seeking any outlet that could satiate it. Desperate people will do anything, even marry one of those insufferable noblemen. But could the noblemen really satisfy a woman's desire? If the court girls weren't taught anything about onanism, were the men? She didn't know but doubted that sexual prowess was a topic that went alongside economics and politics.

She knew her theory was also flawed because she was apparently the only court girl who had derived any gratification from the night sender's visit. Therefore, she would be the only one motivated by physical pleasure, or would she?

Vivianna's face entered Rose's mind. She had been so preoccupied with her own desire she had forgotten about her encounters with Vivianna. Outside the library, the girl insinuated that she knew where to find information, though it was Rose's assumption that she meant information about the night senders. When Vivianna recited her story the night of Rose's party, she elaborated more than the other girls. Rose remembered her saying that she experienced a culmination between her legs, just as Rose did, a fact none of the other girls articulated in their accounts. It was clear that Vivianna knew something, and Rose was now desperate enough to seek her help.

12

That morning, Anne was waiting for Rose at breakfast.

"Good morning, child." Her tone was rosy, which always made Rose nervous. It usually meant her mother had something for her to do that she would not find appealing.

Rose sighed. "Good morning, mother."

She sat down opposite her mother and selected a blueberry muffin from the basket of freshly baked goods in the middle of the round maple table. It was still warm to the touch, the smell intoxicating. Rose inhaled the delicious treat, licking the melted blueberry remnants from her fingers.

"Must you do that at the table?" Anne's tone was reproachful.

Rose ignored her and reached for another muffin. Her mother's hand lifted, threatening to smack Rose's away from the basket. Ultimately, Anne refrained, placing it back on the table. Rose surmised from her restraint that Anne was about to ask her for something appalling.

"I have someone for you to meet." Her mother smiled brightly, but her enthusiasm was not catching.

Rose's teeth clenched. She had considered that the purpose of the night senders may be to force marriages but hadn't fathomed the possibility that her mother would try to arrange one for her just two weeks after her eighteenth birthday.

"His name is Charles Devano, and he's a wonderful man only four years older than you. His family is quite well known in the import/export industry.

Why they're even responsible for importing all of that wonderful chocolate you love so much." Anne gleamed at Rose like she was offering her a coveted gift.

Rose sat, silently eating her muffin, bran this time and stared at her mother blankly.

"Rose?" Her mother prompted. "Don't you have anything you'd like to say?"

Without looking up from her muffin, Rose responded in a cool, even tone.

"Unless you are interested in me purchasing any of that wonderful chocolate for you, mother, I have absolutely no interest in meeting this Charles Devano."

Anne's smile faded. "And why on earth would that be?"

Rose was heated now. She was still angry with her mother after their last argument.

"Because I'm not about to let you pawn me off on some detestable nobleman. I have no interest in being courted by a man I've never met solely for the purpose of marrying because we'd make a suitable match. I'm eighteen years old for Heaven's sake! I want to live my life, not get married!"

Her mother pursed her lips in disapproval.

"Yes, Rose, you are eighteen years old. And yet this is quite a juvenile outburst. No one said anything about marrying this man. I simply asked you to meet him."

Anne's insinuation that she was still a child ignited her fury even more.

"I refuse to meet him!" Rose was screaming now. All of the pent up sexual frustration she couldn't comprehend was rising to the surface, along with her urge to defy the expectations placed upon her by the court. "You cannot force me, and I will not meet him!"

Rose moved to get up, but Anne grabbed her by the forearm across the table.

"Listen to me, child," she demanded. "You are my daughter, and you live in Dover. We are bound by tradition, and you will follow it."

Rose yanked her arm, but her mother had a firm grip.

"Oh, and one other thing, young lady. I spoke with Mrs. Weston the other day, who was excited that my daughter has decided to take her courtly duties so seriously. You and I both know that's a fallacy. I don't know what you're up to, or what you were really searching for in that library, but mark my words, I will find out. So I suggest you cease this fruitless search immediately before you find yourself in even more trouble than you are right now."

Rose glared at Anne. "Mother, the only mystery around here is you." She pulled her arm abruptly, breaking loose from Anne's grip.

Rose stalked out of the dining room to find peace in the one place she could always count on as a sanctuary.

13

For the past two weeks, Roosha had barely left the cave. He knew he needed to put the idea of seeing Rose far out of his mind, yet every time he made his way out of the cave, he felt pulled towards her. He couldn't understand what it was about this girl that had such a magnetic force over him.

Roosha had several interactions with Avidan, all of which had been abnormally brief. He sensed that Avidan was distancing himself from him after their conversation on the hill. This further indicated to Roosha the seriousness of the situation Avidan refused to discuss with him. It also served as strong evidence that Roosha needed to steer clear of Rose despite how wrong that felt inside him.

"Roosha!" Someone was yelling his name from the corridor outside his small cave. "Roosha!"

He stepped out into the stone-carved hall and followed the sound of the voice. It sounded like Avidan.

"Avidan?" He yelled back.

Avidan was waiting for him at the end of the passageway.

"Felonious has another assignment for you tonight." Avidan grasped Roosha's shoulder and pulled him in close. "Make sure to stick to protocol." Avidan gave Roosha a hard, meaningful look and then disappeared down the hall. Roosha went off in search of Felonious, disappointed that he would be visiting someone other than Rose.

14

Rose stood in the barn, grooming her beautiful black mare, Carmera. The horse came into Rose's life when she was eleven years old and had been her closest companion ever since. Rose appreciated the animal's pure, peaceful nature. Carmera didn't judge, gossip, or scheme. The mare didn't have any preconceived notions of Rose's wanting to gallop across the forest for hours to feel the freedom of escape and the rhythmic movement between her legs. Her love was pure and unconditional.

"Am I interrupting?" A familiar voice called out, one that Rose recognized.

"Good morning, Vivianna," Rose responded politely.

"I was hoping we'd run into each other here at some point."

"Were you now?" Rose asked curiously.

"Yes. I believe we have some things to discuss that are better suited to this more intimate setting than one of the court gatherings." Vivianna tilted her head towards Rose. "Wouldn't you agree?"

"Perhaps." Rose still wasn't sure whether she could trust Vivianna, so she decided to proceed cautiously. Vivianna gave her a seemingly genuine smile.

"Well then, let me ask you, how was your nighttime visit?" Her suggestive tone insinuated that she already had an answer in mind.

Rose's body tensed up. Carmera shifted nervously next to her, picking up on Rose's sudden change in mood.

"Why would I tell you anything about that? Aren't you one of Savannah's bidders?"

Vivianna laughed. "Oh, Rose, you don't have to make yourself a subject of ridicule the way you do to be different. I find it much more peaceful to let them think I'm like them and reserve my original thoughts and opinions for myself."

This explanation took Rose by surprise. It appeared that Vivianna was smarter than Rose realized. She preferred being the quiet observer who minded her real thoughts, rather than the outspoken target Rose had made herself. But that didn't automatically make her trustworthy.

A full minute passed with Rose continuing to brush her horse in silence. She was desperate to talk to someone about her visit, and about the night senders, but at the same time, she was afraid that revealing too much would work against her.

Sensing her hesitation, Vivianna spoke first.

"Hmm, perhaps it would be more prudent if I were to go first. My first nighttime visit was absolutely lovely and not painful at all. In fact, it was quite pleasant."

Rose froze. Had she heard Vivianna correctly, she wondered. Vivianna specifically said that her first nighttime visit was absolutely lovely. But if she had specified that it was her first, was it possible that Vivianna had received a second visit? That was unheard of, and if that was the case, Rose was determined to know how she had managed it.

"First?" Rose prompted.

Vivianna smiled; she had been sure Rose would not miss that word.

"Yes, Rose. You see, I found my nighttime visit so stimulating I woke up longing to repeat it."

Rose was taken aback. She thought she was the only one who had ever derived any pleasure from the night senders and was relieved to discover she was not alone.

"But how? How did you manage to secure a second visit?"

"That morning at breakfast, I told my mother that after my visit, I had now been seeing women in a new light; that I fancied them more than men. I told her how Betsy, one of our maids, had the most supple little breasts that I suddenly wanted to feel pressed against my own."

Rose burst out laughing, and so did Vivianna.

"You should have seen her reaction! All of the blood drained from her face. Her dark skin faded so much I thought it would turn white!" She snorted. "My mother didn't say a word to me the rest of the day, but she must have sent some urgent message because my night sender was back that night."

Rose's side hurt from how hard she was laughing. The thought of her own longing for a second visit made her laughter subside.

"How did you keep this from Savannah? And the rest of the court women for that matter?"

"I knew the last thing my mother would want was a rumor circulating that I preferred the company of women, especially considering she already had a suitor lined up for me. There was no way she would risk telling anyone. Based on her ability to arrange my second visit in such a covert fashion, I believe my mother must have a direct line of communication with the night senders. Otherwise, I don't know how the other ladies of the court wouldn't know ... unless they were sworn to secrecy on the subject."

Rose thought Vivianna's words over. If her mother had a direct connection to the night senders, perhaps that's how Vivianna had access to more information on them.

"But what about Savannah? She's the queen of gossip. I couldn't even keep my erotic book from her, and that was buried beneath hay in the barn loft, which is not a place you would ever expect to find Savannah."

"You just have to know how to handle her. Whenever I'm with Savannah, I always keep her focused on her favorite subject, herself. When she was asking too many pointed questions about my nighttime visit, I noticed she was wearing a new pair of shoes. I popped my head up with a bright smile and exclaimed how much I adored them. That compliment instigated a twenty-minute monologue on where the shoes came from, who made them, how much they cost, and how a lady must always sacrifice comfort for style. While I bore the boredom of learning all about her shoes, her attention was entirely redirected, ceasing all questions about my visit."

"Brilliant." Rose's eyes were filled with admiration. Clearly, Vivianna possessed a cunning nature, one from which Rose could learn.

"What happened the second night?"

"He went through the same ritual, this time biting me on the other side of my neck. All I know is that it sent the same delicious pulsating waves of pleasure all over my body." Vivianna smiled sheepishly. "I've never felt as alive as I felt after that first bite."

Rose knew what Vivianna meant. She had felt the exact same way. She was still shocked that another court girl responded so strongly.

"I understand what you mean," Rose said wistfully. Vivianna nodded. "The very next day, I awoke to my mother sitting at the foot of my bed. She had been waiting for me to wake up so she could tell me she had the loveliest nobleman for me to meet."

"Are you talking about your husband, Edmund?"

"Yes, Edmund indeed." Vivianna looked down at her wedding ring and turned it around her finger. "When she introduced me to him, I thought he was very nice. Clever and quite funny. I also knew she was expecting this match to work, and I thought that if I agreed to it, then at least I would have a husband to please me every night. That perhaps then, there would be no need for a night sender."

"How has that been?" Rose inquired tentatively. Despite her doubts, she still wanted to know whether the noblemen had received some training that would teach them to give pleasure the way the night senders did.

Vivianna's smile faded. Her green eyes that moments before had been beaming with excitement now seemed far away. Rose sensed that the answer to her question would confirm her intuition about the noblemen. Vivianna's eyes refocused. She looked Rose directly in the eye.

"Wanting, actually."

Rose felt a great deal of empathy for Vivianna at that moment. She had been married to Edmund for almost three months already. Rose couldn't imagine how difficult it must be to lie with a man night after night knowing what real satisfaction feels like, and not experiencing it with him. Before she could respond, Vivianna changed the subject.

"Now, to the task at hand. What do you know about the night senders?"

"Not much," Rose admitted. "My mother didn't tell me anything other than they would bring me great pain, and that it was imperative I keep my mask on during my visit. As we both know, she was wrong about the pain. I also know from my own research that the timeline is odd. Dover has been around for over three hundred years, but the night senders only seem to date back about a century. I want to know who they are, where they came from, and what their purpose is."

"Very astute of you to pick up on the dates." Vivianna nodded her head in approval. "I grappled with the same questions, not knowing what to do about them, that is, until one fateful day in the library."

Rose's eyes burned with curiosity, wanting to hear every detail of what Vivianna was about to tell her.

"Growing up, I had always wanted to see the basement of the library, but my mother said it was no place for a child. The one time I snuck down there, she made every attempt to scare me off. She told me all of the books were cursed ... that evil spirits lurked within them, ones that preyed on young girls." Vivianna twisted her face into a demonic expression, her eyes wide and possessed.

Rose tittered, only because it seemed appropriate. Her mind was too fixated on the night senders to really concentrate on Vivianna's backstory.

"At ten years old, the threat seemed real enough to keep my curiosity at bay. But now I realize that there are ghosts down there, not scary ones, but ones with stories, quite fascinating ones, I'd imagine."

Rose leaned in closer, her expression bewildered. Were these stories of the night senders, she pondered.

"What do you mean?"

"There are three diaries in that basement, ones I'm convinced are connected to the night senders."

Rose gasped. "How do you know that?"

"The other day, I agreed to help my mother transfer old books to the basement below the library when a group of women needed her assistance on the main floor. She gave me her set of keys and told me to start without her. When I reached the basement door, I noticed that one of the keys she gave me was significantly different from the others. I had never seen it before. It was long and black with a red wing inscribed on it. Downstairs, the afternoon light poured in from a narrow window, illuminating the room. I put the books I was carrying on the bottom step and inspected the odd space. It wasn't eerie the way my mother described it; it was intriguing. Worn, rickety shelves lined the walls, housing ancient books with yellowed pages. Their musty stench permeated the air. In the center was a disorganized pile of boxes and antiquities. In the far corner, I saw a red trunk. It seemed to stand out somehow. I went over to it and brushed a thick layer of dust off the top. There was a wing symbol etched into the wood that matched the one inscribed on the key. Quickly, I pulled out the key, placed it in the lock, and turned it. The chest creaked open slowly, dust flying into my face. Inside were three ancient looking leather-bound books. I picked one up carefully and flipped it open. It was a diary written by a noblewoman. I scanned through a couple of pages as quickly as possible, but then I heard footsteps approaching the top of the stairs. I immediately closed the book, put it back exactly where I had found it, and locked the trunk. By the time my mother walked into the room, I was sorting the books she had asked me to bring down there."

Rose looked at her, flabbergasted. She didn't know where to begin. Could Vivianna have discovered the only source of history that would provide any explanation on the night senders?

Rose fumbled for words, finally putting a coherent question together. "Did you see anything about the night senders written in the books?"

"No. I didn't want to risk my mother walking in on me while I was anywhere near that trunk, so as soon as I heard footsteps, I stopped reading. But I'm sure they will tell us something important." Her tone was confident.

"What makes you so sure?"

"Logic. What are we told about the night senders, aside from the fact that we should fear them?" She looked at Rose expectantly.

Rose sifted through any detail she had heard from her mother, or any other ladies of the court until her eyes lit up, understanding of Vivianna's train of thought.

"That they have enormous wings!"

"Exactly!" Vivianna mirrored her enthusiasm. "Also, what purpose is there in keeping three diaries in a locked trunk in the basement of the library? Mind you, a library run by a woman who seems to have direct communication with the night senders. It must be to hide them, or better yet, to keep their contents secret."

Rose couldn't argue that Vivianna had a valid point. It wasn't the only plausible explanation, but it was a theory with merit. And she wanted to find out if Vivianna was right.

"Does your mother have any idea you saw them?"

"Of course not! Like I said before, Rose, you don't always have to wear your emotions on your sleeve. When my mother found me, I was perfectly calm, the way she had left me. I gave her back the keys without waiting for her to ask, and when she asked me how the book sorting was going, I replied in my usual way. Sometimes observing without reacting warrants much more felicitous results." Vivianna gave her a sly smile.

Rose was impressed. Clearly, she had underestimated Vivianna in many ways. Not only was this girl different from the rest, but unlike Rose, Vivianna was smart enough to maintain a poker face. She never gave herself away, earning the trust of the other court girls and keeping her affairs private. Rose needed to learn how to be more like Vivianna.

"So then how do you plan on us gaining access to these diaries?"

"That I'm still figuring out. My mother is the only one I know who has the keys to that room and the trunk, and she guards them well. But she also always needs help in the library, so that may be our best option."

"We could volunteer," Rose exclaimed. "There's a whole chapter in that abhorrent book your mother gave me about the importance of charitable use of a court lady's time."

Vivianna looked at Rose, assessing her.

"If we do this, our efforts must be furtive. We cannot do anything to arouse suspicion. My mother cannot have an inkling that we are looking for anything, nor must we give Savannah any indication that our relationship has changed. Believe me, if she suspects anything, she will cause trouble. You'll have to control your reactions Rose, especially around her."

Rose's lips curled into an offended pout. She didn't appreciate Vivianna's implication that she was incapable of hiding her emotions. Rose opened her mouth to speak, but Vivianna spoke first.

"This is exactly what I'm referring to. Your facial expression just now indicated you were displeased with my assertions. You must learn to control your expressions, Rose. Otherwise, we don't stand a chance of pulling this off."

Rose could feel her face automatically starting to rearrange itself and concentrated on remaining smooth and expressionless. She looked at Vivianna straight-faced.

"I will get myself under control. I want us to follow through on this mission."

Vivianna surveyed Rose carefully and then nodded in approval.

"Much better. I'll speak to my mother about helping in the library and then let you know the next step in the plan."

"Okay," said Rose, again trying to suppress all emotion from her words. It felt unnatural, but she understood why it was of great importance.

Vivianna nodded curtly.

"I'll see you tonight, at Amelia's party. Not a word, nor an inclination to anyone." She looked at Rose sternly and then exited the barn.

"Curses," Rose muttered to herself.

She had forgotten that Amelia's birthday was so close to hers. She disdained the idea of attending this soiree. Amelia Delacorte was

Savannah's closest friend, if one could consider her a friend. To Rose, Amelia seemed more a competitor than a crony, stealthily vying for Savannah's position in the group, making her more unbearable.

Rose ran her hand along Carmera's neck and contemplated. She had been so eager to learn more about the night senders that she agreed to team up with Vivianna without considering if she could be fully trusted.

But at the same time, Rose had no other option. There was no one else she could talk to about the night senders, and she had no way of accessing such valuable information on her own. It was either work with Vivianna or manage to forget about them altogether, which Rose could not do. Finally, she was on the path to discovery, and she refused to turn back, even if that path was laden with thorns.

15

Rose traipsed up the steps to Amelia's abode, clutching a bouquet of fresh-cut peonies that Anne had forced her to bring. The flowers were a delicate pink surrounded by baby's breath. It was considered the quintessential arrangement for this affair. Rose had received four of them at her own party and detested the colors. Her favorite flower was a classic red rose. It was bold and beautiful, but still fierce. Its sharp thorns protected the rose from predators, making it more powerful than a fragile pink peony.

Rose was grateful her mother had acquiesced to her request for roses at her own party. However, it was only after Rose identified that it would be ludicrous not to let her choose the flower she was named after. Anne conceded, albeit begrudgingly, and stipulated that they could not all be red. Rose agreed, provided none of them were pink.

At the top of the stairs was a large red entryway flanked by two ornate pillars. In the center of each door was a sizable solid-gold knocker shaped like a crown. Rose grimaced at the sight of them. They were far too garish for her taste.

Rose hesitated, stricken with apprehension. In the past two weeks, she had been able to avoid answering questions on her night sender visit. She attended to all of her courtly duties and left quickly after so that Savannah could not corner her, but tonight that would not be an option.

At a party with only twelve attendees, Savannah would have a multitude of chances to approach Rose, not that it mattered. Traditionally, the girls who were already eighteen would voluntarily recount the tale of their visit, as was done at her party. In her current state, Rose worried she would crack under interrogation, and did not want to do anything to jeopardize her new mission with Vivianna.

Knowing her fate was inevitable, she grasped the repulsive crown and knocked on the door, hoping no one would answer.

"Good evening, Miss Woodburn, I presume." The maid greeted her politely. She must have been the last to arrive. "Please come in. All of the other ladies are in the salon."

The house was even more opulent on the inside, though it was hardly noticeable amidst the hundreds – possibly thousands - of flowers. Every surface was bursting with lavender. There were lavender arrangements on every table, and petals strewn across the wood floors. The scent was usually calming to Rose, but in this amount, it was overwhelming, bordering on noxious.

Rose made her way to the salon, where the girls were chatting in groups of two or three. Vivianna was speaking to Amelia, making it an opportune time for Rose to rid herself of the flowers she was holding, not that Amelia needed any more.

"Well, well, Rose Woodburn. So you made it to my party after all." Amelia's voice was thick with derision, but her nose made it difficult to take her seriously. The tip was flat and pointed slightly upward. It reminded Rose of a pig, which is perhaps why Savannah sometimes referred to her as piglet. Supposedly it was a term of endearment, though Amelia's hefty frame made the nickname all the more unflattering.

"As you made it to mine." Rose matched her tone.

"You've been disappearing so quickly lately we all thought you must be ill. At least, more so than normal."

"Not quite." Eager to change the subject, Rose held up the bouquet. "These are for you. They'll stand out nicely against all of this uniform purple." Rose extended her hand with the flowers, but Amelia made no move to take them. Instead, she glared back at Rose.

"Have you forgotten your etiquette lessons entirely, little Rose?" Amelia exuded condescension. "You're supposed to leave gifts for the hostess with the maid. I cannot leave my guests unattended to put those weeds in water right this second."

"Of course." Rose felt her face contorting and focused on regaining her composure. She smiled, but it was forced, her mouth exposing too many teeth. She was sure it must have appeared a bit mad. "Would you excuse me?" Rose nodded at Amelia and Vivianna and then turned on her heel, intending to march straight out. She slammed the bouquet onto an end table jammed with purple blooms and had her hand on the knob when she was intercepted by Savannah.

"Why, Rose, you're not leaving so early, are you?"

Rose froze, unsure of what move to make. She debated the consequences of her actions both ways. Undoubtedly, Anne would be made aware of an abrupt departure, and this unbecoming behavior would raise her suspicions. If she stayed, Rose risked having an outburst, which would make her even more of a spectacle. Already tense, she refused to be catechized by the girls.

"Surely, you're finally going to regale us with the tale of your nighttime visit," Savannah insisted, her attitude patronizing. "And, of course, let us take a look beneath that scarf of yours."

The blood gathered furiously beneath Rose's cheeks, threatening to reveal her anger and embarrassment. She opened her mouth to speak when a voice called from behind them.

"Savannah, thank God, I found you. Amelia requires your audience immediately."

"What does little piglet want now?" Savannah muttered. She took off towards the salon, pausing in the archway. "Oh, and Vivianna, do make sure Rose graces us with her presence at story time."

"Of course, Savannah," Vivianna responded obediently.

Rose shot her a look of betrayal. Once Savannah was through to the other room, Rose reached for the door once again.

"What are you doing? You can't just leave," Vivianna urged.

"Oh yes I can, that is, unless you plan on stopping me," Rose challenged.

"If you want any chance of gaining access to those diaries, you will stay here and tell the story. Notice I said the story, not your story." Vivianna eyed her carefully. "Don't put up a fight, Rose, just tell the version they do and be done with it. Consider it a test of how well you can manage your emotions. Don't react to anything they say, and if you feel yourself succumbing to emotions, breathe deeply before responding."

Rose followed suit immediately, filling her lungs to capacity and then slowly releasing the air. She knew Vivianna's advice was sound. All she had to do to survive the party was tell them exactly what they wanted to hear; that they were right. There was no reason to let passion get the best of her. These girls weren't worthy of the truth. She inhaled again, the flow of oxygen relaxing the muscles in her face, and allowed Vivianna to drag her into the other room.

"Why Rose, we've been waiting for you!" Savannah motioned for her to sit on an ottoman in the middle of the group. Rose reluctantly eased onto the green velvet. "We're all greatly anticipating your story." Savannah snatched Rose's scarf, exposing her smooth skin, and almost choking her in the process. She sat down with the other girls, contempt plastered across her face as she stared at Rose's neck.

Rose glanced briefly at Vivianna, who gave her the same stern look she had in the barn. Rose shifted uncomfortably, keeping her eyes on the floor.

"Well, Savannah, I'm afraid there isn't much to tell." Rose's voice was soft. "It was just as you said. The creature bit me on the neck, and it was fairly painful." She loathed lying about the pain and perpetuating this falsehood but understood it was for the best.

"And where are your bite marks, Rose Woodburn? I don't see any marks on your neck." Savannah glared at her accusingly.

"I don't have any. It's rather uncanny." At least that part was accurate, Rose thought to herself.

"So, you admit you were wrong to doubt me the other day?"

Rose looked at Savannah's smug expression, dissent bubbling inside her. She refused to admit she was wrong to question Savannah. The girl was already a tyrant. If no one ever challenged her, her behavior would worsen, perhaps approaching that of a merciless dictator. Rose swallowed her disdain and spoke slowly, her words measured.

"I was wrong to assume you were lying about the bite. Clearly, you were not lying about that aspect of the experience."

Savannah's eyes narrowed to slits. "And which aspect of it was I lying about, Rose?"

Rose shrugged. "None of it, I suppose. An opinion isn't necessarily right or wrong." She unknowingly twisted her mouth into a smirk.

Savannah started to fume. Her fists were balled up tightly, her nails cutting into her palms. She opened her mouth to unleash her wrath but was interrupted by a procession of servants carrying a cake and a group of male minstrels bearing violins and flutes. The handsome musicians charged into the salon, kneeling at Amelia's feet and serenading her with birthday praises. With the girls thoroughly distracted, Rose seized the opportunity to sneak out discreetly.

ROSE ARRIVED HOME SAFELY, proud of herself. Though she failed to maintain perfect composure, she had not given away any vital information. Hopefully, no further suspicions had been aroused in Savannah than were ordinarily present. Managing to get under Savannah's skin in the process had also given her a sense of satisfaction, albeit a childish one.

Rose gazed over the city and sky from her balcony, inhaling deeply. As she exhaled, she released the longing that had eaten away at her for days; released the need for another midnight encounter. Shutting the doors behind her, Rose slipped into bed without performing her ritual. She drifted to sleep, at peace with the notion that hopefully soon, with Vivianna's help, she would learn more about the night senders.

16

Roosha soared through the night sky on the way to his next assignment, Amelia Delacorte. He was already dreading the experience, as he could only assume this girl would be no different from the standard court girls.

At exactly midnight, Roosha flew in through the girl's window to find Amelia lying in the middle of her large bed, her limbs clamped tightly together. She was clutching a cross in her right hand and held it firmly against her chest.

Roosha couldn't understand the fear that had been instilled in these girls. It was as if this adolescent before him waited for some blood-sucking demon to attack her in the night. Instead of applying reason where he could see none, Roosha decided to finish his task as quickly as possible. He would leave the girl in peace and extract himself from this depressing situation.

Roosha took a couple of soundless steps toward the bed and then leapt lightly onto the girl so that she was restrained beneath him, but not crushed under his weight. He looked down at her, and a wave of both guilt and disappointment came over him.

Her body was shaking so hard he could hear her teeth chattering. Avidan was right; the mind is a fortress even magic cannot penetrate. Roosha knew that even if he used all of his powers, there was no way he could break through the deep-set fear implanted within this girl. In this case, he felt it would have been more merciful to leave her be, but he was bound by law to complete his assignment.

Without delay, he bit into her neck. Her fearful gasps fell directly upon his ear. He could smell the beads of perspiration gliding down her temple. They reeked of terror. She shook violently, her body thrashing, and her lungs gulped for air as if she were taking her last breath. Roosha remained on top of her, pinning her arms down until her convulsions subsided, and she passed out.

Once she was asleep, his duty was fulfilled. Roosha stood up and walked over to the window. He sat perched on the ledge, contemplating. This is such a waste of our abilities, he thought to himself. Here we are with all of these enhanced features designed specifically to deliver ecstasy. Yet, we're stuck using them on a class of women who are taught to fear bodily pleasure as if it were the means to a slow and agonizing death. Meanwhile, he knew that it was the other way round; that a life lived without physical contentment was a slow and agonizing death. That fate was part of being a night sender.

He thought of Rose, who was dying to experience more physical gratification, and how he was forbidden from returning to her. It made no sense to him. Why should he deny the one court girl who had a chance to live a full, impassioned life the gift of sensual satisfaction? He knew it would cause him physical pain, but that would be far easier than the mental anguish of "torturing" her petrified counterparts. At that moment, he knew his decision was made.

Roosha stood up on the ledge, his resolve unwavering. He was done abiding by absurd rules that served no purpose. He leapt through the window, allowing his wings to carry him to the one place he had wanted to go for what seemed like an eternity now, Rose's bedroom.

17

Roosha landed silently on Rose's balcony, firmly planting himself on the stone platform. He couldn't believe he was finally back there. Roosha peered through the glass doors and saw her lying in bed. She wasn't wearing the mask.

Despite his earlier resolve, he was wary of her actually seeing him, considering how different, or downright monstrous, he would appear to her. The last thing Roosha wanted was to frighten the girl. If she screamed, it could put them both at risk of discovery. The image of Rose's parents barging into the room made him shudder. Roosha scanned the immediate area, finally spotting the mask on her bedside table. Perhaps, if he could reach it before she awoke, he could safely fasten the silk over her eyes.

Roosha tested the handle on one of the balcony doors, pulling it downward. It was unlocked. As he eased it open, the door creaked slightly. His eyes immediately shot to Rose's face, but she did not stir. She must be asleep, he concluded.

Roosha entered slowly, stopping at the foot of Rose's bed. He wasn't feeling his normal assuredness. For the first time, he felt nervous, unsure of what to do next. The night senders were only prepared to follow a strict protocol. Enter quietly, unseen by anyone. Once inside, they were to position themselves over the girl so that she was gently, but firmly pinned against the bed. Then they bit into her neck, releasing their powers. Once the girl had fallen asleep, or more likely, passed out from fear, they were to leave, again unseen. He had broken that particular part of the protocol with Rose. She was very much awake when he bolted out the doors. But never before had a court girl begged him to stay, and so he fled, afraid of the ramifications if he remained in that room a second longer.

But now, as he stood before Rose, there was no protocol to follow. He would have to decide how to proceed. His first objective was to affix the mask to her beautiful face. He leapt quietly, landing alongside her night table. He draped the white cover carefully over her eyes.

The smooth silk glided across Rose's skin, rousing her from her sleep. Her eyes blinked, each time opening to the wall of white. She hoped she was dreaming again. Her hands instinctively moved to her face, probing the soft fabric beneath her fingertips. Roosha's body tensed. He was unsure what he would do if she attempted to remove it.

Rose's heart started beating faster. She remembered going to sleep without the mask on that night. And to her knowledge, there was only one entity that would have crept into her room so late to affix it to her face. She breathed deeply, inhaling his scent. It was the same musky aroma that had previously tantalized her nostrils, only more potent.

She smiled, aware that he was in the room with her. Finally, her night sender had returned. Again Rose filled her lungs, sending a flow of fresh air to the parts of her body that coveted his attention, regions that had been raging with an uncontainable fire since their first encounter. As she released the air through her mouth, the flames calmed, and her body relaxed, knowing it was about to be satiated.

Rose yearned for a glimpse of this creature, but fought the desire, placing her hands back on the bed without disturbing the mask. The vivid memory of his abrupt departure from the last time she attempted to remove the mask compelled her to behave. She refused to do anything that might make him leave.

When Roosha saw that she wasn't resisting the mask, his posture relaxed as well. He wasn't ready for her to see him.

"Thank you for coming back," Rose beamed.

Roosha paused, surprised that she was talking to him, and taken aback by the sincere gratitude in her voice. His first inclination was to respond, but he doubted that speaking to her was wise. He envisioned how furious Avidan would be, knowing that not only had Roosha returned, but he'd also revealed to Rose that the night senders could understand and communicate with humans.

"May I ask your name?" As soon as she said it, Rose felt silly. Why would I presume he has a name, she thought to herself. She didn't know what kind of creature it was, how it came to exist, or even what it looked like. All she had ascertained from grabbing its arm was that it had soft skin and a muscular build.

"Do you even have a name? Can you speak?" Again she felt somewhat ridiculous for trying to converse with the night sender. At the same time, she sensed there was something very human about this bringer of pleasure. It also occurred to her that if Vivianna's mother had successfully delivered a message to them, the night senders must understand some language, presumably English.

Roosha decided he wasn't ready to speak with her. Instead, he placed one of his fingers over her lips to silence her. The touch of his skin warmed her lips. She felt the urge to devour his finger the way she did those delectable blueberry muffins but worried that if she were too forward, he would flee. As he continued tracing his fingertip around her full lips, all thoughts were temporarily driven from her mind. Her attention was consumed by the tingling sensations swirling around her.

Roosha climbed firmly on top, careful not to put any weight on her. Instead of biting her neck, he licked the base of her earlobe to her collarbone. His tongue emitted subtle vibrations that tickled her skin, turning her entire body into an erogenous zone. Rose felt a rumble of pleasure build in the sensual cavern between her legs, like a formerly dormant volcano preparing for an eruption.

Rose's hands moved to cup her sensitive breasts. Following her motions, the night sender slid the straps of her gown down to her sides, revealing her supple chest. Her nipples were already at attention. His eyes marveled at the soft, creamy flesh beneath him that was so longing to be touched.

He placed one hand above each of Rose's breasts. Her back arched as her breasts were drawn to his hands. They were abnormally warm, as if he'd just held them over an open flame. The heat made her chest more tender and sent a rush of warmth throughout her entire body.

The night sender traced his tongue from her collarbone to her breasts, slowly encircling each nipple. Rose gasped. His tongue had suddenly turned incredibly cold and felt like ice against her skin. He flicked it back and forth over her nipples, each flick delivering sharp pangs of pleasure. The alternating hot and cold sensations titillated her skin, eliciting unruly moans of ecstasy.

The last thing Rose remembered was feeling out of control, her body convulsing without the consent of her mind while his tongue induced further arousal. Then the world went dark.

The next morning, she awoke to a body ripe with sensual desire, hoping what she'd experienced the previous night was only the beginning.

18

"Where were you last night?" Avidan was standing in the dark hall outside of Roosha's stone cubicle.

"Greetings, Avidan. How are you, friend?" Roosha was feeling elated from his encounter with Rose, despite Avidan's accusatory tone. Avidan didn't return the pleasantries.

"Your assignment was at midnight, yet you didn't check back in with Felonious until three hours later. Where were you?"

"Checking up on me, were you, my dear friend?"

Avidan's expression remained unrelentingly stern. Roosha's elation subsided as his protective instincts took over. Despite the camaraderie he usually felt with Avidan, Roosha was unsure of his trustworthiness. He dared not put Rose at risk from his decision to break the laws of the realm.

"I went for a long flight to dispel the dejection from last night's assignment. It was abysmal. The poor girl was so terrified it felt like a full-on assault, not a gift."

Technically, Roosha wasn't lying. The experience with Amelia was regrettable and reminded him of the atrocities he committed in his previous life, the ones that had condemned him to the realm of the night senders. The memories made him shudder. Avidan looked at him, unconvinced.

Roosha had, in fact, gone for a more extended flight than he planned. When he left Rose's room, his tongue felt engulfed in flames, and his head throbbed. He flew until he reached an area where he could rest safely. A full hour passed before he regained enough composure to check in with Felonious without arousing suspicion.

"All right, then." Avidan sighed. Roosha heard the skepticism in his voice. He gave Roosha a wary look, thick with implication, but Roosha did not care. He had been enthralled by Rose that night and had no intention of letting anything, or anyone for that matter, prevent him from seeing her again.

The next seven nights, Roosha returned, each time pleasuring Rose until she gave in to the throws of orgasm and passed on to oblivion. Then he would leave, with her in a state of ecstasy, and him in a state of agony. Physically he felt like a masochist needlessly inflicting pain on himself. But in his heart, he believed he was finally doing something worthwhile with his punishment and abilities. He was also developing a fondness for Rose that transcended the physical realm, and it was that fondness that beckoned him to her bed each night.

19

"You've been in an awfully good mood lately." Rose's mother peered at her like a jeweler scrutinizing the gem he was about to purchase for the glaring flaw he knew he would find.

Rose had been a model lady of the court for the past week, practically skipping to all of her classes and meetings, and attending to her duties without complaint. She even managed to be somewhat pleasant with Savannah. Most mothers would relish seeing their daughter in such a cheerful, agreeable state, but Rose's joy only provoked wariness in Anne.

"Don't you want me to be happy, mother?" Rose gave her a genuine smile. Even though she knew her mother would never approve of the source of her happiness, the contentment Rose was feeling was from an authentic place.

"Why, Rose, what mother wouldn't want to see her daughter happy? The problem with you is that usually, it's the wrong things that make you happy. And considering nothing new has occurred in your life that I'm aware of, outside of your sudden enthusiasm for your courtly duties, I'm beginning to think you may be hiding something from me."

Rose was familiar with this tone. It was Anne's way of letting her know that she would be carefully watched from this point forward, that her mother would uncover any and all secrets. Rose felt a sharp pain in the pit of her stomach. The past seven days had been the best of her life. She could not do anything that would jeopardize her now nightly visits. She thought quickly under Anne's glare and devised a solution, or better yet, a distraction. It was the only concession she could think of that might placate her mother enough to call off the scrutinous search into the real root of Rose's happiness.

"I assure you, mother, I'm not keeping anything from you. I do have something to share, though. Frankly, it surprised me so much I've been ruminating on how to discuss it with you."

"Do go on." Anne's expression was unreadable. Vivianna would have been impressed, Rose imagined.

"Well, mother, I've been thinking about what you said last week, and maybe it wouldn't hurt to just meet this Charles Devano…"

Especially if I get some imported chocolate out of it, Rose thought to herself. She wondered what it would be like to have a delectable truffle melting on her tongue while the night sender licked her neck.

"Why, Rose, that's a splendid idea!" Anne was smiling now. "I'm glad you've come to your senses a bit and realized there's no harm in at least meeting the man. He does come from a wonderful family."

Rose was about to roll her eyes when she remembered what Vivianna instructed about controlling her blatant facial expressions. She closed her eyes and opened them with what she hoped was a neutral expression.

"Right, of course, mother. No harm in meeting a person." Rose tried not to make her words sound forced. She clung hard to the notion that this was the best way to keep her night sender safe. Charles would be nothing more than a pawn, a means of keeping her mother distracted from Rose's mood and affairs.

"I'll set up dinner with his family right away." Seemingly excited by this impending social engagement, Rose's mother waltzed jubilantly out of the room. Just as Rose let out a sigh of relief, Anne popped her head back in the doorway.

"Oh, and dear, I am still fully aware that you are up to something. The idea of meeting Charles is surely not the source of your notable glow." Her mother gave her a knowing glance and then disappeared.

Rose swallowed hard and sunk back into the couch. She would have to be very careful.

20

After her encounter with her mother, Rose retreated to the stables to calm her nerves. As she stroked Carmera's neck, she thought of how much elation the horse brought her, and how her mother had tried to ruin that too. At the age of eight, the ladies of the court began their equitation training. They were expected to become skilled riders. In Rose's opinion, it was the most practical skill the girls were taught. From her first ride, she developed a passion for the sport. Rose felt completely free on top of the horse, knowing the animal could carry her far beyond Dover's limits and the limitations of her societal position.

She begged her mother for a horse. Anne promised that if Rose attended her classes and showed excellent discipline in her studies, she would consider getting her a horse when she was a few years older. Rose had been disappointed, but not discouraged.

For the next three years, she arrived early to all of her riding classes and always wanted to be the last to dismount. The five hours per week she spent in the saddle were never enough for her. She was an excellent equestrian who had a way of connecting with her horse. Initially, Rose rode a dapple-gray pony named Cinnamar, who she loved, but she still longed to ride one of the larger, full-size horses.

One day, Rose was out in the fields surrounding Dover picking wildflowers and playing with the other court girls. At that time, she had amicable relationships with almost all of them, though not Savannah, who, at eleven years old, already had a superiority complex. But even then, Rose was still more of an independent soul and went off on her own, exploring the fields. It was there that she came upon a beautiful black mare. Strangely, Rose thought, the horse was entirely on its own - no bridle, no saddle, no rider, and no herd.

Not knowing what to think, Rose remained hidden in the bushes about ten feet away from the animal. The horse's ears flicked in her direction, a sign that it heard her rustling and was aware of her presence. The animal listened but didn't move. Rose was taught that horses were flight animals, so she didn't want to spook the mare and have it run away. She waited quietly and patiently until its ears and posture relaxed. The horse went back to grazing, and Rose cautiously took a few steps closer, and then kneeled down, her eyes on the grass.

The horse raised its head. Rose remained motionless. The animal curiously ventured a few steps toward her. Rose kept her hands at her sides, making sure not to make any abrupt movements that would startle the animal. After a few moments, the mare gingerly approached her. Rose held still as a statue. The horse sniffed her hair and nudged her shoulder with its head. She looked up, absorbed by the massive height of this black beauty. Slowly, Rose raised her head to the horse's nostrils so it could familiarize itself with her breath. The mare nickered, a sign of friendly affection. Encouraged, Rose lifted her hand and placed it gently on the horse's neck, stroking its shiny coat. The animal didn't flinch. The two of them remained there, enjoying each other's presence.

Sometime later, Rose heard her name being called. She had lost track of time, and the other girls were searching for her.

Rose stood up and said to the mare, "Please stay here. I'll come back looking for you later." Then she turned and headed back to where the other girls were playing. The horse trotted alongside her, which exhilarated Rose.

The mare followed her all the way back to the barn that day, where her mother was waiting. When she saw the creature, Anne was displeased. Rose begged for permission to keep the horse, but Anne abhorred the idea of Rose having some sort of "wild" beast about which they knew nothing. She demanded that Rose take the mare back out to the fields and leave her there. Distraught, Rose collapsed on the floor of the stables, bawling. Taking pity on the child, one of the barn hands, an older woman named Carmera, offered to return the horse to the fields so that Rose didn't have to endure the pain of letting her go. Anne agreed and promptly dragged Rose home.

The next day, Rose was depressed and decided to visit Cinnamar in the barn. When she entered the stables, the beautiful black mare was standing in the stall at the end of the row. Flabbergasted, she ran over to greet the horse. The elderly woman, Carmera, was beside the animal waiting for her. She told Rose she would help her train the horse to see if it was rideable. Carmera reasoned that Anne's objection had been to the horse's "wild" nature and that if Rose could learn to ride her, perhaps her mother would agree to let her keep the animal.

Rose eagerly agreed. She promised to listen and follow instructions without question, a first for her. Carmera immediately charged Rose with naming the horse. She sifted through options in her head but decided the horse was too special to merit a common name. Rose trusted that the mare's rightful name would present itself in due course. Carmera did not object.

Together, Rose and Carmera spent months working with the animal until she could perform every trick and stunt better than any of the other horses in the barn. But even after witnessing the steed's talents, Anne was still reluctant, doubtful of the horse's abilities. Rose was convinced her mother's objection stemmed more from the animal being trained by a barn hand, which infuriated Rose.

One week later, the old woman died, and Rose was so despondent over her death that Anne finally conceded and let her keep the horse. Touched by Carmera's empathy and willingness to help her, Rose named the horse after her. From that day forward, the two were inseparable.

Rose was only halfway through brushing out Carmera's long black mane and still consumed by reverie when her train of thought was interrupted by the sound of approaching footsteps. From the clip clopping of heels, Rose was sure it was a woman.

"Hello, Rose," called a familiar voice.

"Hello, Vivianna, how are you?"

Vivianna walked closer until she was right outside Carmera's stall.

"Fine, thank you. And you? I noticed you've been quite sprightly lately, since after Amelia's party." Vivianna grinned at her.

Rose was torn. She expected Vivianna to notice her change in demeanor. The girl had already proved to be very observant. Rose considered opening up to Vivianna about her night sender visits more than once in the past week. But each time she debated sharing her secret, she opted against it, unsure whether she could trust Vivianna with such sensitive information.

"Well, after our last meeting, you told me to act normal, and I'm a very passionate person." As she heard the words aloud, they sounded much less convincing than they had in her mind.

Vivianna smiled coyly at her. "That you are. But not when it comes to your courtly obligations. Being so agreeable in carrying out those duties is not like you at all."

"Just because I'm less obstinate doesn't mean I've become agreeable. Perhaps I'm only placating my mother so that she doesn't pry into our library endeavors." Internally, Rose felt relieved. Her justification was not preconceived, and yet still seemed to her like a plausible explanation.

"Hmm, but you must admit you haven't been the same this week. Beyond your newfound attitude, your cheeks are constantly flushing deep pink. Your features seem softer, and your skin is positively glowing."

Rose gaped at Vivianna. She never realized just how attentive this girl was. Admittedly, Rose hadn't registered all that much change in herself. She was more focused on how amazing she was feeling and had not realized there'd been such a noticeable difference in her outward appearance. Her mother must have caught sight of the same changes. The glow was partly why Anne dismissed her excuse about Charles. Rose considered her cheeks turning pink and reasoned that it must happen naturally when she thought about the night sender, which was often.

Rose felt the warmth spread beneath her cheeks and was suddenly extremely frustrated. Any hope she had of maintaining a neutral face and demeanor vanished in that instant. She was angry with her cheeks for constantly giving her away, enraged by her inability to hide her emotions, and embittered with her mother for continually standing in the way of her happiness.

"You and my mother should have been detectives!" Rose screamed. "Are you both so innately bored with your own lives that you feel the need to take heed of every detail of my appearance and behavior?" Rose was breathing hard but felt better after the release.

Vivianna started laughing.

"Oh, Rose, I see we have a lot more work to do if you are to gain control of your reactions."

Rose abruptly closed her mouth and focused on regaining her composure. She realized then that Vivianna was more interested in testing her after their conversation last week, and what happened at the party, rather than interrogating Rose. She was about to apologize for her outburst, but Vivianna spoke first.

"I did indeed notice significant changes in you because I am more observant than most. I did surmise that there was a reason for these changes, though I didn't know what that reason may be. Your outburst confirmed that there is a reason and that it's sensitive, something your mother certainly wouldn't approve of. I'm not going to ask you what it is because clearly, you don't yet want to disclose that information. The bigger issue at hand is getting your composure under control because we may have an opportunity to get into the basement of the library very soon."

Rose's face brightened. "What do you mean? How?"

"There is a children's book festival at the library next Thursday. I've already informed my mother that you and I would love to help out. She was delighted by the offer."

"That's great news!" Rose was excited the plan was finally taking shape.

"It gets better. At dinner the other night, she complained that they have so many children's books she doesn't know what to do with all of them. I suggested she store some of them in the basement of the library and that we could bring them up gradually throughout the festival. She thought that was a brilliant idea. So it would appear that we will have some access to the basement. The trick will be getting into that trunk."

Rose's eyes were alight with inspiration. It was really happening, she thought to herself; the plan was coming to fruition. And with a festival full of children running around, Rose was hoping Mrs. Weston would be thoroughly distracted and unable to keep close tabs on them.

"This is perfect, Vivianna! The festival is the right opportunity!"

"My, my, if it isn't Rose Woodburn and Vivianna Weston, now Chamberland thanks to dear old Edmund."

Rose cringed. She knew that grating, high-pitched voice that had been etched in her nerves long ago.

"Hello, Savannah." Vivianna greeted her politely.

"Why, Vivianna, are you doing your charity work for the week, spending time with this miscreant?"

Vivianna smiled. "You know I have a soft spot for the downtrodden, Savannah."

"Mm, yes. Like when you adopted that wretched one-eyed cat."

Rose winced at the mention of the animal, but Vivianna's face remained neutral.

Tomtom had been Vivianna's beloved pet from the time she was twelve years old and had only died seven months ago. Vivianna found the small tabby abandoned in a well and nursed him back to health. She fell in love with the cat and refused to let him go. It was the only time she was subjected to severe ridicule by Savannah, and the reason she had punched her in the face, one of Rose's fondest memories. None of the other court girls were there, but Rose was. The three of them were thirteen years old, and out in the garden at Vivianna's house playing hide and seek.

It was Rose's turn to seek, and so she closed her eyes and counted to thirty while Vivianna and Savannah hid. When Rose opened her eyes, she looked around the vast expanse of herbs and flowers. Standing tall in the center of the yard was a delicate Weeping Willow. From beneath its contorted branches and draping wall of greenery, Rose saw a scrap of yellow fabric, the same shade as Savannah's dress. She ran over and tagged her from behind. Rose exerted more force than she'd meant to, knocking Savannah into the dirt. Vivianna emerged from behind the cascading water fountain laughing uproariously.

"What's so funny?" Savannah snarled at her.

"Your dress! It's caked in mud. Now you're bright as the sun and dull as the dirt all in one!" Vivianna had a penchant for rhyming at that age.

"You think you're so clever, don't you?" Savannah fumed. "Let's see how clever you are when that mouth of yours won't save you."

Savannah snatched Tomtom from his grass-bed and held him over the edge of the well, threatening to send him back to where he came from. Vivianna watched in horror as Savannah gripped the cat by the back of its neck, the poor animal wide-eyed and squirming. Tears poured down her face as she pleaded with Savannah to leave Tomtom alone. Savannah cackled so hard that her arms dropped to her sides. Tomtom was able to wriggle out of her grip and safely back to the ground. As soon as his paws hit the grass, Vivianna lunged at Savannah. She tackled her to the ground and punched her square in the jaw.

Savannah tried to scream, but Vivianna cupped her hand over her mouth. Savannah's legs thrashed out, but she was pinned securely to the ground, Vivianna's knees kneading into her rib cage. She leaned over Savannah with a menacing look in her eyes.

"If you ever come near Tomtom again, I will permanently disfigure that beautiful face of yours." There wasn't a shred of humor or jest in Vivianna's threat.

That was the only time Rose ever saw Savannah terrified. When Vivianna finally let her up, Savannah ran as fast as she could from the yard. As far as they knew, she had never breathed a word to anyone about what happened that day. Savannah was more agreeable with Vivianna after that incident and meaner to Rose, who had been nothing more than an innocent bystander.

"Why, Savannah, do you really want to discuss Tomtom?" Vivianna challenged.

A brief look of fleeting terror registered in Savannah's eyes. She immediately changed the subject.

"What's this I hear about a festival?"

"Just a reading event they're having at the library next week for the children," Vivianna answered coolly.

"We're volunteering," Rose offered. "Vivianna is graciously helping me fulfill my charitable hours."

Vivianna shot Rose a sharp, inflamed look. Rose realized right away that she said something she shouldn't have. Savannah's devious smile confirmed that sentiment.

"Well, isn't that just the sweetest thing, and certainly an opportunity I cannot afford to miss. Vivianna, tell your mother I'll be there to help as well."

Vivianna tried to salvage the damage Rose had done to their plan. "Savannah, that is more than kind of you, but this won't really be your type of charity event. There'll be little children all over the place. Lots of noise, and mess, and stickiness."

"Nonsense, Vivianna. If the two of you can handle it, I'm sure I'll be just fine. See you at the festival." Savannah turned on her heels and strutted out of the barn.

Vivianna glared at Rose. "Why did you do that? You never, ever tell Savannah anything!"

"I was just trying to offer an explanation as to why you would be here in the barn talking to me. You said she wasn't to know our relationship had changed, so I was trying to help!"

"She didn't know anything!" Vivianna sounded a bit exasperated. "I wasn't doing anything out of the ordinary. For all she knew, I could have been going around at my mother's behest, informing each of the court girls about the festival. There was no need to offer her any type of explanation. She had no knowledge until you served her the information on a silver platter."

"I'm sorry! I didn't mean to screw it up!" Rose felt the same way she did in many of her arguments with her mother, like a small child acting out.

Vivianna took a deep breath and was calmer when she spoke. "Okay, now we have Savannah to contend with at the festival. Hopefully, it's just her, and she doesn't rope the other girls into volunteering as well. She's just one obstacle. We will not let her deter us from completing our mission."

Rose listened with respect and admiration. Vivianna sounded like an army captain surveying her losses and preparing a new battle plan. She decided she needed to take instruction better and allow Vivianna to lead.

21

"There you are, Rose!" Her mother was frantic. "Oh, dear." She looked Rose up and down disapprovingly. "I see you spent the better part of the day with that horse of yours!"

"Her name is Carmera," Rose gritted through her teeth.

Anne ignored her comment and continued with urgency. "Quickly, my dear, into the bath! We've a special night ahead of us. Charles Devano will be joining us for dinner."

"Pardon me?" Rose wasn't sure she heard her mother correctly. "Didn't we just agree this very morning that I would meet Charles? And now you're telling me he's coming here tonight?"

"Yes, my dear, do keep up!"

"But how? So soon?" Rose was in such a state of shock; it rendered her unable to articulate her outrage.

"I spoke with his mother this morning. It turned out Charles had a cancellation in his plans for this evening, so naturally, I seized the opportunity to invite him for supper. These are busy people, Rose, with a bustling social calendar. You don't squander an opportunity like this." Anne seemed very pleased with herself.

Rose stood, staring at her, speechless. She wondered how the best week of her life had changed direction so rapidly in less than twenty-four hours.

"Hurry now, Rose! Go and get ready! Anne ushered her up the stairs. "Charles will be here at seven-thirty, and it's already half-past five. I've taken the liberty of selecting a suitable outfit for the occasion. The dress has been laid out on your bed, along with appropriate accessories. No, deviations, please."

Rose grimaced but decided not to put up a fight. All she had to do was wear whatever drab outfit Anne had picked out for her and try to be somewhat pleasant to this Charles character, at least in front of her mother. By midnight she would be tucked in bed with this awful day behind her, ready to receive her night sender.

After much yelling from Anne to make sure she was ready on time, at a quarter past seven, Rose descended the stairs and joined her mother in the sitting room. Her mother appraised her appearance with a satisfied smile. Rose wore the dress Anne had chosen, a yellow and white striped silk gown corseted at the waist. The skirt flowed out gradually until it made a giant hoop around her ankles that swished as she walked. Her brown waves were half up and half down, with some stray curls framing her heart-shaped face.

In place of her usual red pout, Rose had painted her lips a delicate pink, the only shade her mother had left on the vanity. She felt much more girlish than she preferred but reminded herself that this charade was simply a means to protect her nightly visits.

"You look beautiful, my dear."

"Thank you, mother." Rose wished her mother had been that chuffed by her appearance on her birthday when Rose looked much more herself.

"Now, remember to be on your best behavior. Do not embarrass me in front of our special guest." Anne's voice was smooth, but the look she gave Rose was sharp.

"Of course not, mother. I wouldn't dream of it." Rose hoped her tone masked her sarcasm, as she was practicing. She decided that afternoon that mastering Vivianna's approach would be both fun and fruitful. Rose smiled at her mother and was met with a skeptical glare.

THE CLOCK STRUCK HALF-PAST EIGHT, and her mother's guest had not yet arrived.

"Could we eat now, mother? I'm famished."

"Of course not, Rose! It would be incredibly rude to start eating when our guest isn't here."

"Isn't it rude to be one hour late to a social engagement without giving due notice?"

Anne winced, and Rose knew she had made a relevant point.

"Yes, but perhaps something happened that prevented him from arriving in a timely fashion. We must give Charles the benefit of the doubt."

The words hit in the same manner as Anne stabbing a knife in her back. Rose couldn't comprehend why her mother had more empathy for this perfect stranger than she did for her own daughter, and herself for that matter.

"He was supposed to be here an hour ago, mother. Perhaps he's not coming after all." Rose didn't mean to sound too hopeful, though she relished the idea of this man her mother speaks so highly of abandoning a social commitment. That wouldn't be proper at all. And maybe then her mother would deem him unsuitable and leave Rose be.

A loud banging pierced the silence; the brass doorknocker thudding hard against the thick wood.

Rose felt a knot in the pit of her stomach. She thought she had avoided this dreadful dinner. But it appeared she would be dining with Mr. Devano after all.

Anne's face grew brighter with each knock. She smoothed her dress with her hands, making sure it wasn't wrinkled from sitting. It infuriated Rose that she was so excited about entertaining someone who had rudely shown up an hour late. She couldn't understand why Anne's rules of etiquette seemed not to apply to Charles.

The maid answered the door and announced Mr. Charles Devano III, who wore an elegant three-piece brown suit. He had shaggy blonde hair, a strong jawline, and blue eyes full of charisma. Rose could see how many women would find him attractive, but she was more interested in the massive box of chocolates Charles held under his right arm than in the man himself.

"Good evening, Mrs. Woodburn!" Charles' tone was magnanimous. "Thank you so much for your generous invitation to dinner this evening." He took Anne's hand gently in his and planted a cordial kiss behind her knuckles.

"Oh, Charles, the pleasure is all mine. Please, call me, Anne."

Rose wasn't sure if her mind was playing tricks on her, but she could have sworn she saw her proper mother blush.

"Allow me to introduce my daughter, Rose Woodburn." Anne gave Rose a light push on her lower back when she failed to step forward at her introduction.

"Rose! It's an honor to meet you. Your beauty is far superior to that of the flower."

"Yet, my thorns are just as sharp." Rose's smile faltered from the impact of Anne's elbow digging into her side.

"Funny! I do love a humorous gal. Quite the challenge they are," Charles opined.

"You have no idea." Anne smiled tightly.

"I trust you ladies are both doing well this fine evening, hopefully even better now that I've arrived." He extended both arms, one to Rose and the other to her mother, and escorted them to the sitting room.

"Actually, Charles, I'm quite famished."

Rose's mother shot her a sharp look of disapproval.

Charles brows furrowed in confusion. "Am I late?"

"Of course not!" Anne interjected immediately. "Pay no attention to my daughter, she can be quite rude at times." Again Anne looked at Rose with the wrath of a humiliated host.

"No, I'm sure it's my fault, I could have sworn my mother said you had invited me for half-past eight, but I tend to have a terrible memory."

"It was half-past seven, not eight," Rose said smugly. Anne glared at her reproachfully. Rose knew she was worried about offending Charles.

"No matter at all. The important thing is that you're here, and we are so delighted to have you. Isn't that right, Rose?" Anne's expression indicated that she would make Rose's life miserable if she dared disagree.

"Of course, mother." Rose's attempt at enthusiasm fell somewhat flat. Vivianna would be disappointed in how transparent she was being, she thought to herself. Rose would have to focus if she were going to get better at being unreadable.

"Well, ladies, I do apologize. Far be it from me to keep two lovely women waiting. I've brought some of the delicious chocolates my family imports. I hope they will make up for my tardiness. Rose, I hear that foreign truffles are your favorite." He grinned at her.

That was before the night sender, Rose mused to herself. She also knew who had shared that bit of information with Charles. She wondered what other personal tidbits her mother had conveyed to Mrs. Devano.

"Yes, I do adore a good chocolate. Thank you for bringing such a large box."

"It was the least I could do for such a beautiful creature as yourself." Charles handed her the box with a warm smile.

When she lifted her head to meet his eyes, she smiled back naturally, surprising herself. Charles seemed to have an uncanny ability to make those around him feel at ease, yet her senses cautioned her to keep her guard up.

BY THE TIME THEY FINISHED with drinks and were sitting down to dinner, it was ten o'clock, and Rose was getting antsy. She needed to be in her bed with her mask on by midnight to make sure she didn't miss her night sender. But her mother's immense fascination with Charles was becoming more of an obstacle as the evening progressed.

"Oh, Charles, do tell us more about yourself!" Anne prompted. Rose couldn't deny that she was slightly jealous by how much of an interest Anne took in Charles compared to the amount she took in her own daughter.

"You are too kind." He was perfectly polite. "I feel like I've told you so much already. I'm not sure what more there is to say." Charles placed his dinner napkin in his lap.

"What are you passionate about?" Rose interrupted abruptly.

"Excuse me?" Charles looked up from his lap, a bit confused.

"Rose, dear, you know it's horribly impolite to interrupt." Her mother put a very harsh emphasis on horribly.

"I'm terribly sorry, mother." Rose selected a warm roll from the basket in the middle of the table. She tore the flaky crust apart, the aroma wafting up to her nose. The smell made her mouth water. "It's just that you seem quite intrigued by learning as much as possible about Charles, so I thought I'd help the process along by inquiring as to what he is passionate about." She spread a generous amount of butter on the roll, earning a sideways look from Anne that went unnoticed by Charles. He seemed oblivious to their silent exchanges.

Charles nodded, pondering the question. "Well, let's see. I must say I excel at the family business. I'm an excellent negotiator. You should see what I've done in terms of restructuring some of our current contracts. None of our counterparts want to go up against me in negotiations." His delivery exuded a hint of arrogance.

"With all due respect, Charles, I didn't ask you what you excel at, I asked you what you were passionate about." Rose took a sip of cabernet, savoring the full-bodied varietal.

"Well then, I must admit, Rose, I'm not entirely sure what you mean." Charles stabbed a piece of filet mignon and brought it to his lips.

Anne gnawed at her salad, observing the exchange between them. Her posture was tense.

"What do you love doing? Not because you're good at it, or because you have to do it. Passion does not require purpose. What do you enjoy doing just because it excites you or makes you feel good?"

Anne put her knife and fork down abruptly, the metal clanging against the wood table. "Rose, dear, leave the poor boy alone. Not everyone is as unbridled as you are. Some people understand what is expected of them and have the discipline to adhere to it. Charles, I'm terribly sorry. Please tell us more about your negotiation abilities."

Rose rolled her eyes and hoped her mother didn't notice.

"No, it's quite all right, Anne. Rose, I don't believe the two are mutually exclusive. I believe one can be passionate about what they're good at, just as one can excel at what impassions him." He gestured towards Rose. "I've heard you're an excellent rider and that you've quite a passion for horses. Is that not true?"

Rose took a long swig from her wine goblet. "That is true. But no one forced me, it was my decision."

"I hope you're not implying that a passion cannot be something you were forced into."

"And if I am?" She challenged.

"Again, I would contend that the two are not mutually exclusive. It was your mandatory court lessons that exposed you to riding, was it not? You were expected to ride, and still, you fell in love with the sport. I was groomed for negotiation, and I love it. Does the fact that my passion allows me to be the man my family expects of me detract from that passion?"

Rose's cheeks flushed deep pink. She hadn't considered Charles a man of critical thinking. "I suppose I can see why you enjoy negotiation."

Anne smiled smugly.

Rose observed Charles more carefully now, wondering if his fervor extended to the bedroom. Would his kiss contain the confidence and conviction of his words? Would kissing his thin lips arouse her the way the night sender did? She pictured herself kissing Charles, his moist tongue making its way into her mouth, flicking its end against hers. The vision aroused her sensual inclinations, which were already heightened from the wine.

BY THE TIME DESSERT WAS BROUGHT OUT, it was half-past eleven, and Rose had become visibly impatient. Anne had already told her to stop fidgeting three times. But Rose couldn't help it. She refused to miss her nightly visit. She was starting to feel sensitivity in new areas of her body and refused to lose even one night.

"Rose? Rose?" Her mother's sharp tone brought Rose back to reality, which unfortunately was still at the dinner table. From the way they were looking at her, she had clearly missed something.

"Yes?" she prompted, though she wasn't sure whether she should be addressing Charles or her mother.

"Charles just issued you a wonderful invitation to join him for a walk in his family's garden next week." Her mother looked at her expectantly.

Rose looked at the clock in the corner of the dining room. It was now a quarter to twelve. Rose sighed. While she detested the idea of spending an afternoon alone with Charles, she knew it would take far less time to acquiesce to his invitation than it would to politely decline. It would also save her from her mother's wrath. Desperate to be done with the evening, Rose feigned the slightest enthusiasm.

"I'm sure that would be lovely."

"Splendid!" Clearly, her mother was more excited than Charles.

"Wonderful, Rose. I'll call for you next Thursday at noon. You'll love the garden on my parents' estate. And perhaps my mother will join us for tea."

"Lovely." Rose tried to conceal her dread at the thought of having tea with two Devanos.

"Oh, this is divine. You kids will have such a grand time together. Now, why don't we celebrate by opening up those truffles Charles was kind enough to bring?"

Rose squirmed in her seat. The clock was now at thirteen minutes to midnight. She could feel her window of pleasure slowly slipping away from her.

"Perhaps we should save them, mother. I'm quite full after that delicious meal."

Anne looked at Rose with evident suspicion. "I've never known you to refuse a chocolate, even after engorging yourself."

"Can't a girl simply be full, mother?"

"A girl, yes, you, no."

"Ladies, it's quite all right. I didn't realize it was this late. I really should be going." Charles tapped the face of his gold pocket watch. The back was engraved with his initials.

Rose was relieved at his words and felt her body physically relax. By her standards, this was the best thing Charles had said the entire evening.

"So soon?" Her mother ventured, disappointed.

"I'm afraid so, Anne. I've got some business to attend to in the morning."

"And we wouldn't want to keep Charles from his business, now would we mother? Especially when he so excels at it."

"Of course not, dear." Anne's tone was polite, but Rose could tell that she was seething underneath that smooth exterior.

"Well, then, I'll be off. Thank you for a lively evening, ladies." Charles winked at Rose.

"Let us at least escort you out, Charles," Anne offered graciously.

Rose glanced at the clock. When she saw the time, her foot automatically started tapping impatiently beneath her dress. There was no way she was going to make it to her room by midnight at this rate.

As they entered the front vestibule, the maid went to fetch Charles' coat.

"It really was wonderful to have you, Charles," her mother cooed. Rose felt an eye roll coming and managed to stop it midway.

"It was lovely to be here. We must do it again sometime."

The maid helped Charles into his coat, and they bid him a final farewell. As soon as the door shut behind him, Rose wasted no time.

"Goodnight, mother." She gave her a quick kiss on the cheek and turned on her heel to leave.

"Not so fast, dear."

Rose stopped reluctantly. Why was her mother doing this now? Rose reasoned that remaining polite would inevitably get her upstairs faster.

"Yes, mother?"

"You've been incessantly fidgeting for the past hour. Is there somewhere you have to be?" Anne gave her a pointed look.

"Of course not, mother. I'm simply tired. It's quite late."

"I see." Anne stood with her arms crossed tightly over her chest.

It was apparent her mother was unconvinced. Rose needed to redirect the conversation before Anne started probing.

"I spoke with Vivianna today. Her mother needs volunteers for a children's event at the library, so I offered to help."

"That's very noble of you, Rose. Though it has absolutely nothing to do with your behavior at dinner."

Rose sighed. She wondered why Savannah was so much easier to distract.

"Can we discuss it tomorrow, mother?" Rose forced a yawn. "I really am drained."

"It doesn't matter when we discuss it, Rose. Just know that whatever it is, I will find out." Anne gave her one final icy glare and then walked away.

Without a second thought, Rose bolted up the stairs, desperate to make her nightly visit.

When she entered her room, the fire the maid prepared was burning low, but still lit. The rest of the space was shrouded in darkness. She looked around and saw nothing. The balcony doors were closed, and the room appeared empty. Rose glanced at the clock on her bedside table and saw it was already fourteen minutes past twelve. Her heart sank as she realized she must have missed him.

22

Roosha was standing in the far corner of Rose's room, observing her. He had arrived at midnight, seen Rose's bed empty, and decided to wait. He passed the time exploring her bedroom to learn more about this creature that enraptured him.

Roosha had just positioned himself out of sight when she burst through the door. He was amused by her frantic demeanor. As her eyes darted from corner to corner, it was apparent she was searching for something, which he thought might be him. His chest fluttered at the possibility.

"He's not here," Rose whispered., tears forming in her eyes. "How could I have missed him?"

Roosha smiled, her sentiment confirming the validity of his theory. His elation quickly gave way to confusion. Roosha still wasn't accustomed to having such strong emotional reactions. He couldn't understand why the dejection in her voice made his chest ache.

Rose wanted so badly to summon anger. She wanted to be angry with her mother for keeping her at dinner so late. She wanted to be angry with Charles for his tardiness and loquacity. But she couldn't bring herself to be angry because at that moment she was too disappointed. She couldn't fully comprehend the sorrow she felt at the idea of not seeing her night sender. Rose slid down onto the floor, her back pressed against the side of her bed. Her head dropped to her knees, tears streaming down her face.

Roosha felt agonized, and he knew it wasn't because Rose was experiencing pleasure. It was because he couldn't stand to see her in pain.

"You didn't miss me, Rose. I'm here. I've been waiting for you."

Rose's head popped up, her eyes wide with astonishment.

Roosha himself was also in a state of disbelief. The words had poured out of his mouth without his conscious consent. From the wild look in Rose's eyes, he wasn't sure if he had made a ghastly mistake.

Rose didn't know what to think. Her body was processing so many different emotions simultaneously. There was the elation of knowing that her night sender was in the room with her; that she had not missed him. She was also dumbfounded that all this time, he could speak, understand her, and chose not to, despite her prompting. And more interestingly, there was the immediate shift from her insatiable desire for physical pleasure to wanting to know this mystical creature that constantly put her in a state of ecstasy.

Roosha didn't know what to do. He feared that the longer Rose remained silent, the more terrified she must be. He wanted to speak, to see if she was all right, but he worried that she might scream and wake the rest of her household. He decided to take a chance and was prepared to leap out the terrace doors if she did.

"Rose? Are you all right?"

The sound of his voice brought Rose back into the present moment. She was surprised by how alluring it was. It was a deep baritone, though still tender, and somehow familiar. So many questions brewed in her mind, it threatened to overflow. She wanted to speak to him but found herself stammering.

"You ... you ... you can talk?" Her tone was laden with shock.

"Yes."

"But ... but the other day ... the other day ..."

"I didn't speak with you the other day because I was afraid it would scare you." He decided not to convey all of his own trepidations that had also stopped him from speaking.

"But the other six days ..." Rose was frustrated that she couldn't finish her sentences.

"I've never done this before, Rose. I didn't know how to proceed." He spoke softly, sincerely.

"Done what, exactly?" She knew it was an obvious question, but she still wanted to hear the answer directly from his lips.

"Visited a girl more than once." Roosha wanted to say more but didn't know if he should disclose that he was forbidden from seeing her. He feared if she knew he had broken that sacred law, she would send him away.

"Oh." Rose had so many questions she wanted to ask, that now it was she who was unsure how to proceed. "What made you decide to visit me again?"

Roosha paused. He knew he should have anticipated that question. Now he had to decide exactly how to answer it.

"Because you're the only girl who's ever asked me to."

Rose's heart fluttered in her chest. Never before had she taken such pride in her uniqueness.

"Well, thank you. I'm glad you came back."

The words sounded mundane. She cursed herself for failing to adequately express the magnitude of her exultation. Roosha, on the other hand, was relieved by her words. Visiting Rose had become the highlight of his existence.

"As am I."

Rose felt the warmth beneath her cheeks and knew she was blushing. She wondered if he was close enough to witness the changing hue of her cheeks. She still had no idea where he was, though his voice sounded like it was coming from somewhere near the terrace doors.

"Do you have a name?"

"Yes. My name is Roosha."

"Roosha?" She repeated the word as he had enunciated it. To Rose, it seemed an odd name.

"Yes."

"Do all of the night senders have names?" She peered across the room, searching for him.

"Yes."

"Do you have a surname?" Rose scanned from the balcony to the fireplace, her vanity, and over to the bed but could not pinpoint Roosha.

"No. We only go by one name."

"Can I see you?" The words rushed from her mouth, giving away her real yearning. Rose's eyes were alight with curiosity. She was still peering hard through the darkness, trying to catch a glimpse of Roosha.

In the shadows, Roosha hesitated. Again, he knew that once he started speaking to her, she would want to see him. He remembered how Rose had tried desperately to rip off her mask the night of his first visit. And while she was different, he couldn't imagine her embracing his monstrous form.

"I don't know if that's a good idea, Rose."

"What makes you say that?"

"We look very different from your kind. And the last thing I'd want is to frighten you."

Rose was burning with intrigue. "You couldn't possibly frighten me, Roosha."

The sound of her melodious voice pronouncing his name made him feel an emotion he had never felt before, desire. He heard the longing in her voice, which in turn had him wanting. The pleading look on her face infused him with the courage, or perhaps the foolishness, to expose himself. He was starting to realize that a life lived with insouciance was much less complicated. He couldn't fathom how humans operated everyday factoring emotions into their decision-making process.

"All right. But all I ask is that you don't scream. If you scream, I will have to leave immediately."

The thought of him leaving disturbed Rose. She swore that no matter what this mysterious creature looked like, she would not utter a sound.

"You have my word."

Roosha took a deep breath and then stepped cautiously towards the hearth. He placed a fresh log on the embers, rekindling the fire. As the flames gradually revealed this marvelous creature to her, many words crossed her mind, intimate descriptions of his striking form, but scary was not among them.

Rose felt a longing between her legs as she took in the statuesque form before her, resembling a mythical warrior, one who would have been revered as a god. From his waist up, he was a man, his torso lean but chiseled. His angular face was devastatingly handsome, framed by long, wavy black hair like an Andalusian steed. Roosha had two legs, exactly like a horse, only thicker, with hooves at the base. A black loincloth rested over his manhood, though it was evident from the bulge beneath that his girth was on par with a stallion. Attached to his shoulder blades were enormous crow-like wings.

But what most captivated Rose was his skin. It was a very deep blue, as dark as the night sky. And above his pelvis, where a human naval would be, his skin glowed a deep amber. She saw the same orange when she finally met his eyes.

Rose held his gaze, but words escaped her. He looked nothing like she thought he would, nothing like the gruesome image circulated by the court.

Mesmerized by the amber glow emanating from his naval area, she reached her hand out in front of her and took a step towards him.

Roosha jumped back suddenly, landing farther away from Rose, and closer to the balcony, with a tiny thud. Rose looked up at him, a bit bewildered by his retreat.

"I'm sorry, did I do something wrong? I didn't mean to frighten you, Roosha." She retracted her hand.

"You didn't, I…" Roosha looked pensive. "Your mother is coming. I'll be back tomorrow night at midnight."

Before Rose had a chance to react, Roosha had already leapt from the balcony and flown off into the night. A second later, Rose's mother opened the door without so much as a knock.

"Rose? What's going on here?" She peered around the room carefully, inspecting every corner.

"What do you mean, mother?" Rose was still too stunned to come up with anything better, so she strove for nonchalance.

"I was walking down the hall, and heard a noise that definitely came from your room."

Rose thought as quickly as she could. "I dropped something, mother."

"What did you drop?"

Rose looked around but couldn't make out anything on the floor in the darkness.

"Um, me. I was about to sit on the bed, and I missed it. I caught the edge and then slid down the side and landed softly on my bottom. I'm terribly sorry to have disturbed you." Rose smiled sweetly.

Anne looked at her suspiciously.

"Why aren't you in bed? I thought you were utterly exhausted from dinner."

"I decided to read for a bit." Rose eyed her nightstand. Thankfully, there was a small book on it.

"In the dark?"

"I wasn't reading in bed, mother. I was sitting beside the fireplace. That's why I just added a new log for more light." Rose pointed to the burning wood.

Anne hesitated, taking one last thorough glance around the room.

"All right then, goodnight, Rose."

"Goodnight, mother."

As soon as Anne shut the door, Rose felt relieved. A deep breath came whooshing out of her chest. That was a close call, she thought to herself. She and Roosha would have to be more careful. Now that she had just started talking to him, she was even more determined not to lose him.

23

The next day, Rose found herself at tea with the court girls, though she couldn't remember getting there. Her mind was adrift and entirely focused on her next encounter with Roosha. She relished knowing his name. It was personal, and it made him all the more real. He did exist, and she knew him by name.

All she remembered from the morning was her good fortune in avoiding Anne at breakfast. Surprisingly her mother had already left the house by the time Rose came downstairs, probably another trip to the florist. The arrangement of white roses was wilting. After the close call during the night, Rose was grateful for a relaxed morning without the scrutiny of Anne's penetrating stare.

Instead of indulging in the fresh scones in front of her, Rose had rushed back upstairs, thrown on her green sundress, and exited the house before her mother returned. She thought about ditching the court gathering to spend some time with Carmera but decided against it. Now she was at her obligatory affair, though she was hardly present. Rose stared into her mint tea, contemplating why Roosha's skin glowed in that one particular spot.

"Rose? Hello? Rose?"

A small cookie came flying at her, landing in her hair. Rose's hand instantly reached for the remains of the cookie and hurled them back at Savannah.

"What is your problem now?" Rose growled.

Savannah lifted her plate like a shield.

"There's no need to get violent, Rose," she shrieked innocently as if she weren't the one who initiated macaroon warfare. "I simply noticed you've been acting stranger than normal. You haven't said a word all morning." Her tone was accusatory, not concerned.

"I should think that would make you happy, Savannah. It provides you even more opportunity to talk about yourself." Rose smiled, pleased with her own retort.

"You know, Rose," she sighed. "Just this once I'd rather hear about you. You seem quite preoccupied lately. And I think I know the real source of that preoccupation." Savannah grinned triumphantly.

Rose immediately glanced at Vivianna for direction, but Vivianna discreetly shook her head. She seemed to have no idea what Savannah meant. Rose's eyes grew wide as Roosha's face flashed across her mind. Quickly, she shuffled through all of their recent interactions, unable to pinpoint how Savannah would have found out about Roosha. Still, nervous beads of sweat trickled down the back of her neck.

"Do tell, Savannah. Don't leave us all in suspense here." Rose's voice masked her apprehension, but inside she was trembling. She no longer wanted to be a source of conversation for the court girls. She yearned for the privacy Vivianna managed to procure.

Savannah's smile turned devious. "Well, a little bird told me that you had dinner with a Mr. Charles Devano last night."

Rose let out an internal sigh of relief. Savannah had no knowledge of her night sender, which was all that mattered. Rose was irritated by how fast gossip traveled in the tiny town of Dover, especially amongst court members. She wondered how Savannah had gotten wind of their dinner when it had only happened hours ago.

Rose was about to roll her eyes at the implication that Charles could occupy that much space in her mind when she realized a golden opportunity had just presented itself. Charles was the perfect decoy, a way of keeping Savannah's suspicions focused on the wrong target. If

Rose started talking about Charles, Savannah would attribute her change in behavior to him.

"Why, yes, Savannah, I have been caught up fantasizing about Charles," Rose lied.

Savannah folded her frail arms across her chest. "So, when are you all getting engaged?" Her tone was bitter.

Her words felt like a lightning strike, shorting Rose's system.

"For heaven's sake, Savannah, we've only had one dinner! And we weren't even alone, it was chaperoned!"

"So what? Henry and I only had two fabulous dates before he placed this beautiful ring on my finger."

Savannah flashed her giant emerald engagement ring and matching wedding band as if no one had seen them the first thousand times. The other girls made appropriate remarks of admiration, whereas Rose grimaced. To her, wedding bands always looked more like finger cuffs, a limitation of freedom based on obligations, not love.

"Well, Savannah, I'd prefer to get to know him better before making such a life-altering decision."

"Life-altering? Oh, Rose, this is when life really begins, you'll see. Well, I mean unless, of course, Charles comes to his senses and realizes he needs more of a proper lady." Her tone was dripping with condescension. Amelia snickered behind her.

Rose's eyes flitted to Vivianna, who gave her a subtle eye roll. Savannah was too entertained by her own voice to notice the quick exchange.

"When are you seeing him again, Rose? Or did you scare him off with how you devour those truffles his family imports?"

Rose scoffed. "I see you're not as privy to current gossip as you think. It just so happens I'm seeing him Thursday at noon for a walk in the gardens."

As soon as she said the words, a frustrated expression appeared on Vivianna's normally neutral face. Savannah glared at Rose, her cheeks a sullen crimson. Rose knew she'd be thoroughly insulted by the implication that she wasn't aware of all the latest gossip.

"Well then perhaps I should have dear Henry educate Charles on exactly what he's in for. Maybe then he'll wisely rearrange his schedule before Thursday."

"Go right ahead. He did seem quite taken with me at dinner, though."

Savannah scowled at Rose, her dagger eyes radiating contempt. Abruptly she stood up.

"Ladies, we are finished with tea." She snapped her fingers and authoritatively shouted, "now!"

One by one, the girls followed her out in a single file line. Vivianna was the last to stand. Once the other girls had made their way out of the room, Vivianna tossed a piece of paper at Rose and joined the back of the line. Rose grabbed the crumpled paper and opened it. Inside, Vivianna had written a note.

Meet me in the library in 15 minutes. DISCREETLY.

Rose glanced at the clock. It was a quarter to twelve. She leaned back in her chair, putting her feet up and settling into an unladylike position. Sipping her tea, she indulged in her daydreams of Roosha.

24

Vivianna was waiting inside the front entrance to the library at exactly noon. As soon as Rose walked through the door, Vivianna grabbed her arm and pulled her into the children's section, which was empty.

"Why did you agree to meet Charles at noon on Thursday?"

Rose was surprised by the abruptness of Vivianna's question. It wasn't like her to openly show this level of frustration.

"He suggested it at dinner, and so I acquiesced."

"And so you acquiesced?" Her tone was incredulous. "Since when are you agreeable to a suggestion like that?"

"Since I'm trying to keep my mother from launching an in-depth investigation into what I am doing."

"And what is it exactly that you're doing?" She eyed Rose speculatively.

Rose paused. She knew Vivianna was smart enough to know that something was going on with her outside of their library scheme. But Rose still wasn't positive that she could trust Vivianna implicitly, and Roosha was too important to warrant that kind of risk. Rose was in a quandary. She debated whether to outright lie to Vivianna or to admit that she was withholding information from her.

"I'm not doing anything she likes. My mother detests my wardrobe, my mannerisms, how I eat my desserts, my horse, and my attitude. She would definitely not approve of what we're planning. So, in short, I'm trying to do one thing to placate her enough to keep her out of my business, at least temporarily. Why do you have such a problem with my seeing Charles on Thursday anyway?"

"Because Thursday is the library event!"

Rose gasped. She had forgotten that the children's event was also on Thursday.

"What time is it?"

"It's from noon until three o'clock."

Now Rose was the one feeling immensely frustrated. She knew that if she canceled on Charles, she would put her mother on high alert, especially after what happened last night with her impatience at dinner followed by the conspicuous thud in her room. She didn't want to let Vivianna down, especially seeing as she was equally, if not more anxious to learn about the night senders.

"What if I come at the end of the event?"

"There might not be any books left to transport to the basement, in which case we would have no reason to be down there, and my mother wouldn't give us her keys."

"I can't come before. My mother will have me primping for my inane date with Charles for at least a full hour beforehand." Rose pressed two fingers against her temple. "How can we make this work?"

Vivianna shrugged. "I don't know, but we'll have to figure something out. With Savannah there, we definitely need two people to pull this off."

"Speaking of Savannah, was it me, or was she extra vicious with me today? Throwing the cookie and then those dagger eyes she gave me at the end before dismissing everyone from tea?"

Vivianna laughed.

"What's so funny?"

"You really do stay out of the gossip mill, don't you, Rose?"

Rose gave her a confused look.

"Charles Devano was Savannah's first choice for a husband. She's fancied him for years and loves the Devano family's extravagant lifestyle. Her mother set up a tea with Charles right after her night visit, and apparently, it was a disaster. No one knows exactly what happened at tea, not even her lemmings. Afterward, Charles must have told his mother she was awful because Mrs. Devano informed Savannah's mother that her son would no longer be courting her. Savannah was humiliated."

Rose's initial chuckle instigated a fit of giggles, a needed break from all of the mounting tension.

"That must have been some shock to her inflated ego."

"I think that might be an understatement considering she already had Mrs. Devano etched into her notebook four years ago. I saw it in our etiquette class."

"And to think, she's perfectly welcome to him! I have no interest in Charles aside from distracting my mother."

"No interest at all? He is quite handsome."

"Yes, he is, just ask him." Rose grinned. "He does enjoy a good debate. Perhaps Savannah couldn't keep up with him."

"Hopefully. It's about time someone challenged her. Amelia tries, but her performance tends to be pitiful."

"Why is it you've never challenged Savannah?" Though it was on her mind, Rose hadn't meant to verbalize the question. She considered it too familiar, something you would only ask a friend. Rose had never regarded any of the court girls as friends, but as they shared in this exchange together, Rose felt a certain camaraderie with Vivianna, which made her comfortable enough to ask.

"Because it's not worth it."

"What do you mean it's not worth it? You're smarter than she is. You could dethrone her majesty and become the leader of the group."

"Is that what you would want, Rose? If you were in my position."

"All I want is to be left alone, whether in your position or mine." Rose sighed, imagining how peaceful life would be if the court, Savannah, and her mother let her be.

"Exactly, Rose! That's what I want as well, and it's what I have attained. Challenging Savannah only leads to arguments, schemes, and drama, none of which I fancy. I don't question her; I redirect her attention until she switches targets. Although, your brashness in answering her questions may jeopardize my strategy."

"Sorry about that," Rose muttered.

She considered the high percentage of unconscious decisions she made. It was Vivianna who had achieved what Rose wanted, not the other way around. Perhaps if she behaved more like Vivianna, Rose would be in a more advantageous position at home and with the court. It was time for her to become less reactionary and much more observant.

25

Roosha sat on the edge of the water, feeling calm. He was grateful that he hadn't frightened Rose by revealing his speaking abilities and appearance all in one night. It was her genuine acceptance and fascination that had instilled this calm within him. For the first time as a night sender, he didn't feel like the monster that had condemned him to this fate.

If only Rose knew, he thought to himself, what he really was, there was no way she would want to see him again. He was more a beast in his previous life than the one he resembled now.

Roosha looked up to the night sky. It was almost midnight. Soon he would see Rose. The thought made him excited and anxious at the same time. Usually, his job was easy. He went in unseen, with no interaction with the girl. Not only had Rose heard his voice, but she also peered into his eyes, seeing a part of him no other woman had, which made him nervous about pleasuring her. And nervous was an unfamiliar state for him.

ROSE SAT AT HER VANITY, staring into the mirror. She had painted her lips a deep red and was now questioning her decision. Her usual elation in anticipation of Roosha's visit had devolved into timidity, which didn't make sense to her. He had already seen her half-naked, writhing in ecstasy, yet here she was masking her natural parts in an attempt to make herself more presentable.

They already had a significant physical connection, with Roosha giving her not only her first but every orgasm she had ever experienced. But after hearing his voice and looking deep into his eyes, she felt more exposed somehow, as if tonight he would be seeing her naked for the first time.

ROOSHA LANDED QUIETLY on the balcony. The doors were slightly ajar, and there was soft candlelight emanating from inside Rose's bedroom. He paused before entering to remind himself to breathe. He had managed to calm himself on the way over by focusing on every aspect of flying that he could think of, his wingspan, the cool breeze blowing against his skin, the darkness around him, the empty streets, and the shape of the moon. These thoughts left no room for speculation or worry about what the night would entail. And while this strategy had worked to get him to Rose's abode, his nervous energy returned in full force as he stood only steps away from her.

On the other side of the door, Rose was pacing back and forth across the room. It was one minute to midnight, and she didn't know how to position herself for Roosha's arrival. It seemed a silly notion to be concerned with, but still, it occupied her mind, making her antsy.

She thought it would be ludicrous to be lying in bed, waiting for him. Surely, they would talk before engaging in any sensual endeavors? But what if he didn't want to talk? Rose wasn't sure how she felt about that proposition. Could she still accept an arrangement based solely on physical pleasure now aware that Roosha could communicate with her? Rose shook her head, trying to clear all of these thoughts from her overactive mind. She knew she was getting too far ahead of herself. She hadn't even seen him since learning that he could speak, so there was no sense contemplating how it would impact their relationship.

The doors to the balcony opened slowly. Rose's head shot up, her body freezing in place. She was standing at the foot of her bed when Roosha stepped through the doors. He ventured closer to Rose, careful not to make a sound as he moved. Rose's eyes were locked on Roosha's, their orange glow mesmerizing her.

"Good evening," she managed.

"Hello, Rose." Roosha stopped a couple of feet from her. With the sound of his voice, her timorous energy dissipated.

"I'm glad you came back." Rose smiled shyly. She wondered why she felt so girlish under his gaze.

"So am I." Roosha's inflection was even, but his posture was stiff.

"Shall we sit?" Rose motioned to the edge of the bed. She felt silly, though their awkwardness seemed to automatically trigger her etiquette lessons. Her mother would have been proud, though simultaneously disapproving of her company. Rose was disappointed, as she had just sworn to no longer react unconsciously.

Roosha glanced at the inviting sheets, unsure. He had never thought of sitting on a court girl's bed before. Though logical, the idea was foreign to him. Sensing his hesitation, Rose sat first and motioned for him to sit beside her. Roosha complied, leaving the same two feet of space between them. Rose looked at him, her eyes burning with curiosity.

Amused by her eagerness, Roosha prompted, "You look like you have much to say, Rose."

"I'm sorry, I don't mean to stare. I just have so many questions." She looked down, her cheeks a bit flushed.

"You mean about what I am?"

"No, not exactly. I'm more interested in who you are."

Roosha softened at her words, his posture relaxing. Despite his monstrous form, this girl was still treating him as if he were a man beside her, not a monster. She wasn't afraid or reproachful. She seemed to accept him just as he was. He wondered if she would still be able to do that if she knew his history.

"I haven't given much thought to it since I became a night sender." Roosha shook his head. It was true. Since being changed, he identified with being a night sender, as opposed to being Roosha. Perhaps, not believing himself worthy of his own persona in this realm after the atrocities committed in his previous life, he had inadvertently created an additional punishment.

"But why not?" Rose looked at him, confused.

"Because as a night sender, we're identified by that classification."

"But you have a name. That's an individual characteristic that already sets you apart from the other night senders."

"Yes, but only in our own realm are we referred to by name. To your kind, we are simply night senders."

"I see. How are we referred to in your realm, us girls that you visit?"

"Much the same, I suppose. We only learn your names to know whom we must visit. Otherwise, you are all referred to as the court girls."

"And that's how you see me? As just one of the court girls?"

Roosha met her eyes, surprised by the suggestion.

"No, not at all. I see you only as Rose. Though that also stems from how significantly different you are from any of the court girls I've encountered."

Rose smiled, flattered. "Wonderful. And I see you as Roosha, significantly different from any of the other night senders, just because you are you."

Roosha was taken aback. Who was this amazing woman before him? His desire to know her was growing stronger.

"You, my sweet Rose, are something else."

With the back of his hand, he gently caressed her cheek. Rose turned beet red, the blood flushing to that area. A tingling sensation surged to her lower region. All Roosha had to do was touch her, and her body became one giant clitoris. But this time, Rose didn't want to succumb to her sensual desires right away. She wanted to know this creature, who was anything but monstrous to her.

"How long have you been a night sender?"

"Eighteen years."

"Will you be one forever?"

"No. We eventually die too, like your kind." Roosha added that last part in the hopes that it would quell her curiosity a bit. He didn't want more questions on their lifespan, or how they came to be, as he was sure that would lead to a discussion on sentencing, and how the events of their previous human life determined their current one. He wasn't ready to share his past with Rose. He wanted to enjoy her acceptance of him for a while longer before his past atrocities drove her away.

Rose was disappointed by the thought of Roosha no longer existing at some point. She had countless questions but decided to limit how many she would pose that night. She didn't want Roosha to feel like he was undergoing an interrogation.

"How did you become a night sender?" Rose examined her inquiry. It wasn't the question she intended to ask, but somehow her mouth released the words in that formation. The two questions emblazoned in Rose's mind were who the night senders were and what their purpose was. But in carefully watching Roosha's reaction, she sensed she had touched on a significant matter.

Roosha tried not to look alarmed. The one question he was dreading, and she gave it to him straight. He wasn't ready and cursed his foolhardy lack of preparation. He was shrewd enough to have anticipated she would ask that question and should not have returned to her room without an answer prepared. His mind scrambled for a way to deflect her inquiry.

"Don't they teach you anything about us?" Roosha feigned incredulity, as Avidan had explained to him many times that the court girls were taught fear over fact, or rather, fear instead of fact.

Roosha's words pinched the thorn already in Rose's side. He had unknowingly asked the one question that could provoke her enough to divert her line of questioning.

"They don't tell us anything!" Rose had to concentrate on controlling her voice, as it naturally got louder anytime this subject arose. "They tell us we'll get our nighttime visit at midnight on our eighteenth birthday. We aren't told the true purpose of this visit, nor anything about your kind. We're simply warned we should be deathly afraid of the night senders, that you'll inflict great pain on us, and that we are forbidden from enjoying the experience in any way, which doesn't even make sense!

But of course, no reason or explanation is provided for any of these commandments."

Rose's cheeks flushed with anger. She didn't realize the extent to which she was furious with her mother, the court ladies, and the entire system itself.

Roosha watched her, astonished. He wanted to know how this girl managed to maintain her passion and sense of self in a society that worked so hard to strip her of it.

"Why weren't you afraid?" Roosha prompted. "The first night I visited you."

Rose's face changed, her expression growing thoughtful.

"Because I was, and have always been enlivened by the unknown."

Her bright eyes burned into Roosha's. He couldn't explain why, but at that moment, his lips were drawn to Rose's.

Roosha leaned in and gently pressed his tender lips against hers. With the tip of his tongue, he slowly parted her lips, opening up a new realm of desire. As their mouths connected, his tongue caressing hers, Rose's mind started to blur. Never had she tasted anything so mouth-watering, so ambrosial it made her truffles seem plain as porridge. All of the questions she had lined up faded away word by word. She was consumed by the moment and focused only on the magnetic energy between them.

As the kiss grew deeper, Rose's mind drifted further into darkness. All she saw were dancing colors of light, which she viewed as their two spirits joining in rapture. At some point, Rose's body turned limp, and the dancing colors gradually faded until ecstasy transported her to a peaceful slumber.

AS ROSE WAS WAKING UP, Roosha's pain was finally subsiding.

When Roosha's lips caressed Rose's, the discomfort began. Stabbing sensations pursued his lips relentlessly as if someone had taken a set of sewing needles and was using his lips as a pincushion. But as his pain intensified, he knew Rose's desire grew, which was the only thing that kept him going. As she reached her hand around the back of his head to pull him closer to her, he reminded himself that he was created to give this kind of pleasure, and this may be the only chance he had to fulfill that purpose. With his tongue, he licked her lips, willing them open. As their tongues intertwined, Roosha's chest tightened, fighting the escalating pain. By the time Rose passed out from pleasure, Roosha was on the verge of passing out from the agony.

26

Rose woke up glowing. She stretched her arms wide across the width of the bed, basking in how divine she felt. A loud knocking on her bedroom door interrupted her peaceful solitude.

"Rose! Rose, dear," her mother called. "Do get up, we're going shopping!" Her mother's voice was overly cheerful. Rose surmised that this shopping venture was related to her impending garden walk with a certain nobleman.

Rose was about to make a sarcastic remark but held her tongue. She thought of Roosha and reminded herself what was at stake and held steady with the plan to placate her mother.

"Wonderful, mother. Just give me a few moments to get dressed."

TOGETHER THEY WALKED THE SMALL, colorful streets of Dover. The weather was crisp, but the sun was high in the sky, its rays warming their skin. Rose hadn't been out in the city recently and enjoyed the bustling of different people around her.

All of the small shop owners were busy at work, crafting, creating, and organizing things to sell. They passed by the cobbler shop, with its oversized shoeshine chair outside, the florist, whose storefront looked like an enchanted garden, and the redolent bakery. Rose found it torturous to walk by without entering, as the smell of freshly baked bread wafted through the windows and called to her taste buds. She paused for a brief second, her nose turned in the direction of the door, but her mother kept moving, and so she reluctantly followed. Next, they passed Mr. Frazgo's candy store, with its ornately designed blue and gold shutters. Typically, the candy store would have been an irresistible temptation, but the sight of Devano imported truffles in the window served as a deterrent, reminding Rose why they were out shopping. Besides which, Roosha was now her favorite flavor.

After winding through three more sinuous streets of alternating pastel colors, her mother stopped in front of a small three-story yellow building with giant eight-foot windows. Rose looked up and could tell from the second-floor display that they had reached their destination. In the second-floor window were four puffy, whimsical looking dresses, and one elegant green number that stood out. The sign above the door read, Mrs. Taddy's Taylor.

Anne was eyeing the frilly lavender dress in the center with admiration. Rose took a deep breath and reminded herself that Roosha was her motivation to remain cordial right now.

"Shall we?" Anne tilted her head towards the narrow staircase that led to the shop entrance. Rose smiled weakly.

"Of course, mother."

Her mother opened the door to the shop. Inside, an explosion of color greeted them. Rose felt they were entering the inside of a rainbow. The shop was adorned with bright, vivid hues in every direction, from sunshine yellow to pale pink, sky blue, violet, mint green, orange sherbet, wispy white, eggplant purple, and a slew of others. The walls were painted a neutral cream, though you could barely see them. At least twenty-five mannequins were lined tightly together throughout the tiny square shop, each bedizened in elaborate garments and fanciful accessories. Rose sighed, knowing she wasn't getting out of there anytime soon.

From behind one of the mannequins appeared a plump and jolly woman, her messy blonde bun bouncing as she stepped forward clumsily.

"Greetings, ladies, and welcome to my humble shop! How may I help you today?"

"Good afternoon, Mrs. Taddy, I presume?" Her mother sounded sedate in comparison to this buoyant woman.

"Yes, ma'am, that's me. And you'll find Mr. Taddy downstairs at Mr. Taddy's Taylor, although I doubt you'll be needing his services today!" Her delivery was loud, cheerful, and bursting with energy. Rose's mother seemed a bit overwhelmed by it, which made Rose smile.

"Ah, no, I don't believe we will need your husband's services this morning. What we do need is a dress for my daughter." She gestured towards Rose. "She has a significant social engagement coming up soon, and we must make her look presentable."

Mrs. Taddy's eyes lit up. "Who's the lucky chap?"

Anne looked insulted. Rose knew she considered the woman's nosiness offensive. She recalled the words her mother had instilled in her since she was old enough to formulate questions, "a proper lady never pries."

"Not that it is any of your concern, but the lucky gentleman is Charles Devano, of the family that imports our delectable Dover truffles."

Rose bit her lip to suppress a laugh. Her mother's delivery was dripping with such superiority; she found it comical.

"Oh! So then I guess you've found yourself a real sweetheart there, eh honey!" She winked at Rose. "Get it? Because he imports sweets." Mrs. Taddy guffawed at her own joke. Rose found her laughter contagious. Unamused, Anne remained stoic.

"Well then, dear, let's have a look at you." She took Rose by the hand and twirled her around once. "Beautiful hourglass figure. We'll make you look so ravishing it won't be the chocolates he'll be wanting to bite!"

"Excuse me, madam." Rose's mother gave the woman an admonishing glare. "That's no way to speak to a proper young lady."

Mrs. Taddy ignored her and addressed Rose.

"Let's see what we've got for you, love. What colors do you prefer?"

Rose liked Mrs. Taddy. Not only was she not afraid of, or even discouraged by Rose's mother, but she also had the courtesy to ask Rose what she preferred.

"Let's go with something pastel," Anne chimed in from the corner. She had already sat down expectantly like she was waiting for the maid to serve lunch.

"She always like that?" Mrs. Taddy whispered to Rose.

"Worse," Rose confided.

TWO HOURS AND THIRTEEN DRESSES LATER, Rose was ready to scream. Her patience had been evaporating like rain off the hot cobblestone streets in summer. By the eighth dress, she was fed up with her mother's commentary, and focusing on Roosha was growing increasingly difficult. Even Mrs. Taddy's enthusiasm waned.

"I just don't know…" Anne's lips were pursed in her typical indecisive posture. Rose knew this look meant nothing was going to satisfy her. Poor Mrs. Taddy looked like she was ready to shred the chiffon fabric she was holding in two.

"I adore the top from the second dress but detest the bottom. And I love the bottom of dress seven, but the top is ghastly."

At this point, Rose didn't even remember which dresses those were. The floor was strewn with bows and gowns, the shop in disarray.

Before Anne could continue her verbal tirade, Mrs. Taddy chimed in, attempting to mask her frustration.

"Tell you what, dears, I'll take the top of dress two and sew it onto the bottom of dress seven for you if you want. I can even have it done tomorrow if that will get you, ladies, on your merry way." While unsaid, the "now" was clearly implied in her statement.

Rose's mother looked thoughtful. Both Rose and Mrs. Taddy scrutinized her expression, hoping that the proposed plan would end this whole ordeal.

"I suppose that will do." Two sighs of relief were let out simultaneously. Rose's mother stood and walked towards the door. "Rose will be by tomorrow afternoon to pick up the dress."

Mrs. Taddy nodded and bid them good day.

ON THE WAY BACK HOME, Rose's mother wanted to stop at the flower shop, Flora & Fauna. It was a majestic place better fit for a fairy tale rather than Dover. The walls were crawling with ivy, and a winding path led through droves of colorful flowers. Rose loved meandering around the greenery while her mother consulted the florist on elegant table centerpieces. She was caressing the petals of a lily when a hand grasped her arm and pulled her behind a wall of cascading green leaves.

"What the...," Rose startled.

"Have you come up with a plan for the library event? It's fast approaching," Vivianna urged.

"Me? You're the master planner between us."

"Yes, but since you refuse to cancel on Charles and I don't have the power to make you appear in two places at once, that significantly limits my options."

"I'm sorry! I absolutely cannot cancel on him now. My mother just spent the past two hours choosing a new dress for the occasion. It's being made for me as we speak."

Vivianna looked frustrated but determined.

"All right then, I'll hold down the fort until you can get there. But do us both a favor and feign an illness or find some plausible excuse for leaving early. I don't relish the idea of operating this quest solo with Savannah lurking."

"I know what you mean; she is a meddlesome nuisance. I will try to get out of the garden as fast as possible, but I have to be smart about this."

Vivianna surveyed Rose strangely.

"I know you are hiding something significant from me, Miss Woodburn. Hopefully, completing this mission together successfully will be the key that unlocks your secrets as well."

Vivianna ducked out of the florist quickly without another word. It wasn't like her to be so candid about her intentions. Again, Rose felt the desire to trust her, to be able to confide her blossoming romance in someone who just might understand her, but fear crept its way back up, lodging its ugly self in her throat, threatening her to keep her mouth shut.

27

Roosha watched the glistening moonlight reflect off the lake. He had been eagerly awaiting his visit with Rose the entire day, which made him feel like a masochist. As he took in the water's calm, he mentally braced himself for another night of physical pain. He knew it would worsen as their bond deepened, but the love growing in his heart far outweighed the toll the pain was taking. He was finally feeling again, and for the first time since his human life, he had a purpose. Roosha refused to give up the source of his love and reason, no matter the cost.

When he arrived at Rose's balcony, she was sitting at her vanity writing. The sight piqued his interest. He was curious about what she was writing. He pushed the balcony door open slowly. Rose jumped out of her chair with the slight creaking sound of the door and waltzed toward Roosha, planting a welcome kiss on his lips. Despite the stab of pain, Roosha still smiled gratefully. He wasn't sure he'd ever grow accustomed to such a warm reception after so many years of court girls greeting him as if he were the grim reaper there to slowly suck the life from them.

"Good evening," Rose gushed.

"Hello, beautiful, Rose. May I ask what you were writing? You seemed quite engrossed."

Rose blushed. She appreciated that he was intrigued by what she was doing. She couldn't remember the last time her mother expressed that level of interest unless it was to blatantly disapprove of or correct Rose's actions.

"I was writing a letter to myself, actually."

"A letter to yourself?" Roosha raised an eyebrow.

"Yes. I've been doing it since I was a child. You see, I've always been an oddity amongst the ladies of the court." Roosha grinned at her for stating the obvious. Rose's cheeks responded for her, flushing a deeper pink.

"My position in society didn't afford the opportunity to travel in other social circles. I've been surrounded by the same group of people since I was a child, all people who never accepted me. I was alone but refused to be lonely, so I learned to confide in myself. Almost every night, before I went to bed, I wrote down all of the thoughts, emotions, and ideas I couldn't openly express to the other girls, or even to my own mother. Instead of keeping a diary, I considered the practice daily conversations with myself. I suppose writing has helped keep me sane."

When Rose finished explaining, she was astonished. She had never told anyone about the letters, and now here she was divulging everything about them to Roosha as if she had known him for years. She marveled at the effect he seemed to have on her.

Roosha was fascinated. "I'd love to read them sometime if you would share them with me."

"Really?" Rose was moved by his request. No one in her life had ever expressed any desire to know her on such an intimate level. Even her mother seemed to avoid having meaningful conversations with her.

"Yes, Rose." His expression was sincere.

"But why?" She shook her head. "They're just random thoughts of mine."

Roosha lifted her chin. "But they're not random. They are your innermost truths, an authentic part of you that could not be shared. I, too, am excited by the unknown, and your mind is a mysterious and enchanting place I am eager to explore."

Rose's cheeks gave away her delight. She couldn't comprehend this magnificent creature being so captivated by her, nor could she adequately express the gratitude in her heart that someone finally appreciated the real Rose, inclusive of her imperfections.

"Yes, I suppose you can read them sometime."

Roosha caressed her cheek. "Thank you, Rose."

She stared deep into his amber eyes. "Won't you tell me something personal about you then?"

Roosha looked at her cautiously. "What would you like to know?"

"How you became a night sender, this wonderful creature whose visit is always the best part of my day; the one thing I look forward to every morning when I awake."

A wave of warmth spread through Roosha. Again, she managed to make him feel human even though he knew he was not. He deliberated internally while her eyes bore into his in anticipation. He could not bring himself to share his story with her. Roosha convinced himself that he didn't want to frighten her, but deep down, it was his own fear that the truth would destroy her image of him and drive her away.

"I don't know, Rose. I only remember waking up like this one day, in this form, and as part of this realm."

Rose hesitated, weighing her options. She didn't want to press, but she was unconvinced.

"Were you always a night sender? Or were you once something else?"

Roosha dithered. He was unsure if Rose knew more than she had let on, or if she was a keen guesser.

"Why do you ask?"

She looked at Roosha thoughtfully, running her hand across his chest, stopping along the right side of his left breast, where a human heart would be.

"You seem so human to me, not like some monstrous creation, but one who once lived as a man."

Her explanation confirmed her perceptiveness. Roosha was now desperate to change the subject. He thought about leaving, but if he fled abruptly, he knew it would fuel her suspicions.

"Rose, I am a night sender through and through. Any past life I may have once lived is but a distant, lost memory." He felt guilty lying to her but reasoned that it was to protect them both.

The flicker of pain in his eyes reminded Rose of her mother. She sensed Roosha was holding back but decided not to pursue the topic further. She would give him time; earn his trust. Rose moved on to lighter subject matter. She inquired about his habits, living situation, passions, and how he filled his days. She learned of his nocturnal nature, the caves he called home, and his frequent flights over Dover and up to the top of the hill to gaze upon the stars. Though still curious about the night senders themselves, her questions had quickly progressed to Roosha individually.

Rose, in turn, shared stories of her riding free atop Carmera and the deliberate way in which she consumed her chocolates. She even let Roosha read the first couple of letters she had written to herself as a child. At the same time, they laid in bed together, her body curled up against his side, where she eventually fell asleep. They had spent the whole night talking.

Roosha gently untangled himself from Rose, careful not to wake her. As he leapt from the balcony, he felt lighter, his body cutting through the air with effortless precision. Inside he was bursting with energy and appreciation. Until now, his whole existence was dedicated to suffering for the sake of another's pleasure. But now, it was he who felt so buoyant, so alive, and not from causing pain. He didn't understand how it was possible.

28

Rose headed downstairs, ready to accompany her mother to the dress shop to pick up her custom garment. Anne was fussing over a delivery from the florist, another arrangement of fresh-cut white roses. No matter how many times she visited the shop, she never deviated from her standard centerpiece.

"Beautiful flowers, mother. Though they would look more striking in red."

Anne smiled wistfully.

"Maybe so, dear, but these are my favorites, the ones you were named after."

"Really, white roses?" Rose was taken aback. Anne very rarely shared something so personal with her. "I knew I was named after the flower, but you never told me why."

"I loved white roses dearly in my youth." Her mother's voice was mournful as if she were revisiting a terrible memory.

Rose watched carefully as Anne caressed the petals softly with her fingers. Her eyes were distant, trance-like. She seemed to be staring at the flowers, without really seeing the flowers. Rose wanted to say something, to ask if her mother was okay, but couldn't interrupt this moment. She seldom saw Anne in a vulnerable state. In the past, any interjection on her part triggered her mother's guarded nature to return in full force. So instead of interfering, Rose clung to this opportunity to observe.

Her mother's eyes welled with moisture. As tears spilled over onto her pale cheeks, Anne's right hand wrapped around the stems of the roses, squeezing them tightly, a sharp thorn digging into her skin. Blood trickled down her wrist.

"Mother, you're bleeding!" Rose rushed over and cupped her mother's blood strewn hand in hers.

"It's quite all right, child." Her tone was even-keeled, her body reactionless.

"Aren't you hurt? The thorn pierced deep." Rose searched her eyes, but they still seemed far away. There was an extended pause before Anne finally turned her gaze towards Rose.

"You know nothing of pain," she snapped.

Anne abruptly withdrew her hand and left the room. Rose remained, again frustrated by her mother's behavior. She thought of chasing after her, forcing Anne into an embrace until she finally cracked and admitted the source of her pain, but her feet remained planted on the floor.

Rose sighed. She knew that pursuing her mother would be in vain. Anne had already retreated back behind her protective walls, the ones she had used to shut Rose out since she was old enough to ask questions. Rather than argue, Rose seized the opportunity to wander the streets of Dover on her own.

THIS TIME SHE ALLOWED HER NOSE to lead her into the bakery, straight to a fresh baguette still warm from the oven. As she savored each bite of the flaky, tender crust, she thought about how much she enjoyed staying up all night talking to Roosha. It had provided a different kind of gratification, one that she had been craving her entire life, a connection with a kindred spirit. Roosha listened attentively and looked at her as though she were the most fascinating person in the world. He seemed charmed by all of the characteristics her peers deemed unacceptably strange. He treasured her for her unique nature, which made her so grateful she had possessed the courage to retain her quirkiness in the face of relentless ridicule and judgment.

"GOOD AFTERNOON, CHILD." Mrs. Taddy was back to her exuberant self. "Where's that lovely mother of yours?"

Rose laughed. She was impressed by how well Mrs. Taddy concealed any contempt towards Anne.

"I'm afraid it's just you and me today, Mrs. Taddy." Rose gave her a wink.

"Wonderful! Oh my dear, it's incredible how pleasant you turned out..."

Rose sensed she was about to add something along the lines of "growing up with a mother like that," but then thought better of it. Rose was grateful she did. Even though she liked Mrs. Taddy, she wasn't about to confide her childhood traumas in the woman, especially when gossip likely spread within the small city just as quickly as it did among ladies of the court.

"I can't wait to see how the dress turned out," Rose lied.

Mrs. Taddy gave her a skeptical look.

"You can't fool me, child, this is your mother's dress, not yours. I saw you eyeing the dark green one in the window yesterday. It's not too late to change your mind."

Mrs. Taddy was observant. Every time Anne was distracted by colors, or fabric swatches, Rose's eyes focused on the emerald gown. It was a stunning combination of velvet, satin, and lace, all in a magical green hue. Rose briefly considered switching gowns. She envisioned her mother's face with a wicked smile. Anne would be livid if Rose returned with anything other than what her mother had approved, a devilishly satisfying proposition. But then Rose thought of her time with Roosha and realized that angering her mother in a child-like fit of defiance would not serve her purpose in any way right now. She took a deep breath and asked for the one the woman had sewn for her. Mrs. Taddy opened the wardrobe behind her desk and pulled out the dress.

"Would you like to try it on, make sure the fit is right?"

Rose surveyed the garment. It was dull and too frilly for her taste. The top was a simple white satin corset with long, sheer sleeves twice the width of her arm. The bottom was a lavender skirt with small matching bows going down the entire left side of the dress, which Rose found hideous. Although, she thought, the less attractive she looked in front of Charles, the better.

"No, thank you. If you wrap it up, I'll just take it home."

Mrs. Taddy began combing through the wardrobe for a box.

"So love, you've got a date with Mr. Charles Devano?"

"Hardly," Rose scoffed. "We're simply going for a stroll in some garden."

"Do you like him?"

Rose sensed a slight edge to Mrs. Taddy's voice. "I can't say I know him well enough to answer that question. Why do you ask?"

Mrs. Taddy hesitated. "I don't want to overstep my bounds. It's just that you seem like such a nice girl..."

Rose was now very interested in knowing precisely what Mrs. Taddy was trying to convey.

"Please speak freely, Mrs. Taddy. Anything you say is strictly between us. You have my word."

Mrs. Taddy looked around as if to make sure they were alone.

"Well, he doesn't seem like a very nice young man. One night, I was here late cleaning up my shop, and I heard yelling out in the street. I went to the window and saw Charles, excuse me, Master Devano. I believe that's the term he prefers. He was next door at the liquor shop and had two big brutes with him. Mr. Porter, the owner, opened the door, and they pulled him out into the street. The two lackeys shoved him roughly against a wall and held him there while Master Devano bellowed about tariffs on the whiskey his family sells the man. I couldn't hear anything Mr. Porter said, but at one point, I saw Master Devano lean in and slap Mr. Porter square across the face. The poor man's head turned so fast he knocked the other side straight into the wall they held him against.

They let go of him, and he almost keeled over. Mr. Porter hobbled into the store, came out carrying two bottles of scotch and left with the two brutes, not by choice. The next day I ran into Mr. Porter in the street. The right side of his face was badly bruised, and he was really shaken up. I've known that man for fifteen years; he's a good person. I can't imagine he did anything to merit that kind of treatment."

Rose stared at her blankly. She had no idea what Mrs. Taddy was going to say, but she certainly hadn't expected to hear something like that.

"Thank ... thank you for shar ... for sharing ..." Rose stuttered.

Mrs. Taddy looked regretful. "Oh dear, I didn't mean to frighten you, I just... oh, I don't know what I was thinking! I'm very sorry, love. Just forget the whole thing. I'll make you a cup of tea."

"No ... no, that's okay, thank you. I really must be going now. Thank you again, Mrs. Taddy."

Rose paid the woman and left quickly with the dress. She grasped the box tightly, her hands shaking the entire way home.

29

That night Rose was especially grateful for Roosha's presence. She had been unable to calm herself since returning home from the dress shop. Ruminating on Mrs. Taddy's disturbing story made her uneasy. She was already dreading the garden walk before the woman's horrifying account of Charles' behavior. Now, she was on edge. She wondered how a man who seemed so charming at dinner could behave in that manner towards an innocent man. By evening, she reached a point where she considered telling her mother but decided against it, figuring Anne would write the woman off as a liar, which she very well might be.

When Roosha arrived, Rose was already at the balcony doors, ready to wrap herself in his warm embrace. Sensing her need for comfort, he held her tightly, gently rubbing her back.

"What's wrong, my sweet Rose?"

Rose dared not disclose anything about Charles or her impending date. Aside from not wanting to hurt his feelings or make him jealous, Rose was also concerned about what Roosha would do if he feared for her safety. And, aware of how careful they had to be, she decided not to risk alarming him.

"I had a difficult day, but now that I'm in your arms, I'm feeling much better." It wasn't a lie; she convinced herself.

"Do you want to tell me what happened?"

"No. I don't want to waste our precious time together by reliving unpleasantries from the day. I just want to be here with you."

Roosha could feel the tension in her body and suspected that hearing about what had her in this state would not be a waste of time. But rather than pry, he decided to help soothe her instead.

Roosha gently brushed his lips against Rose's neck. As his tongue crept lightly along her skin, her breathing turned to gasps, and her heart thudded restlessly.

Roosha continued to the base of her neck, along her collarbone, and finally up to meet her eager mouth. Rose felt so many sensations overwhelming her body. She loved this man, or creature, or whatever he was. She loved Roosha, the only one who knew and understood her. He brought out all of these incredible qualities she hadn't known were in her. Rose grasped the back of Roosha's head, willing his tongue deeper into her mouth.

Roosha's head was throbbing, but he refused to let the pain deter him.

He wrapped his hands around Rose's waist and lifted her onto the edge of the bed. Slowly, he slid his hands up her thighs, pushing back the ends of her gray nightgown. He pulled his mouth away from Rose's, looking deep in her eyes as he kneeled to kiss her other mouth for the first time.

Roosha looked at Rose, love, and sincerity beaming from his eyes. "Remember, you mustn't utter a sound, my sweet Rose."

Rose returned his gaze, her eyes alight with bewilderment, and nodded. She cupped her right hand over her mouth as Roosha eased her back onto the mattress. He placed the backs of her knees against his shoulders and buried his head between her legs, his coarse mane tickling her inner thighs.

Softer, pinker flesh greeted his eager tongue, already moist with anticipation. Roosha licked her pleasure center's outer region, marveling at the beauty of her labia with its supple fullness equivalent to that of her upper lips. Roosha sucked on them gently, her juices dripping onto his tongue as he eased it into her moist cavern.

Rose gasped, and her lower back arched, bringing her closer to Roosha's face. Flicking the tip of his tongue upwards, Roosha's oral muscle brushed firmly against her swelled wall of pleasure. Rose's eyes closed, her hand clamping down tighter over her mouth. She could not think or concentrate, lost in the throes of ecstasy. Roosha's tongue burned, but her muffled moans ignited his desire to please her.

Sensing he had uncovered her most sensitive spot, he slid his tongue in and out, each time thrusting it up against that same tender area. Rose felt a rumbling building within her as if the walls of her nether region would collapse from the immense rapture. She bit down hard on her tongue to keep from screaming.

Rhythmic contractions enveloped Roosha's tongue until his mouth was flooded with a tantalizing ambrosial flavor. As her sweet juices enticed his taste buds, a sharp pain ripped through his chest, as if someone had plunged a knife through his torso and was now twisting the blade.

30

Roosha laid on the floor, paralyzed. Tonight was the first night he had been physically incapable of leaving after Rose passed out. The searing pain from kissing her lower region rendered him unable to see. Her room, which he knew well, became a blur of darkness. Rather than risk what was now a treacherous journey to the balcony, he remained motionless on the floor at the foot of her bed, praying the pain and his blindness would cease before morning.

Roosha hadn't anticipated how much pleasure Rose would derive from his actions that night. After all, he had never performed such an act on the other court girls, and he was too selfish in his human life to have ever pleasured a woman in that manner. But as his tongue penetrated deeper, his suffering escalated to an excruciating level. Even now, his entire body felt sore, as if he had been beaten mercilessly by a group of thugs. The orange glow from his naval radiated intensely, a flame burning a hole through his abdomen.

At one point, the pain became so unbearable that he questioned his motivations for putting himself through that ordeal. But then he heard Rose's moan, the one that signaled she was on the verge of orgasm. That moan brought meaning to his life. He loved her and would do anything to hear that climactic utter, no matter what he had to endure.

Hours later, part of his vision returned. He blinked several times, assessing his sight. Though objects were still distorted, he could at least make out the general shape of their fuzzy outlines. It was enough to make it back to the cave; at least, he reasoned, it had to be.

Warily, Roosha crawled to the balcony, his hands and forearms struggling to propel him forward. By the time he made it through the French doors, his arms were throbbing. He desperately wanted to stop and allow his body time to recover but knew he could not. Daybreak was fast approaching.

Grabbing the railing, he steeled his body and mind. Muscle ripped and protested as he pulled himself erect, a feat that required all of his energy and concentration. His exhausted body swayed like a weed in the wind. Unsure of his ability to fly, he turned to take one last look at Rose. She was in a deep slumber, her face peaceful. Roosha sighed, instigating stabbing pains in his rib cage. He had to fly. Were he not to return, Rose's serene face would be twisted with anguish, and he to blame, a thought more painful than his current physical agony. He vowed never to let that happen before tumbling over the railing.

Roosha stumbled through the air with great difficulty. Every flap of his wings felt like punching an unhealed bruise. He winced, but pushed forward, the short journey arduous. Fighting his body's desire to succumb to its torment, Roosha focused on the only thing that mattered to him, Rose. Were it not for her, he would have given in to the pain.

Finally, at the clearing, Roosha descended through the trees, crashing beside the lake at the base of an oak tree, his arms wrapped around the trunk for support. Minutes passed before he attempted to move.

Steadying himself, Roosha limped towards the cave, where he intended to remain until the aching subsided. When he reached the last tree before the waterfall, another sturdy oak, he stopped. Roosha leaned against the bark, giving his body a brief respite. There was no way he could limp in front of the others without alerting suspicion. He shut his eyes and again thought only of Rose. He had to be strong for her. Summoning all of his strength, Roosha pushed hard against the tree, lifting himself upright. His arms threatened to collapse under his weight. He stepped slowly and deliberately, clenching his jaw tightly to quell the agony. He was almost through the entryway behind the waterfall when a familiar voice greeted him.

"Hello, friend."

Roosha immediately knew who it was. He turned and balanced himself against the rocks.

"Avidan, how are you, friend?" Roosha sounded out of breath.

"Better than you, I take it." Avidan eyed him suspiciously.

"Oh, I'm fine, dear friend. This is nothing. I had a small collision flying this evening."

"A collision?" Avidan raised his right eyebrow.

"Yes. I got distracted and flew into the edge of a cliff." As soon as he heard the words come out of his mouth, Roosha regretted saying them. With their heightened night vision, the idea of crashing into something was far-fetched. He cursed himself for offering an explanation where silence would have served him better than an implausible excuse.

"Hmm, and what was it that distracted you so?" Avidan folded his arms across his chest.

"My thoughts," Roosha spoke in a defeated manner.

"I see. Well then, my dear boy, I suppose there's only one question you should be asking yourself." Avidan closed in abruptly, his face only inches from Roosha's. "What on earth are you thinking?" His last six words were loaded with implication and accusation. Avidan looked at him incredulously and then took off into the night.

As perceptive as he was, Roosha couldn't be sure of the extent of Avidan's knowledge. But he knew Avidan was no fool and that he had to be much more careful going forward. Rose's safety was paramount. Roosha called Avidan friend, but inherently he knew that only in his darkest hour would friend from foe be revealed.

31

Rose observed herself in the mirror, appraising how hideous her new dress looked. The white bodice washed out her fair skin, and the bows adorning the one side of her dress made her body look lopsided. Despite the ugliness of the gown, Rose was beaming.

Her mind was fixated on Roosha and her newfound capacity for pleasure. Rose had never ventured inside the warm cavern between her legs, had never known, or even fathomed the depths it possessed. She was enamored by Roosha and intent on having him explore this area further with her so that she would know all of her capabilities.

"Oh, Rose, you do look ravishing!" Her mother smiled sincerely.

"Thank you, mother." Rose did not have to fake her cheerfulness today. She was sure nothing could spoil her mood.

"Charles will be so pleased!" Anne clapped her hands together, her fingers resting on her lips as she admired her daughter's beauty.

On any other day, Rose would have immediately rolled her eyes. But today she didn't care. She refused to let Charles or her mother's undue desire to please him affect her. She would go on the garden walk and daydream about Roosha. She planned on putting everything, including what Mrs. Taddy had told her, out of her mind.

Anne's cheerful face grew serious. "I'm not a fool, Rose. I know you aren't looking forward to this date, but won't you give Charles a chance?"

Still facing her reflection, Rose focused on controlling her reaction, not allowing any smirks or eye movements. She kept her mouth shut and smoothed the skirt of her dress with her hands. Anne gently put her hand on Rose's cheek, tilting her daughter's face towards hers.

"He was clever enough to debate you at dinner rather than dismissing you the way most of the other noblemen would have."

"Who are you trying to convince, mother? Me, or you?" Rose's voice was calm, but she could feel her resolve faltering.

"What is that supposed to mean?" Anne's brow furrowed.

"If you know I have no interest in seeing Charles, then why are we having this conversation? Perhaps it's to convince yourself that you're doing the right thing by forcing me into a courtship when you aren't." Heat flushed beneath her cheeks.

"Who knows what the right thing is?" Anne muttered, almost inaudibly, a wistful look in her eyes.

"Excuse me, mother?" Rose's inflection mirrored her confusion from Anne's uncharacteristic utterance. She had expected an argument from her mother.

Anne placed her hands on Rose's shoulders. "I'm simply suggesting that you get to know him. He did bring your favorite chocolates the other night, a thoughtful gesture," Anne offered.

"He's boring," Rose blurted. She shook her mother's hands from her shoulders while silently cursing herself for losing her temper. "And as much as I fancy the chocolates, I most certainly will never fancy him!"

Anne sighed, her blue eyes resigned. "Sometimes, what we find exciting inevitably leaves us disappointed, Rose."

IT WAS EXACTLY NOON when Charles called on her. Rose was surprised by his punctuality, given how late he had arrived at dinner the other week. Perhaps he had been confused about the time after all. Anne looked so delighted to see the man that Rose loathed the idea of giving him the benefit of the doubt.

"Why, Charles, you're on time!" Rose felt a slight kick in the back of her leg, which could only have been from her mother.

Charles feigned a look of distress. "Don't sound so surprised, Rose! I would hardly leave a such a beauteous creature waiting. How unforgivably rude that would be!"

"What my lovely daughter meant to say was that she's been waiting in anticipation of this day and was could not bear waiting a moment longer. She's so grateful to have this time with you." Anne cocked her head to the side and eyed Rose sternly.

Rose forced a cough to stifle her laughter. She shouldn't be surprised that her mother had put her "proper" mask back on now that their company had arrived.

"No one has a way with words quite like my mother! Shall we?"

VIVIANNA PULLED CHILDREN'S BOOKS from the shelves, while contemplating the obstacles she would face that afternoon. There was her mother's watchful eye, discreetly getting hold of the key to the trunk, managing a swarm of small children, and, on top of all that, there was Savannah. Vivianna cringed. She was much more confident about pulling off this mission when Rose was part of the plan, but she was still determined to give it her best effort.

"Vivianna, dear?" Mrs. Weston called, her voice a bit hoarse.

Vivianna turned to see her mother wrapped in a wool shawl. She looked at her curiously.

"Yes, mother?"

"I'm afraid I need to return home. Would it be too much of an imposition for you to manage the children's event without me?"

Vivianna couldn't believe how quickly fortune had smiled upon her. Had her main obstacle just been effortlessly removed from the equation?

"Of course, mother." She cocked her head to the side and surveyed her mother, who had seemed fine this morning. "What's wrong?"

"I'm feeling terribly ill, and I don't want to infect any of the children." Mrs. Weston coughed into her ivory handkerchief.

"I'm sorry to hear that, mother. Don't worry about a thing. I'll take care of everything. Go home and get some rest. I'll check on you as soon as the event is over."

"Thank you, dear." Mrs. Weston held out her hand. "Here are the library keys. The gold one is the key to the basement so that you can store the extra books later."

Vivianna took the keys, elated. Another obstacle was out of her way. Her mother had given her the keys without Vivianna even having to ask for them. She was regaining her confidence in securing the diaries.

"Thank you, mother."

"Of course, dear." Mrs. Weston turned to leave.

Vivianna grinned. Savannah hadn't even arrived yet. She was sure she could go down to the basement right away, remove the diaries from the trunk, and put them in a safe place for later. When Vivianna looked down at the keys, her face fell. She flipped through them three times, only to find that the black key with the red wing was missing.

THE DEVANO FAMILY GARDEN was magnificent. It seemed to be an endless labyrinth of sculptured hedges and lattices overflowing with orchids, ivy, lilies, and delicate wildflowers. It was a place Rose would love to visit often, only with present company excluded.

On the carriage ride over, Charles had bored her with talk of his family's company and their recent acquirement of new wealth through various channels, as if money would somehow make him appealing to her. Or perhaps he just enjoyed bragging about his family fortune, Rose thought to herself.

Now that they were in his territory and away from her mother, Charles seemed to be taking much more interest in Rose's physical appearance.

"I must say, Rose, you are positively glowing today."

Rose observed him carefully. His words sounded polite, but his leer was less than gentlemanly. She nodded curtly without uttering a word to him.

"That's a lovely dress. It suits you quite well, or better yet, your figure suits the dress." Charles' stare moved over every part of her except her eyes. Rose was beginning to feel uncomfortable. Even thinking of Roosha wasn't helping. The more she thought about him, the more she wished he were there to protect her.

This morning, she had been so proud of the glow she woke up with, another advancement in her womanhood, but now she wished she had a way to turn it off, as it seemed to be attracting unwanted advances. Desperate to divert Charles' attention, Rose abandoned her earlier plan and decided to investigate this man.

"Thank you, Charles. I got it at Mrs. Taddy's Taylor in town. Are you familiar with the establishment?"

Charles thought for a moment. "I believe so. My family does business with many small shops in town, so I'm sure I've seen the place before. I must say they do exquisite work." Charles stroked Rose's upper arm, feeling the fabric of the dress.

Rose felt a knot in her stomach. Surely that was too forward for a gentleman. She wished her mother were there to witness his behavior. Maybe then Anne would realize Charles was in no way deserving of a chance. The fact that she had imagined kissing this louse at dinner made Rose ill. Gingerly, she stepped away from Charles and began walking along the pebble path that wound through the garden.

"Tell me, Charles, what is your style of doing business?"

"What do you mean, Rose?" He seemed to be speaking to her breasts.

"Well, you said your family does business with a lot of different shops. How on earth do you manage it all?" Rose thought she might get more information if she acted as clueless as the other court girls were.

"Oh, Rose, my family has systems in place, and standard contracts with each vendor." He brushed a tendril of hair from her cheek. Shyly, Rose turned her face from him and quickened her pace.

"Still, it must be difficult keeping track of each individual shop. There are so many of them."

"No, quite the opposite. We have scheduled days of the month for delivery and payment collection, and a well-organized process ensuring things run smoothly."

"But what would happen if you had a problem with one of the shops? Say it was a scheduled payment collection day, and the shop owner didn't pay you properly. How would you handle the situation?"

Charles looked at her strangely. "You have quite the inquiring mind, don't you, Rose?"

She felt her cheeks flush timidly. Rose couldn't tell from his tone how he meant that comment, but she was disinclined to believe it was a compliment.

"It's just that you make your family's business sound so interesting. I'd like to know more." There was a brief pause. Charles' eyes bored into hers cryptically. Beads of nervous sweat formed in her cleavage and on the back of her neck. "You did say it was your passion...the other night at dinner," she offered meekly.

"Ah, yes! I did." Charles seemed to visibly relax. "Well, Rose, if a shop owner doesn't pay on time, I'll visit him to determine the reason for the delay. If he doesn't have the funds on hand and it's the first time this has happened, I'll attempt to accommodate him with some type of installment plan. If it were to happen again, then my family would, of course, reconsider doing business with that particular merchant."

His words made sense, and he sounded sincere. But Rose couldn't get the image of him assaulting a shop owner out of her mind.

"Would there ever be any additional punishment for not paying?"

"Other than no longer doing business with my family? What could be a worse punishment than that? Our import company is responsible for keeping many shop owners in the comfortable lifestyle they are accustomed to."

"So, you would never resort to any unconventional methods, like violence?" Rose regretted the words the second they escaped her mouth. She could hear Vivianna's voice telling her that she had just revealed far too much information.

A look of shock registered on Charles' face. "Why, Rose, I'm surprised you would ask such a question. Why on earth would you think that? My family adheres to a strict code of ethics in business. There is absolutely no place or purpose for violence. The idea is reprehensible."

Rose's cheeks grew red with embarrassment. She felt like a child being admonished. "I...I'm sorry, Charles," she stuttered. "I don't know what came over me." She looked down at the patch of grass between her shoes.

Charles lifted her chin with his index finger. "Rose, who put that outlandish notion in your head?" Despite his measured tone, a frightening intensity emanated from his stare.

Rose trembled. She dared not mention Mrs. Taddy for fear that, if her account were accurate, it would put the woman in imminent danger.

"No...no one. I've only read about it in books."

Charles waved his hand dismissively. "Rose, books of that nature are a waste of time." He gripped her shoulders firmly, his fingers digging into Rose's skin. "Promise me you'll never say something like that again. It distresses me that you would even think I was capable of any type of violence, let alone in a professional setting."

One by one, the beads of sweat trickled down her chest and back. "Of course not, Charles. I never meant to impugn your family's noble name in any way. It was inappropriate of me to question your affairs. I have no idea how proper businesses operate. I'm afraid that's not something they bother teaching us ladies, and I didn't want you to think I was as frivolous as the other girls." She summoned her most girlish pout.

Rose was embarrassed, not from offending Charles, but from giving herself away so easily without first obtaining proof. Now, Charles was aware of her suspicions and would remain guarded, making sure he revealed nothing of consequence, if there even was anything to reveal. Rose still had no way of knowing whether Mrs. Taddy's story was true. She decided the most strategic approach was to appear an ingénue. Hopefully, placating his ego would prove a more fruitful strategy.

Charles put his hand beneath her chin and lifted her face back up. Now he was looking her in the eye.

"Of course, beautiful Rose. One cannot expect such a lovely creature to know anything at all about the operations of a business, nor should you. Your time is much better spent at home decorating and entertaining."

Rose felt the urge to strike him but refrained.

VIVIANNA'S MIND WAS RACING. The key she needed wasn't there, and she had no idea where it might be. As far as she knew, her mother was the sole person entrusted with the library keys, and she was nearing the exit. Vivianna had to think fast. Desperate, she removed one of the keys from the ring and ran after her mother.

"Mother! Mother, wait!"

Mrs. Weston stopped and turned slowly. "What is it, dear? I need to go lay down."

"I'm sorry, but I believe one of the keys is missing." Vivianna handed the keys to her mother, an innocent expression on her face. Mrs. Weston inspected the ring.

"Hmm. You're right. The key to my desk has apparently disappeared. No matter, the gold one is the only one you need. Have a good afternoon, dear."

Inside, Vivianna was fuming. She grasped at any thought that might present a way to find that key.

"Mother, is there anywhere I could look for the key to your desk? Somewhere else it might be? It would save you the trouble, especially with you not feeling well today."

"That's very kind of you, dear, but it's not necessary." Her mother turned and opened the door to leave.

Vivianna's eyes were wide with disbelief. She couldn't believe her plan was over before it even started. She wondered what she was going to tell Rose.

"It just occurred to me," Mrs. Weston paused, her face still towards the door. "There is a box of lost items in the basement. Every day after closing, I retrieve whatever has been left in the library and add it to the collection. It's possible my key got mixed up in there. You may as well take a look while you're downstairs, dear. My desk key is small and silver with a red stone at the top."

"Yes, mother, I'll find it for you!" Vivianna felt a renewed sense of hope. There was a chance, albeit a slim one, that she may find the key to the trunk. At least now, she had somewhere to search.

BY THE TIME THEY WALKED the entire length of the enormous garden, Rose yearned for their date to end. While acting mindless had succeeded in changing the subject after her stumble, Charles had unfortunately taken the opportunity to return to his leering.

Several times he touched her in seemingly innocuous ways, and each time Rose felt violated. His hand occasionally grazed the small of her back or caressed her long locks. In each of those moments, she stepped to the side, deliberately moving out of his reach, but it did nothing to deter him. His lingering stare continued to make her uncomfortable as if he were willing his eyes to penetrate the fabric of her dress.

Even worse was Rose's evolving internal dialogue. Her experience with Roosha the night before made her feel empowered and excited about her body and sensuality, which she was still discovering. She basked in the glow of her skin, knowing it came from deep within her essence.

But now she was uneasy. The way Charles looked at her made her feel like prey. At first, she thought him the culprit for persisting in his unsolicited attempts to touch her, but as his behavior continued, doubt crept into her mind.

Rose began to wonder if she was responsible for his lewdness. She couldn't help thinking that none of the other court girls must elicit this type of behavior from the noblemen. Was her glow to blame? Was her appetite for pleasure? Was she unknowingly sending out some kind of signal that she desired him? It didn't make sense to her, but then again, neither did his behavior.

When they reached the entrance to the garden, Rose seized the opportunity to make her exit. "Well, Charles, thank you so much for a lovely day. I really must be going now."

"So soon?" He placed his hands in hers, pulling her body closer to his than she preferred.

"Yes, I'm afraid so. You see, I'm late for an event at the library. I wouldn't want to disappoint the children or the other ladies of the court, especially when I volunteered to help." Rose was proud of herself for her smooth delivery in spite of how much her skin was crawling. As a nobleman, Charles should not want to keep her from her courtly duties.

"That's very altruistic of you, Rose. In that case, I shan't delay you. As it is, I've some business to attend to myself." Charles caressed her palms with his thumbs. "My, you have such soft skin, Rose." Instead of kissing her hand, as is customary, he leaned in close and whispered in her ear, "We must do this again soon. I look forward to getting to know much more of you." He kissed her cheek with moist lips, leaving a trail of saliva that felt like poison on her skin. Rose cringed internally. "I'll send for the carriage."

"No," Rose blurted. The thought of spending one more moment with him was unbearable. "It's quite all right, Charles. If you don't mind, I'd prefer to walk. It's not far."

"I suppose that would be fine. An excellent way to balance out your truffle intake." He winked. Rose was too unsettled to process the insult.

"Goodbye, Rose." Charles bowed politely.

"Goodbye." Her voice was high and strained. Rose curtseyed before quickly leaving the garden. As soon as she was sure he could no longer see her, she started running at full speed.

Rose scrambled through thick brush, branches tearing into her new dress. She made it about half a mile before a severe cramp at the top of her right rib cage forced her to stop. Short, shallow breaths heaved through her system uncontrollably. She leaned on a fern tree for support. Gradually, her body slid down the bark, slumping on the ground. Tears welled in her eyes as questions flooded her mind. How could she allow

Charles to behave in that manner? Why didn't she have the courage to say something, anything to him? All she had done was move out of his reach after he'd already touched her inappropriately. His eyes were far more forward than his hands, yet she had done nothing to avert his ogling. She just stood there as he mentally undressed her, probably picturing all of the vulgar things he wanted to do to her, or rather, parts of her.

Rose's cheeks flushed with shame, the tears spilling from her eyes. She had practically condoned his behavior. Rose repeatedly slapped the patch of moss beside her, wishing it were Charles' face.

Sucking in large gulps of air, she attempted to calm herself. She placed her hands on the ground and eased herself to her feet. As Rose's breathing slowly returned to normal, the cramp subsided.

She stumbled down to a stream and surveyed her disheveled reflection in the water. The veins in her eyes were bright red, the skin beneath them puffy. Her hair had come undone, loose ends sticking out to the sides. Her sleeves were tattered from catching on branches, the bottom of her skirt slicked with dirt. She thought of how furious Anne would be when she saw the new dress ruined.

Rose dipped her hands in the water and ran them through her hair, smoothing out the wild strands. She splashed the frigid liquid on her face, the cold shocking her back to reality. There was no time for wallowing. Vivianna needed her at the library, and while she may have let herself down that afternoon, she would not let Vivianna down.

VIVIANNA WAS FLUSTERED. There were so many screaming children wreaking havoc in the library, that it seemed more a child care program than a reading event. She had yet to make a single trip to the basement.

"We're here," a familiar shrill greeted Vivianna.

"We?" Wiping the confusion from her face, Vivianna turned around to see Savannah and Amelia standing in front of her. "Good afternoon, ladies. Amelia, I didn't realize you were attending."

Amelia opened her mouth to speak, but Savannah interjected. "She wasn't until I convinced her what a wonderful cause children's literacy is. Why illiterate children are almost as intolerable as illegitimate children, wouldn't you agree?" Savannah smiled tightly.

"Of course," Amelia chimed in at once. "And I was not about to leave my closest friend unaccompanied." Amelia put her hands on Savannah's shoulders. Vivianna watched in amusement as Savannah squirmed from the contact.

"That's quite noble of you, Amelia, and we could do with the extra help. Why don't you ladies head over there?" Vivianna pointed to a long, oval table covered in newspapers. Piles of brushes, paper, and paint jars were strewn across the center. "You can run our art enrichment program for the afternoon."

Savannah's nose crinkled. "I'm not sure …"

"Though I must say, Savannah, you are a bit overdressed," Vivianna interrupted. "Perhaps you'd prefer a simpler activity, one better suited to your capabilities?" She dangled the question as bait, hoping to provoke Savannah's ego.

Amelia pursed her lips. Savannah wore a dark orange satin gown and matching bonnet. The bodice was intricately embroidered with small pink blossoms. It was an elegant dress worthy of a lavish dinner party.

"Better to be fashionably forward rather than …" Savannah cleared her throat. She looked Vivianna up and down, eyeing her simple frock with disdain. "Comfortably common. Fret not, little Vivianna. My wardrobe will only enhance my capabilities."

Amelia sniggered. "Couldn't have said it better myself, Savannah."

Vivianna smiled widely. "Paint it is!" She led them towards the station where four young children had already opened most of the paint jars.

"Where is Rose?" Savannah asked innocently, though she already knew the answer.

"On her second date with Charles, which I'm sure you are well aware of." Vivianna had emphasized the word second, knowing it would irk her.

"Curious, isn't it, that she chose to break her courtly commitment to you to spend the afternoon with him." Savannah grinned wickedly.

"She made a commitment to the event, not to me," Vivianna replied dismissively.

"And yet, I doubt she would have agreed were it anyone else who asked her."

"Perhaps, or perhaps not. I suppose we'll never know." Vivianna clapped her hands together. "Now, if you'll excuse me, I've an event to run." Before either of them could protest, Vivianna turned on her heel and hastened toward the basement.

ONCE ON THE OTHER SIDE of the heavy wooden door, Vivianna breathed a sigh of relief. She closed her eyes, appreciating how well the wood suppressed the chaotic noise from the main room. Quickly, she gathered herself, knowing time was of the essence. It wouldn't be long before her absence was noticed.

From the top of the stairs, she examined the room. On the opposite wall was a narrow, rectangular window. Its translucent glass allowed just enough of the midday light to navigate the otherwise unlit space. It was as she remembered it, only with more piles of books that her mother must have carried down there prior to the children's event.

Her eyes moved to the far corner, where a glaring shade of red jutted out from beneath a dusty crate. The trunk was still there, unmoved. Vivianna marched straight to the mysterious coffer and pulled on the latch. It was locked. She fiddled with the set of keys her mother had given her. There were six of them, including the small silver one she had arbitrarily removed. Though she presumed it would be a futile effort, she decided to try each of the keys. One by one, she shoved them into the lock, and one by one, they failed to unlock it.

Vivianna rummaged through the crate on top of the trunk. Strewn across its floor were random objects, from lady's gloves, to men's spectacles, and children's toys. There was nothing remotely useful, nor any items resembling a key. She hoped this wasn't the collection of lost belongings her mother had suggested.

Vivianna dug through the other cartons, but they were filled with books and odd antiquities. She yanked volumes from their neat rows and furiously shook them to see if any contents fell from their pages. Growing increasingly frustrated, she began flipping the boxes upside down and dumping the contents onto the floor in heaps. After the fourth box, she gave up. Her arms throbbed, and she was choking from the overwhelming cloud of dust that had been created. She was out of ideas and now had a huge mess to clean up.

"WHERE ON EARTH HAVE YOU BEEN?" Savannah spat at her, livid. The front of her fancy dress was laden with tiny handprints in shades of blue, purple, and gray. Amelia stood beside her, simpering.

"My goodness, Savannah, what happened?" Vivianna feigned incredulity.

Savannah's cheeks grew redder. "Those monstrous little beasts attacked me!" She balled her shaking fists.

"I am sorry about that, Savannah. A child's nature can be quite unpredictable." Vivianna gazed at her sympathetically. "Perhaps you should head home. You may still be able to salvage that lovely dress." The sooner she was rid of Savannah and Amelia, the sooner she could return to her hunt, Vivianna reasoned. Perhaps she could break the lock on the trunk?

Savannah glanced around the library. Vivianna couldn't be sure, but she thought she was searching for something, or more likely, someone, which would explain why she had arrived at the library in formal wear.

"Charles won't be honoring us with his presence this afternoon, you know."

"And apparently, neither will Rose," Savannah snapped.

Vivianna didn't say anything, though Savannah had hit a nerve. She agreed that the date had gone on rather long. Only fifteen minutes remained, and Rose still wasn't there. Most of the children had already left, and Vivianna didn't know where the key might be.

Savannah fidgeted, glaring at the library entrance. "Well, I suppose I should attend to my dress. It is an original design." With her nose held high, Savannah stalked away.

Vivianna glanced at Amelia, who didn't have a drop of paint on her. "Curious, isn't it, that the children spared you."

"What can I say?" Amelia shrugged. "I suppose they preferred a more fashion-forward canvas," she added snidely. "Now, if you'll excuse me, I must escort my dear friend home."

VIVIANNA WAITED PATIENTLY as the library emptied out. Free of both her mother and Savannah's watchful eyes, she would now have the opportunity to safely scour the building, starting with another trip to the basement. Her anticipation was marred by the nerve Savannah's words had pinched. She was angry with Rose. They had devised a plan together. They were supposed to be working as a team to get these journals, and now, here Vivianna was struggling while Rose strolled through a garden with a man she claimed to detest.

That was the part that frustrated Vivianna. She wanted to know why Rose had abandoned their mission to go on a date with Charles Devano. It was clear Rose was keeping something from her, but what secret was so important that it took precedence over their plan? And why didn't Rose trust her with that secret? Vivianna winced. She had put her full trust in Rose the day she confided in her about the diaries, but Rose still had not reciprocated.

Vivianna was about to unlock the basement when she heard the front door swing open again. In her rumination, she had forgotten to lock the entrance.

"That cursed girl," she muttered under her breath. Vivianna removed the key from the cylinder and headed back towards the library entryway. "Did you forget something, Savannah?"

When she reached the front, she saw Rose standing against the door, reigniting her anger. She flounced towards Rose, ready to unleash a barrage of questions. But when she stopped and looked at Rose, her anger dissipated.

Vivianna knew something was wrong. Her beautiful, spirited friend looked like a crestfallen tatterdemalion. She peered into Rose's red-rimmed eyes with concern. Vivianna fingered her ragged sleeves, fearful of how Rose's dress had come into this condition. She pulled her friend into a warm embrace.

"Rose, what's wrong? What happened?"

"I'm okay …" Rose whispered.

"You certainly don't look okay. Was it Charles? Did something happen?"

"I don't want to talk about it."

Vivianna squeezed Rose tighter before pushing her an arm's length away to look her in the eye. "Something is clearly wrong. Did he hurt you?"

"No … I mean, not physically." Rose wiped a tear trail from her cheek.

"Then, how? What did he say to you?" Vivianna shook her shoulders unintentionally.

Rose replayed the events of the afternoon again in her mind and shuddered.

"He just … he … please don't make me talk about it right now. Not here. I just want to go home and take a bath. I came to help get the diaries. Please, let's just do that."

Vivianna decided not to press. "Okay. We'll talk about it when you're ready." She enveloped Rose in another hug before letting her go.

"Have you found them yet?"

Vivianna explained to Rose exactly what had happened throughout the course of the afternoon, including her mother's departure, the failed attempt to find the key in the basement, and Savannah showing up with Amelia and impeding her search efforts.

"Have you looked anywhere other than the basement?"

"No, why?"

"Because it doesn't make sense to me that the key would be somewhere in close proximity to the trunk if the contents are supposed to be well-protected. It seems your mother may want to keep it somewhere closer to her. Have you thought of looking in her desk?"

Vivianna's eyes lit up. "Rose, you're a genius!" Vivianna remembered that the desk key was the small silver one with the red stone, which she had pulled off the ring earlier. "And to think the key I removed from the ring by chance this morning was the key to her desk, and yet I haven't thought to use it all day."

They smiled at each other and headed straight for the giant desk in the back of the library. The expansive unit had eight large drawers, none of which had locks on them. The girls yanked each drawer open and rummaged through them, only to find stationery and books that were on hold.

On the upper level of the desk were four thin drawers. Rose pulled the handle of each one, but they didn't budge. Vivianna produced the small silver key and unlocked the first drawer. Rose watched in anticipation as it slid towards them, revealing its contents.

The first drawer contained two stacks of cash, probably collections from book sales, Vivianna reasoned. She relocked that drawer and proceeded to the next one. Inside were three pairs of mismatched ruby earrings and a gold necklace, none of which she recognized as part of her mother's personal jewelry collection.

"Perhaps this is where she keeps the expensive lost items?" Vivianna suggested.

She proceeded to the third and fourth drawers, but they were empty. Both of the girls were now feeling deflated.

"Where is this cursed key?" Vivianna slammed her hands down on the desk in frustration, knocking the small key onto the floor. As she knelt to pick it up, she noticed something odd beneath the desk.

"Rose, come and look at this."

Rose knelt beside her and followed Vivianna's gaze. There was a tiny compartment in the side of the desk that looked like it opened. It had a lock on it identical to the ones on the drawers. Vivianna eyed Rose, who nodded. She took a deep breath and eased the key into the lock. Slowly, Vivianna turned the key to the right until it could go no farther. As the key clicked into place, a drawer popped out to reveal a red satin pouch. Rose gasped. Vivianna grabbed the pouch, fingering it in her hand before opening it. Inside was the black key with the red wing on it.

"Hmm, now why are two court ladies huddled on the floor? Looking for something?" Shrillness pierced the air like an alarm.

Rose and Vivianna looked at each other, disconcerted. It was Savannah. She must have crept back into the library quietly. Vivianna grabbed the key and shoved it inside her shoe. She looked at Rose and put her finger over her mouth to signal silence. Rose nodded. Vivianna then shut and locked the drawer quietly before popping up from below the desk. Rose stood up slowly behind her.

"Why, Savannah, I didn't expect to see you again so soon. What brings you back to the library?" Vivianna's voice showed no sign of apprehension.

"I forgot my hat." She held up the orange bonnet that matched her dress. "Now, exactly what were you two doing down there?" She eyed them both suspiciously.

"I thought I dropped my earring, but it was a false alarm." The words were out of Rose's mouth before she could stop herself.

Savannah's stare moved from her eyes to her earlobes. "Oh? You're not even wearing any earrings, Rose."

Vivianna stiffened next to her.

"We saw something gold and shiny on the floor, and Rose thought it was an earring. It was a false alarm. Now, if you'll excuse us, Savannah, we're about to clean up the library from the event."

Rose was impressed by the finality of Vivianna's tone. She wasn't asking Savannah anything; she was telling her what was happening.

"Well, in that case, I suppose I should stay and help."

"Thank you for the gracious offer, but that's not necessary. There isn't much to be done, and we won't be long. I need to get home to tend to my ill mother."

"Then I'm sure it would be better to have the extra help for your mother's sake. The quicker the cleanup, the faster you'll see her." Savannah gave them both a sly smile.

"Suit yourself." Vivianna went over to a small closet and came back with a broom and a rag. She handed the cloth to Savannah and the broom to Rose. "The kids were mainly in the front of the library, so that's where the real mess is. Savannah, be a dear and wipe down the tables where the children were doing their lovely artwork." Vivianna smiled knowingly at her. "And Rose, please give the floors a thorough sweeping after all the cookies we gave them."

"And what will you be doing?" Savannah asked.

Vivianna picked up a stack of books from one of the tables. "I'll be transporting these books down to the basement where they belong while Rose regales you with how well her walk with Charles went." Vivianna winked at Rose subtly.

Rose was about to protest, but Savannah had already turned towards her, a mischievous expression on her face.

"Yes, Rose, do tell. I'd love to hear all about your walk with Mr. Devano."

Rose realized that she was meant to distract Savannah, giving Vivianna a chance to procure the diaries. It was the least she could do after all Vivianna had done. Still, Rose felt an unease in the pit of her stomach. She dreaded the idea of even thinking about, let alone discussing her experience and was sure if she had been truthful with Vivianna, she never would have put her in this position. Rose took a deep breath that failed to ease the tension in her jaw.

"Well, I must say... their garden is lovely." She intended to keep her rendition as banal as possible.

Savannah sighed, her foot tapping. "The garden was lovely? Come now, Rose, let's have it. Exactly what happened on this little date of yours?"

Rose gulped. She knew someone like Savannah would never believe the truth. As she thought it, the word truth made Rose pause. She realized she didn't have to share her story. All she needed to do was capture Savannah's attention.

"Well, Charles picked me up in his carriage. He has two of the most magnificent Clydesdales I've ever seen, brown with..."

"Yes, yes," Savannah interrupted, agitated. "Spare me the hippophilia, Rose. What happened in the garden?"

"Well..." Rose stammered. "We strolled arm-in-arm, talking."

"Talking? For two hours, all you did was talk?" Savannah folded her arms across her chest and tilted her head.

Rose felt the flush of blood beneath her cheeks. "Yes. It was quite lovely," she lied.

"Funny, from the state of your dress, it appears your mouth did far more than just emit words." Savannah pointed to the shreds of fabric hanging from Rose's sleeves. "I shouldn't have expected anything less from Scarlet Rose," she breathed, her tone acerbic. "You are and have always been a disgrace to the ladies of the court. Thankfully, poor Charles' imposing reputation precedes him the way your licentious one precedes you. Your seductive nature will not tarnish his good name."

Tears pricked Rose's eyes. She blinked several times, willing herself not to cry. Savannah's words exacerbated Rose's fear that she had brought Charles' sexual advances on herself; that her forbidden affair with Roosha and ensuing sensual awakening made her responsible for its effect on him. That it was her glow that had lured him to temptation.

Savannah was sure to begin a smear campaign impugning the Woodburn name. Rose was already ashamed of herself for her lack of courage with Charles, and now she would bring shame to her poor mother, whose primary concern in life was being proper.

In Rose's silence, Savannah had made it halfway to the basement door. Frantically, Rose chased after her.

"Wait!" Rose called. "Where are you going?"

"Why Vivianna's been gone a while, I want to make sure she's all right."

"She's fine; she's just putting books away." Rose's voice was frenetic.

Savannah ignored her, opened the door to the basement, and waltzed down the stairs. Rose was right behind her, terrified that she had failed Vivianna. Her only responsibility had been to distract Savannah, and instead, Rose had succumbed to her own emotional distraction. Vivianna deserved better.

When they reached the bottom of the stairs, Vivianna was stacking children's books in a box. Rose glanced around the room but didn't see the red trunk anywhere.

"Can I help you, ladies?" Vivianna asked nonchalantly.

Savannah walked right up to Vivianna and inspected the pile of books. Her eyes darted around the room, searching for anything out of the ordinary. Vivianna didn't even flinch. She continued organizing the books as if Savannah weren't there. Rose admired her insouciance.

Vivianna slid two boxes against the wall and then headed back up the stairs. "Ladies, I suggest you follow me unless you want to be locked down here overnight. It gets rather dark after sunset."

Savannah stomped back up the stairs. The three girls finished cleaning up the library in silence under Savannah's scrutinous glare. After every surface had been dusted, polished, or swept, Vivianna escorted them both out and locked up the library. In her hand were two small envelopes. She handed one to Rose and one to Savannah.

"These are thank you notes on behalf of my mother for your generous service in volunteering at the children's event today. She was pleased to have our help, and I know she would want to express her gratitude to you both personally. Unfortunately, as she fell ill this morning and is unable to do so herself, I ask that you accept these cards as tokens of her appreciation. I must go and tend to her now. I wish you both a wonderful rest of your day."

"But…" Savannah was at a loss for words.

"Yes, Savannah? Is there something else?" Vivianna was perfectly polite.

"I suppose not," Savannah pouted.

"In that case, I bid you good day, ladies."

Vivianna turned and walked away, heading in the direction of her mother's house. She didn't look back once. Rose was impressed by how matter of fact she could be. If Rose weren't involved in the plan, she wouldn't have suspected anything. The frustrated look on Savannah's face showed how effective her actions were. Once Vivianna was out of sight, Savannah gave up and left without so much as a goodbye.

Rose leaned against the stone wall and opened the envelope. Inside was a small notecard on which Vivianna had written:

Meet me at the stables tomorrow _before_ sunrise.

32

As soon as Rose returned home, she drew herself a hot bath, refusing the maid's services despite her insistence. Rose intended to scrub the crawling feeling from her skin. Beside the copper tub, she struggled to undo the corset. It would have been easier with help, but she wanted to be alone, the only place where it seemed acceptable to be herself. Rose yanked at the strings, tearing a grommet. Finally, wriggling her body sideways, she was able to slide the dress off, tossing the ripped garment into the corner of the room. She knew she would need a viable explanation for its condition.

Rose stood before the bathroom mirror naked, observing her body. She cupped her supple breasts, stroking her nipples with her thumbs. They quickly hardened beneath her touch. Rose shuddered. Normally, she relished how easily stimulated she had become and loved the way her body responded to her touch and Roosha's. But today, she loathed her sexuality.

She considered how defiled she felt by Charles earlier and why. It was because, as far as Rose was concerned, Charles didn't look at her with respect and admiration; instead, he looked at her as nothing more than a means to satisfying his own manly urges.

Rose settled into the warm chamomile and lavender-scented water. She closed her eyes and inhaled the calming fragrances, attempting to clear her mind. After a few moments, she began to feel like herself again.

Rose pondered Vivianna's message and wondered if she had managed to secure the diaries. She reasoned that there would be no purpose in riding out before sunrise if she hadn't, that is unless Vivianna was now taking extra precaution with their meetings. Thinking about how secretive her two most important relationships were at this point exhausted Rose. She breathed in deeply, allowing her body to sink further into the soothing warmth. She focused solely on breathing in and out and was almost asleep when she heard a knock on the door.

"Rose, dear, may I come in?"

It was her mother. Rose knew she would want to know how her date with Charles had gone, which was the last thing Rose wanted to discuss. But she also knew it made sense to get through the conversation now, ensuring Anne wouldn't check on her later when Roosha was there.

"Yes, mother."

Anne opened the door tentatively and then took a seat on the small hand-carved stool near the tub.

"How was your day, dear?" Her voice was measured.

"Fine, mother, and yours?"

"Just fine? Surely a stroll through the renowned Devano gardens must have been more than just fine, Rose!"

Sure, mother, it was degrading, foul and uncomfortable, Rose thought to herself. She dared not tell Anne the truth, for surely her mother would find a way of justifying Charles's behavior. She might even agree with Savannah that Rose had seduced him with her improper manner. Although it was the dress that he kept complimenting, the one her mother had handpicked.

"They do have a beautiful estate, mother." Rose managed weakly.

"And how was your time with Charles, dear? What did the two of you talk about?

Rose sighed. "Mostly his family's business. But he did make it a point to mention how much he loved my dress." Rose hoped that last bit would help end the inquisition.

Anne's face lit up, her eyes sparkling. "Oh, that's wonderful to hear! I'll have to send a thank-you note to that Mrs. Taddy. You see, my dear, I know what suits that beautiful frame of yours."

"You sure do, mother." Rose's voice was flat, lifeless.

Anne looked at her skeptically. "Are you all right, dear? You don't seem like yourself." She placed her hand on Rose's forehead. "Are you feeling ill?"

Rose was surprised her mother noticed any difference in her demeanor. "I'm all right, mother, just tired from the events of the day. I went straight to volunteering at the library after my walk."

"I see. Well, in that case, I will leave you to rest. I'm so happy for you, dear. He's quite a catch, that Charles!"

Rose nodded, staring vacantly at the wall. Her mother smiled tightly before turning to leave. As she placed her hand on the knob, she noticed the balled up dress on the floor. Anne's face faded to white as she took in the frayed edges and torn fabric. Her fist clenched the metal tightly, panic pulsing through her system. She turned back to Rose to ask her what happened, but her daughter had already drifted off.

Anne hesitated. There were several possibilities that would explain the garment's condition, unrelated to Charles. Knowing Rose, she may have gone riding after her library endeavor and was hiding it from Anne to avoid admonition. Or perhaps the children were more rambunctious than anticipated. No matter how many plausible explanations Anne thought up, none of them quelled her apprehension. For Rose's entire life, she extolled the value of acting appropriately to protect her and spare her from a pain of tragic magnitude. Yet it appeared that by inadvertently forcing her daughter into this courtship, she might have failed to protect Rose from not only an improper act but a lascivious one.

As Anne closed the door behind her, she leaned back, pressing her backside against the thick wood and crumpled to the floor. She squeezed her eyes shut and took a deep breath, her chest shaking as she exhaled.

33

That night Rose waited on the balcony for Roosha. She found the cool air refreshing, especially in light of how stifled she felt. The sight of his wings soaring gracefully towards her elicited a sense of security within her after her jarring day.

Roosha landed quietly, his enormous form covering almost the entire balcony. Without a word, Rose threw herself into his arms, breathing in his familiar muskiness.

"Good evening, my sweet Rose. Is everything okay?" He stroked her back.

Rose buried her face in his chest. "Yes. I'm just...on my monthly cycle." Rose was grateful her period came while she was in the bath. Though she had thoroughly scrubbed her skin, her body still felt marred by her afternoon with Charles. She didn't want to be intimate with Roosha in that condition. He deserved far better.

"I see," Roosha responded softly. He picked her up and carried her over to the bed, laying her gently on the mattress.

"Roosha?"

"Yes, Rose?"

"Will you still stay with me...even if I only want to cuddle tonight?" She looked up, her eyes imploring him not to leave.

"Of course, Rose. I won't leave you." He caressed her forehead.

Rose sighed, relieved. The noblemen tended to distance themselves when their wives were bleeding. She didn't know if her cycle would have the same effect on Roosha. He slid into bed next to her, cradling her body against his.

"Will you please wake me before you leave?"

"If you wish, but why must you be up at such a late hour?"

"I'm meeting a friend for an early morning ride," she yawned. "I have to be at the stables before sunrise."

"In that case, I'd like to escort you if you'll allow me." Roosha felt a knot in his stomach and assumed it was a nerve in anticipation of her response.

Rose squeezed him tighter, her lips spreading into a smile. "I would love for you to escort me." She was relieved by his offer.

"All right, then." Roosha kissed the top of her head. He was grateful that Rose had only wanted to cuddle; otherwise, he probably would have been unable to safely fly with her. His pain from the previous night had taken most of the day to subside, so he was also thankful to spare his body a day of agony.

Rose fell fast asleep in his arms, the place where she felt safest. Roosha watched her sleep, reveling in how much he cherished her love. He still didn't comprehend how she could possibly love such a monster, but the feeling she restored in his heart was all that mattered. There was no other place in the world he would rather be than next to her.

AS DAWN APPROACHED, Roosha hated to wake her but honored her request. Rose quickly changed into her jodhpurs, boots, and overdress, and was ready to go. She left a note on her pillow, letting her mother know she was out riding in case she decided to check on her at breakfast time. Rose headed towards the door.

"Where are you going, Rose?"

"To meet you downstairs, in the courtyard, so that you can escort me."

Roosha smirked, amused by her misunderstanding. "Rose, I cannot walk through Dover. Don't you think I would stand out a bit?"

She furrowed her brow. "Then how do you mean to escort me?"

Roosha motioned towards the balcony.

Her eyes lit up in exhilaration. "You mean to fly me to the stables?" Rose struggled to keep her volume low.

Roosha nodded, thrilled by her excitement.

As they stood on the balcony, Rose looked up towards the silver moon and couldn't wait to be slightly closer to it.

"The easiest way is for me to carry you in my arms. Place your hands tightly around my neck so that I know you are secure." Roosha's tone was severe, as he already cautioned that her safety was paramount.

He scooped her up, his left arm under her knees, and his right arm curved around her lower back. He stepped onto the ledge and gave Rose a stern look. She quickly threw her arms around his neck, and then they were off.

Roosha leapt off the balcony, and as he did, his black wings expanded fully across. Rose had never seen them extended before and marveled at how massive they were. They must have spanned ten feet across.

He soared through the air gracefully, like a bird. The cold wind brushed against her face, invigorating Rose. They flew far above all of Dover's tallest buildings, rounding the clock tower as they headed toward the stables. Roosha moved fast, but Rose felt perfectly at ease with him.

Above them, the sky looked like blue velvet dotted with diamonds. Rose marveled at how well Roosha blended in with the night sky, his skin almost the same deep blue. She had the urge to spread her arms like they were wings of her own, but she dared not remove them from around Roosha's neck as she worried that might alarm him.

All too soon, Roosha began his descent. Again, Rose cursed the tiny city of Dover, wishing there was a greater distance between her home and the stables. Rose forewarned Roosha that Vivianna would be there, so he quietly set her down fifty feet from the barn.

"That was incredible!" Rose threw her arms around Roosha. "Thank you so much!" She gazed up at him, her brown eyes beaming with gratitude words would fail to convey.

Roosha brushed his lips against hers. "Be safe, my love," he whispered in her ear before launching himself towards the sky, knowing he needed to return to the cave before sunrise.

Rose stumbled all the way to the barn, her knees trembling from his kiss.

34

Vivianna was already in the stall with her horse saddled when Rose entered.

"Good morning, Rose. Are you ready to ride?"

"Good morning. Yes, I am most certainly ready."

Rose quickly groomed and tacked Carmera, and then the two of them were off into the dawn. They rode out most of the way at a gallop, putting as much distance between themselves and Dover as possible. As the sun began to rise, they gradually slowed to a walk before stopping in a lush valley with a small stream where the horses could drink.

Once they secured the mares to the trunk of a fallen oak, Vivianna settled into the grass alongside the water, the morning dew dampening her dress. Rose joined her.

"Rose, I must tell you, I have some disappointing news."

Rose's heart skipped a beat and then doubled in pace.

"I'm afraid Savannah interrupted me before I was able to remove all of the diaries from the chest."

A lump welled in Rose's chest. "You mean our mission failed?"

Vivianna lowered her head. She plucked a couple of blades of grass from the ground.

"Well, we failed to meet the objective we set out to meet."

Tears pricked Rose's eyes. "It's all my fault. First, I abandoned our plan to go on that awful date with Charles, and then you only needed me to do one thing, distract Savannah, and I couldn't even do that! I'm so sorry, Vivianna. I never meant to let you down." Or anyone else, for that matter, she added silently.

Vivianna's brow furrowed. "Rose, what did happen yesterday? You seemed quite unsettled after your date, and that may be putting it lightly."

At that moment, Rose didn't care whether she could fully trust Vivianna. She needed to confide in someone, and so the story, along with the pent up emotions, came pouring out of her, the vivid memories making her fidget uncomfortably. She shared with Vivianna Charles' carnal stares, his unwanted touch, his brazen commentary on her figure, and how he had taken it upon himself to invade her personal space and kiss her cheek at the end of the date.

Vivianna listened intently.

"Is it me? Has my love of pleasure made me too sexual? I can't imagine any of the other court girls being treated in such a manner." Hot tears streamed down Rose's cheeks.

Vivianna's eyes widened in disbelief. "Of course, it's not you! How could you even think that? Don't blame yourself, Rose. From what you're telling me, you didn't do anything to encourage his behavior. You dressed and acted like a proper lady of the court, and yet he didn't treat you as such. Some nobleman he is, leering at you like you should be displayed in a butcher shop window."

"So, you don't think my glow seduced him?"

Vivianna looked perplexed. "What do you mean?"

"Well, yesterday, when you had me distract Savannah, it did not go well. She took one look at my tattered dress and accused me of seducing Charles. She even called me Scarlet Rose again. I'm sure she's already informed the entire court of this indiscretion."

Vivianna crossed her arms tightly, fury emanating from her emerald eyes. "Leave Savannah to me. Had I known the ordeal that you went through, I never would have left you alone with her."

"Still, Vivianna, please be honest with me. Am I giving off some come hither energy? I feel responsible... perhaps I stirred up some uncontrollable lust within Charles?"

"That doesn't matter!" Vivianna unleashed, incredulously. "Rose, I realize you are different from the other court girls, but your passion and enjoyment of physical pleasure do not give any man the right to disrespect you. It was incumbent upon Charles to remain a gentleman, regardless of any urges he may have felt in his breeches. Besides, you're not the only one who enjoyed your visit from the night senders, remember?"

Rose nodded. "So, Edmund never treated you that way during your courtship?"

"Most certainly not. And if he did, I would have slapped him."

Rose laughed. "In that case, I wish you had been in the garden with me yesterday."

Vivianna smiled and put her hand on Rose's shoulder. "Rose, you are a fierce woman, you don't need me to slap anyone for you. I'm sure you'd get much more satisfaction doing it yourself anyway."

"He made me feel like a helpless little girl yesterday." Rose shook her head, loose strands of mahogany falling over her face.

Vivianna lifted her chin. "You allowed him to. You have to know that your glow, as you put it, does not give him, or any of those other silly boys the right to treat you like anything other than a lady of the court. Unless, of course, you want one of them to at some point." Vivianna winked.

Rose brushed the hair from her face, revealing a grin. "How is it that you're so strong, Vivianna?"

"Because I choose to be a survivor, Rose, one who navigates two different worlds. I know what the court society expects from me, and I make sure to deliver on that. But quietly, out of everyone else's sight, I make sure to embrace and satisfy my own needs, ones that they surely wouldn't approve of and should know nothing about."

Rose felt the urge to ask how Vivianna satisfied her desires but suppressed it. She couldn't ask Vivianna to divulge her secret when Rose still refused to entrust the girl with her own.

"Does Edmund fulfill any of those desires?"

Vivianna sighed. "No, but he's a good man."

Rose looked down, fingering the blades of grass. "Do you love him?"

Vivianna bit her lip. "I've grown to love him, but I've never been in love with him. Though you're well aware that love has nothing to do with court marriages, far less does passion." Vivianna dug more grass from the dirt and tossed it into the flowing stream.

"Right."

They sat in silence for a few moments. Rose admired how well Vivianna could survive those dual roles, one in the position that was expected of her, and the other being true to herself, whatever that meant. Rose couldn't fathom the idea of a passionless marriage. It sounded as appealing as being slowly choked to death, the air steadily departing your lungs, skin turning blue as life leaves your struggling body behind. Death must feel merciful at that point.

"Well then, shall we move on to the good news?"

Rose raised her head, a line of confusion on her forehead. "What do you mean, the good news?"

Vivianna smiled coyly. "I take it you weren't listening to me all that carefully, Rose. I said I was unable to secure all of the diaries."

Rose nodded, understanding.

"I did manage to get my hands on the first one."

35

Vivianna removed an ancient-looking leather-bound book from her saddlebag. Inscribed along the binding was the Roman numeral one. Vivianna settled back into the grass next to Rose. She undid the leather tie that held the book closed and placed it in her lap. Vivianna grasped Rose's right hand in hers. They looked at each other, a sense of friendship forming between them, and opened the book to reveal yellowed pages, all written in the same handwriting. The first entry was dated one hundred and eleven years ago. They both took a deep breath and began reading.

On this day, together, the ladies of the court gathered in our private meeting room to mourn the death of one of our beloved sisters, Renata Fierston, who committed suicide three days ago. She was found hanging from a tree in her parents' garden, wearing her wedding dress, the shredded fabric stained with fresh blood. Her mother, who discovered her body, found a note tucked into the neckline of her dress, which she brought to our gathering. She placed the note in the center of the oval table for everyone to read. In her final message to us all, Renata wrote, 'My story shall be heard. My suffering shall not be repeated. Do not look for me sisters, for I will find you.' There was dead silence, except for the crackling of the fire in the hearth behind us.

To say that none of us knew what had happened to Renata would be a farce, which is undoubtedly why everyone seemed to have the same unease in the pit of our stomachs. The crackling grew louder, sparks jumping from the flames. The symphony of red and orange captivated but did nothing to assuage our apprehension. No one could look away from the fire. Smoke began forming, morphing into different shapes. As the cloud grew, it moved outward from the hearth and into the room.

Frightened, we all stepped back, our gaze still fixated on the gray vapor engulfing the space. Some of the girls ran for the door, but it was locked. We were trapped in the meeting room with ominous smoke swirling around us. The fear was palpable. The gray cloud moved until it had corralled us into a circle, the smoke at its center. From the grayness emerged a person, or at least, the shadow of one.

Before all the ladies of the court stood Renata in otherworldly form. Terrified gasps and muffled sobs reverberated around the room. Her mother dropped to her knees in tears at the sight of her daughter, whose black eyes radiated rage. Not one of us knew what to say. We all stared, motionless at the figure before us, what seemed some demonic version of our former sister. When Renata finally spoke, her voice was fierce and laced with bitterness.

She spoke of how, on her wedding night, her nobleman husband, Harrison Devano, brutally forced himself upon her. A virgin petrified and unknowing, she had begged him to wait, as she was not ready. Her hesitation angered him. He yelled at her, the scent of whiskey strong on his breath, demanding that she fulfill her wifely duties. But fear paralyzed her. When she shrank away from him, he grew more incensed. He turned her around, grabbed the sides of the corset, and tore the bodice apart, exposing her breasts. Then he pinned her down, forcing his way beneath her chiffon skirt. His violent penetration ripped through her delicate entryway. The pain was blinding.

When he was finished with her, he kissed her atop her forehead, rolled over, and went to sleep. Renata crawled out of bed and onto the floor where she lay crying, bleeding, shaken, and alone. She didn't sleep. Instead, she waited until she could gather enough strength to stand. It was the middle of the night when she could finally move, and under cover of darkness, she slowly limped until she reached her parents' house.

She banged on the door, her fists pounding rapidly until the maid finally answered. Startled by Renata's appearance, the maid fetched her parents. Only her mother came downstairs. Renata fell into her arms, begging her mother to take her back. When she described the violent assault, her mother was unmoved. She explained to Renata that a woman's first time was always onerous. It was customary for her husband to expect her to be ready for fornication. After all, they were to have children as soon as possible. She promised Renata that it would get more comfortable, that the worst was over, and sent her back to her marital abode.

The next day, Harrison was perfectly cordial at breakfast. Not a word was said about what transpired in the bedroom. That night, they attended a social gathering together, an engagement party for another couple, and Harrison was a perfect gentleman. He complimented her dress, spun her around the dance floor, and attended to her wine glass, making sure it was always full. But when they returned home, his demeanor changed. He was rough, relentless. She was no longer a noble lady, but an object with which he could do as he liked. This time he faced her as he shoved his manhood deep inside her, aggravating the soreness from the night before. The pain was excruciating.

This pattern continued for the next two weeks. Renata grew more withdrawn with each passing day. The other ladies of the court looked at her oddly, noticing the changes, the dark circles beneath her eyes, how rarely she smiled, and the tightness of her jaw when she did. But none of them ever said anything.

On three separate occasions, Renata addressed the ladies of her generation, desperate to find someone who understood her plight. These three women will not be singled out in this account. Renata described the incessant pain that sometimes made it difficult to sit comfortably, and the emptiness of her relationship. They quickly dismissed the subject of physical relations with their husbands as inappropriate, chastising her for having the gall to bring it to their attention. They'd all witnessed Harrison's gentlemanly behavior towards her in public. Some went as far as advising her to count her blessings that she had such a charismatic husband. They admired his charm and wit, not knowing it was all a façade. He was the shell of a nobleman, not the embodiment of one. And she had become a shell of a woman, in a relationship where the only part of her that held value was the narrow cavity between her legs.

Again she pleaded with her mother for help, confessed that she was losing herself. But her mother assured her she would adjust to her new role in life as Renata Devano, wife of Harrison Devano, and that she would find her purpose once again when she became pregnant. Bone-weary, Renata became resigned to her fate.

Two months passed, the nightly abuse not giving way to a baby. Harrison grew frustrated and accused Renata of being defective, as if she were a machine. She barely spoke anymore and had become thin, her collar bones far too pronounced. Still, the ladies of the court, her mother included, acted as though nothing was wrong.

Another month passed with no conception. Enraged, Harrison threatened that he would have to take her twice each day. Renata could take no more. The thought of him brutally forcing his way inside her twice each day unhinged her. She would rather be dead than suffer this decrepit existence.

That night, after he finished with her and drifted to sleep, she got out of bed and slipped on her torn wedding gown, the contemptible frock that had started it all. She traipsed through the darkness until she reached her parents' house.

Renata didn't go inside. She opened the gate to the garden, a place that had always been warm and safe for her until she turned of age, and everything changed. From the day of her eighteenth birthday, her parents' sole focus had been on ensuring she was presentable, a prize for a suitable nobleman. All of her court classes focused on maintaining a noble home and being a dignified wife, subservient to her husband's needs. Nowhere in the court teachings was there any instruction on making herself happy. And there was certainly no instruction preparing her for what was expected of her on her wedding night.

Devastated, and unwilling to live the rest of her life as another man's vessel, she hung herself from the tree she used to climb as a child. But before dying, she swore she would be back to help the future ladies of the court. She vowed that her death would serve a greater purpose than her life had. Then she proceeded to tell us about her creation, the night senders.

Vivianna looked at Rose, who was as pale as a ghost.

"Devano ... Harrison Devano? Charles' great grandfather was the one who drove this poor woman to suicide?"

Vivianna stroked Rose's back. "It's okay, Rose. It was over a hundred years ago. It has no bearing on the current generation." Vivianna said the words in comfort but wasn't sure she believed them. "Let us keep reading. We're about to learn what we've long desired to know ... how the night senders were created, and why."

They were giant, winged creatures built like a combination of man and horse. Their skin was a blue as deep as the night sky so that they could travel unseen under cover of darkness. Their bellies glowed an amber color, magic that heightened their abilities to pleasure women, for that was their purpose. Renata, who now called herself Madeira (mother of the night senders), created them for two reasons: punishment and pleasure.

The night senders were to provide a self-awareness and discovery process foreign to the ladies of the court. They were to help them connect to their sensuality once they came of age. On the eve of their eighteenth birthday, at the stroke of midnight, the night senders would visit each of the court girls and use their abilities to gently awaken their bodies to all of the erotic energies they contained. She warned that the night senders must be a sacred secret, one that the noblemen must never uncover.

All of the pleasure delivered by the night senders would be felt only as pain to them, for to be a night sender is a punishment. In their previous lives, the night senders were terrible men, rapists, and murderers of women now being forced to pay for their crimes and the pain they inflicted. The role of the night sender is as a servant of women. They have been gifted the ability to arouse the greatest feelings of ecstasy in a woman, but they, in turn, can only feel the equivalent of that ecstasy in agony. It is a penance for all they have done in their previous lives. Madeira inscribed the word of the night senders on the table for all to read:

If you have chosen to be the deliverer of pain in one lifetime, in your next, you shall be forced to be a deliverer of pleasure. And another's pleasure will deliver pain unto you. For that is the cycle of life, the way of ensuring balance and harmony. Create pain for others, and eventually, you will suffer that pain yourself.

Rose's heart was pounding fast. She rocked her body back and forth, all the words she had just read whirling through her mind like a tornado. Vivid images of Renata's bloody corpse dangling from a tree, a tragic suicide induced by Charles' ancestors, made her queasy. Would this be her fate were she somehow forced to marry Charles? Then there was Roosha. Could it be true? Was her sweet Roosha a rapist or murderer, at least in his previous life? Rose keeled over onto her side, still rocking.

"Rose? Are you okay?" Vivianna put her hand on Rose's elbow, steadying her.

Rose looked up at her with bewildered eyes. "I'm not sure. This is a lot to take in."

"It's definitely not what I was expecting." Vivianna sounded more curious than anything else, like a detective unraveling a great mystery.

Renata's lifeless face crept back into her mind. "Is that what your marriage is like?" Rose's voice was small, a petrified undertone to it.

Vivianna shrunk back, affronted. "Heaven's no!" Her voice rose two octaves, her mouth agape. It was the first time Rose had seen her look flabbergasted. "Edmund has never forced himself on me."

"That's good to know." Rose's voice was shaky. "I don't remember my father being violent with my mother, but I was only four years old when he died, so I'm sure there's plenty I missed."

"What made you think of that?"

Rose smiled wistfully. "You've never seen my mother outside of a social engagement. Most of the time, she's not really there. She's withdrawn; she barely smiles. I thought maybe ..."

"That maybe Renata's experience is common?"

Rose stared at the ground. "Yes."

Vivianna stroked her back, not knowing what to say to her friend. There were no words that would offer consolation, no definitive answer she could supply. She knew nothing about Anne personally.

Uncomfortable, Rose changed the subject. "What ... what else is in the book?" Rose asked meekly.

Vivianna flipped gently through the next pages. "Individual accounts of the initial visits from the night senders. They must have met as a group after each girl's right of passage to recount and record the night's events. It seems quite different from where we are now. The court appears to have been more of a sisterhood back then."

Rose nodded. "What were the visits like?"

"Let's read some and see." Vivianna eased her back up, propping Rose's head on her shoulder.

It's January 12th, and Madeline Archer was the first to receive a visit from the night senders. Last night we met in support of her impending experience.

Though Madeira did not make a personal appearance, she sent a gift with a note for Madeline.

The note read:

My Dear Madeline,

Congratulations on your eighteenth birthday celebration, and on being the first woman in history to receive a visit from the night senders. I assure you there is nothing to fear. They cannot and will not hurt you. Consider them your humble servants, who will aid you in your transition to womanhood. Through their magical, gentle touch, you will be able to step into your feminine power, a feat no man can take from you.

In the box, you will find a silk sleeping mask. It is your choice whether you want to look upon these wondrous creatures or maintain an air of mystery from behind the mask.

And remember, the noblemen must <u>never</u> *know of the night senders' existence.*

Yours,
Madeira

Madeline chose to wear the mask. Despite Madeira's assurances that she was safe, she was too apprehensive to sleep and was awake when her night sender arrived at the stroke of midnight. Sensing her trepidation, the night sender spoke to her, calming her nerves. His voice was soothing, like a lullaby, his words reassuring her that she was in control. She could tell him to stop at any time. Once Madeline was at ease, the night sender delicately addressed every part of her naked body, kissing and stroking in such ways that enlivened her spirit. Her mind was adrift in a sea of pleasure. Eventually, she felt the walls of her virginity cave in with ease, releasing her from the confinements of girlhood.

The next day, Madeline was glowing. She was grateful for the visit and assured the other girls that they would enjoy their awakening as well. Two months later,

Madeline was engaged and eagerly awaiting her wedding night, as Madeira hoped she would be. She wanted the girls to have the pleasant experience she was denied.

On February 8th, Allison Michaels was the next to receive her visit. Madeira sent the identical note and gift to Allison, who also wore the mask. After her visit, she reported the same experience as Madeline, emphasizing how much she enjoyed the night sender's touch.

On February 27th, Viola Jameson was the third to receive a visit. After the fulsome accounts by both Madeline and Allison, Viola decided to forgo the mask Madeira had again provided. She wanted to be the first to lay eyes on these fervent creatures. That night, she waited up in anticipation of seeing the creature that would enter through her balcony doors.

At exactly midnight, a giant shadow appeared outside her room, one with a wingspan that extended across the entire balcony. Taken aback, Viola plopped onto the edge of her bed. The night sender entered slowly, greeting her by name. His voice was comforting yet arousing. As he approached, she saw that he was half-man, half Pegasus. His lower body was that of a horse's back legs and his upper body that of a man, brawny and bursting with muscle. His skin was far darker than her own chocolate tone, with a blue tint that camouflaged with the night sky.

She marveled at his distinguished face. He was the epitome of a mythical warrior, an air of mystique about him that made her blush with desire. At the base of his torso was a circle of orange. Viola described it as a glowing energy field.

The night sender approached, caressing her cheek with his hand. He stared deeply into her eyes and advised her that if she closed them, it would heighten her other senses, enhancing her experience. Unable to resist his mesmerizing gaze, she obliged.

The night sender crawled on top of her, his lips brushing against every part of her body, even suckling on her nipples, which grew hard at his touch. His tongue alternated between hot and cold sensations, torturing her most sensitive parts. Viola's body was flushed with heat, her moist cavity dripping.

Before he finished, the night sender positioned his torso directly over hers. Viola briefly opened her eyes and saw that his glowing energy field radiated down, transferring the amber waves to her body.

Afterward, when the night sender stroked her skin, running his finger over her breasts, her body was on fire. The slightest touch made her burn with desire. Her entire body had become an erogenous zone, one giant clitoris. Convulsions between her thighs gave way to ecstasy again and again, until her body could take no more, and drifted off into the most peaceful sleep of her life.

Rose raised her head, frustrated. "But this doesn't make sense! Why isn't there anything in here about biting into our necks? How is it that they were able to spend so much time with each of the girls, focusing on every part of their bodies? And why were they permitted to choose whether they wanted a blindfold? And ..."

"I don't know," Vivianna interrupted. And I'm sure you have fifty more questions lined up, Rose, ones neither of us can answer." She flipped through the next few pages. "There are accounts by at least twenty other women here, and they all seem to say the same thing; they loved their visits."

Rose put her fingers on her temples. "But if they were taught to love their visits, why were we taught to fear ours?"

"Again, an excellent question, Rose. I surmise that the answers to all of your well-thought inquiries probably lie in the second diary."

"Which we don't have."

"Not at this very moment."

"Does it say anything else in there?"

"Yes, there's another accounting after the girls' stories."

Rose sighed. "Let's read it."

With all of the girls now having been physically awakened, they've asked the same question of the court; can the visits from the night senders continue beyond one night? They enjoyed knowing the pleasure their bodies are capable of and want to learn more about their sensual power. We've spoken to Madeira about their request. She sees no harm in allowing the night senders to continue to aid the girls in their self-discovery. The girls will now be able to receive the night senders at other times after their birth night, should they so choose. But Madeira warned that once a girl was married, she was forbidden from receiving visits from the night senders.

Rose was fuming. "This is absolutely ridiculous! How could it have been so different back then? Why are we punished now when the girls back then were encouraged?"

Vivianna was calm when she spoke. "Rose, remember there were two other diaries in that chest. This one documents the beginning of a powerful new tradition. Surely you don't think everything went as smoothly as it appears in this first journal? Otherwise, what reason would there be for a significant change in tradition?"

Rose knew that Vivianna had a point. There were one hundred and eleven years between when that book was first written and where they were now. An entire course of events had transpired about which they knew nothing. But for Rose, it felt personal. She would have been accepted and embraced in the court society they were reading about in this first book. Instead, because of how things had changed, she was the outcast, often persecuted by her fellow "sisters" and pigeonholed as Scarlet Rose, the seductress.

"We have to get the other books." Rose's statement was just as much a demand.

Vivianna stroked her hand. "We will."

THE GIRLS RODE BACK at a furious gallop. As Rose's eyes focused only on the path ahead of her, her mind assembled all of the questions she needed to ask Roosha that night.

36

"Good evening, mother." Vivianna sat on the edge of Mrs. Weston's bed.

"Vivianna?" Mrs. Weston barely opened her eyes.

"Yes, it's me, mother. I'm here." Vivianna stroked her mother's forehead, which was damp with perspiration. "How are you feeling?"

"Better." Her voice was groggy.

"I came by yesterday to return your keys, but you were sound asleep."

"Was I?" Mrs. Weston struggled. Her eyes were now fully closed; the blanket pulled up to her chin.

"Yes. I left them on your night table, see?" Vivianna picked up the keys and jiggled them, the metal clinking together.

"Great," she mumbled almost inaudibly.

"The event went well. At least, the children all seemed to enjoy it."

"Mmhmm." Her mother's labored breathing gave way to snoring.

Vivianna eased herself off the bed slowly, not wanting to wake her mother. The mattress shifted slightly, but her mother did not stir. Vivianna extended her hand to place the library keys back on the night table but stopped only inches from relinquishing them.

She observed her mother closely, leaning in near her face. Mrs. Weston appeared to be sleeping soundly. Vivianna's eyes moved to the enormous Grandfather clock on the wall opposite the bed. Its gold pendulum ticked rhythmically, like her mind. The time was only half-past seven. Edmund would be heading to poker shortly, not to return home until late. If she kept the keys, she could visit the library that night.

Again, Vivianna gazed at her mother. The woman would be livid if she knew what her daughter was thinking.

"But she won't know anything," Vivianna all but muttered to herself.

She leaned down and kissed her mother's forehead. Clasping the keys firmly, Vivianna headed straight for the library.

WRAPPED IN A GRAY CLOAK, Vivianna slinked through the castle grounds quickly, her cat eyes alert. It was imperative that no one saw her, as there were enough prying eyes at the library the day before. She knew the route from her mother's house to the library well. Mrs. Weston had been running the library since Vivianna's grandmother died eight years ago. Together, they had made the short walk many times. The sinuous stone pathways wound through courtyards and gardens rich in trees and shrubbery. Normally bustling with castle dwellers, they were now empty, as none of the nighttime social gathering spots were in close proximity to the library.

As she rounded the final corner before the library, Vivianna froze. Her ears perked up, listening intently to the sound of high-pitched voices. There were women, maybe two or three, she surmised, headed her way. Vivianna crouched behind a blackthorn bush and waited. Footsteps slowly drew closer. She could hear the voices clearly now and recognized them.

"You should have seen her yesterday at the library," Amelia sniggered. "An adorable little girl accidentally spilled a morsel of paint on her, and she was ready to beat the poor darling."

They were talking about Savannah. Vivianna recalled at least five sets of multi-colored handprints mashed onto her dress. So why was Amelia lying, she wondered.

"That's terrible! I do hope she didn't actually strike the child," Genevieve exclaimed.

Vivianna peered carefully through the thick brush, eager to see how astute an actor Amelia was, but it was too dark to make out their facial expressions.

"Well, of course, I thwarted her!" Amelia declared pompously.

"You had the nerve to challenge Savannah?" Genevieve's words were filled with awe.

Vivianna rolled her eyes. The tiny blonde was as beautiful as she was gullible, and Amelia was taking full advantage.

"Well, someone has to. She's not as perfect as she lets on, you know."

"What do you mean, Amelia?" Genevieve asked with bated breath.

Amelia turned her head to the left and then to the right, making sure they were alone. "Did she ever tell you what really happened on her date with Charles? The reason his family royally dismissed her?"

Vivianna's mouth fell open. Could this be the leverage she needed to prevent Savannah from spreading rumors about the garden walk, sparing Rose from court-wide mortification?

"No! Do tell, Amelia," Genevieve gushed. She leaned in close to Amelia, anxiously awaiting this piece of juicy gossip.

Vivianna closed her eyes, hoping to heighten her sense of hearing in case Amelia lowered her voice.

Amelia paused, a wicked grin spreading across her lips. "Oh, I will, when the time is right."

"Promise I'll be the first to know," Genevieve pleaded.

"Of course! You have my word. But you mustn't say anything to the other girls, not yet."

"Oh, I won't." She slid her thumb and index finger across her closed lips.

Amelia wrapped her arm through Genevieve's, and the two merrily made their way down the pathway together. Once they were out of sight, Vivianna stood and let out the snort she had been suppressing.

"The word of a liar," she murmured. "What's that worth?" Still, Vivianna was grateful for the hearsay. Perhaps she could bluff Savannah into silence.

Once inside the baronial building, Vivianna lit the candle she hid beneath her cloak. She had never been inside the library after dark. The main hall was ominous, with its grave silence and rows of shadows cast by countless books. Were someone lurking, it would be nearly impossible to know. Vivianna shivered at the thought.

Hurriedly, she retrieved the black key from beneath her mother's desk and headed straight for the basement. The room was pitch black, and the glow from her candle only illuminated what was directly in front of her. Slowly and methodically, she descended the stairs, making sure one foot was firmly in place before lifting the other. She cupped her hand around the flame so that its light was not visible through the narrow window.

Vivianna inched forward, brushing against boxes of books until she was in front of the trunk. She crouched down, holding the candle next to the latch. It was unlocked, which was not how Vivianna had left it.

Cold droplets of sweat pooled on the back of her neck. Someone else had been down there, and she didn't know who, or more importantly, when.

Abruptly she turned, nearly extinguishing the candle in her haste. She cradled the flame, protecting it, and spun slowly, nervously searching her surroundings. The room was still. Only the thudding of her heart permeated the silence.

There didn't appear to be anyone else in the room. Vivianna sighed, releasing the breath she had been holding, which did nothing to ease the tension in her body. The door to the basement had been locked, she realized. Unless the person managed to lock himself in that room, which wasn't possible because the door only locked from the outside, no one was in the basement with her. Though the person could still be in the library, she shuddered.

"But the winged key was in its secure location ... where I left it," she breathed. "So whoever opened the trunk is already gone...unless there's another key." Her brow furrowed.

Discovering the diaries had created more questions than answers. She knew she had no way of knowing whether she was alone. All she had now was a choice. She could stay and open the trunk, or she could flee. Vivianna's hand trembled, the orange glow flickering.

Having already come this far, she decided to at least open the red box. She placed the candleholder on the floor, and carefully, with both hands, lifted the heavy lid. Only one of the diaries remained.

Vivianna ran her finger along its leather spine. Etched into the side was the Roman numeral three. Whoever had come before her had taken the second book. Perplexed, Vivianna considered different possibilities in her mind, though none of them seemed to make sense. Was this person trying to prevent her from reading the diaries? She shook her head. If that were the case, then why would she have left the third one in there? Perhaps there was something special about the second book? Something she wasn't supposed to know? Who was this person anyway? And why would she want the diaries? Could there possibly be someone else on a similar mission to her and Rose? She doubted any of the other court girls possessed that much fortitude or interest in the night senders. The more pressing concern was whether this mystery person knew of their mission.

Vivianna eyed the third diary, intrigued. She had no way of answering any of those questions now, but she did have the opportunity to read the third diary, and its contents may provide answers or at least clues. She picked up the book and hesitated. If she brought it home with her, this person, a looming threat, would know she had returned. But if she read the diary now, and then put it back, leaving the trunk precisely as she found it, there was a slim chance of covering her tracks, at least temporarily.

Vivianna took one last glance around the room before settling onto the floor. Gingerly, she flipped the leather cover open. Her cat eyes grew wide, her pupils eclipsing her green irises. As she stared at the title page, the blood drained from her face. The inscription read: *The Case of Anne Elizabeth Woodburn.*

The diary was about Rose's mom.

37

That night Rose was sitting in her vanity chair anxiously awaiting Roosha. She was wide awake, her mind overflowing with questions. She didn't know what to think after what she had learned that morning.

Her mind was at war with her heart. She struggled to accept that as a man, Roosha must have been either a rapist or murderer, if not both. How could she love a man who had committed such atrocities? She needed to know what he had done. She needed to understand the cruel individual he once was to see if she could love him still. Each time she released a thought of that nature, she felt a stab of pain in her chest, as though her heart were being slighted by her vicious mind.

When Roosha finally emerged from the sky, she understood her heart's contention. She greeted him with a warm embrace, the pain in her chest easing at his touch. Intuitively, she knew that it didn't matter what Roosha had done, or who he had been. All that mattered was who he was now, the man she loved.

"Are you all right, Rose?"

"Yes…"

Despite her knowing, her mind was still fighting its own demons. It demanded to know why he never told her about his past and feared that he would lie to her now if she asked. The ego required both information and truth that the heart did not.

"Roosha, I once asked you how you became a night sender."

"You did," he affirmed, afraid of where Rose was heading.

"You never told me."

Roosha hesitated. "It's not something I thought you'd want to know."

"If I didn't want to know, I wouldn't have asked." Her reply was more indignant than she intended.

Roosha sighed. "Rose, sometimes we think we want to know the answers to certain questions, but we don't realize that knowing them may do us more harm than good."

Rose grimaced. She was reminded of her mother's withholding information from her under the premise that it was for her own good. She folded her arms across her chest.

"Isn't it up to me to decide what information I want to know?"

"Yes, of course," Roosha affirmed softly. "But once you know it, you cannot unknow it. You may lose the calm sea of bliss that ignorance has had you sailing on and be thrust into rough waters you weren't prepared to navigate."

"If I cannot manage rough seas, then perhaps I am not worthy of the journey."

Roosha's eyes bore into hers. He admired her resolve and her determination to experience far more of life than her limited court world offered. But her confidence did not alleviate his fear that if she knew the truth, she would rebuke him for his dark past.

"You don't have to prove anything, Rose."

"And neither do you." She looked at him sternly. "Nor do you need to hide anything."

Roosha shifted uncomfortably. "Rose, you don't understand. I was a horrible, vile monster!"

Rose placed her hand in his. "Perhaps that is who you were then, but it certainly isn't who you are now. You've been made to do your penance, and you are. You cannot continue to condemn yourself for who you were in another life. You are Roosha, the warm, tender man who has opened my life and my heart to a glorious world I would not have known otherwise."

Roosha caressed her cheek. "You seem to know more than you let on, my sweet Rose."

"I have my ways." She smiled weakly.

He didn't know how she had come to learn that life as a night sender was a punishment, but refrained from asking. The less he knew, the better. It prevented him from revealing more than she needed to know. Now he had a choice to make. Should he tell Rose the truth about his horrible history and risk losing her?

He searched her eyes. They were beaming with empathy and encouragement, willing him to share the darkest part of himself with her. Roosha closed his eyes. It was time he summoned the courage Rose had displayed.

"My sweet Rose, I only pray you still want my affections after what I'm about to tell you."

Rose fingered his coarse waves. "Roosha, there is nothing you could ever say that would drive me away. I love you." Rose realized that despite how long she had felt this way, this was the first time she had said the words aloud. Lifting onto her tiptoes, she kissed his lips tenderly.

Roosha was beside himself. She loved him. The elation from hearing those words was indescribable. His heart swelled with gratitude for this magnificent woman before him.

With a renewed sense of purpose, he took a deep breath and began his story. Rose listened intently without interruption.

"My name was Daniel Cleafer. I was born an orphan. My mother died during my birth, and my father, or whoever was there when I was born, must have given me away because I grew up in an orphanage for boys. It was awful there. Never enough for everyone - food, blankets, clothes. Sometimes we shared, and sometimes you had to fight for your share. From a very young age, I learned that if I didn't take care of myself, no one would do it for me. When I was twelve, a couple of other boys who were older than me - Jax and Lionel - decided to leave in the middle of the night and fend for themselves. I went with them. We traveled from town to town, making our way by stealing from people and shops. We had no home and no interest in settling down. Usually, we slept in the woods. The three of us would split up in the daytime to pickpocket and pillage. Then we'd bring everything we'd stolen back to the woods and share the spoils of our efforts. I excelled at stealing. I was much faster and more tactful than those two. They started calling me phantom because no one could see me coming, or knew what had happened until long after I was gone. With my superior skills, I set my sights on superior goods. While Jax and Lionel were hitting bakeries and lifting coins off unsuspecting villagers, I was able to steal gold coins and trinkets from jewelry stores. It was in a rich town called Davensport that I made my best haul. There were two jewelers in that town, and between them, I was able to steal one hundred troy ounces of gold. When I returned with my loot, Jax and Lionel were waiting for me. Lionel, who was much bigger than me at the time, attacked me from behind and then held me against a tree while Jax grabbed the gold. They beat me unconscious and then absconded with my spoils."

Rose winced. She abhorred the image of Roosha being harmed.

"I swore one day I would find them and seek revenge." Roosha sighed, hesitant to continue. Rose squeezed his hand.

"It was ten years later when I happened upon Dover. I was still stealing. I never bothered to learn any other way of life." He shook his head disapprovingly.

"While I was inspecting the town to make my mark, I saw Lionel standing outside of the cobbler shop. He was dressed nicely, and on his arm was a beautiful woman. He looked disgustingly happy, whereas I was alone and miserable and still holding onto my grudge. I vowed to take that from him in some way, to leave him the way he had left me, with nothing and no one. I followed them. I learned that she was his fiancé and discovered where each of them lived. I observed their routines, following them like a demonic shadow. A week later, I struck. I decided I would take what was to be his before he had the chance to enjoy it, the way he and Jax had done to me." Roosha squeezed his fists tightly, his face twisted. "And I would make him watch," he whispered.

Rose swallowed hard, her body rigid.

"I kidnapped the girl and brought her out into the woods. I tied her to a tree, gagged her, and left her alone while I fetched Lionel. I broke into his home while he was asleep, beat him senseless with my eager fists, and dragged him into the woods. Once he came to, I made him watch while I forced myself on her. I was drunk with rage and power and had no regard for anyone or anything other than my revenge. Lionel begged me to stop, begged for mercy, begged me to take him instead. But all I wanted was to hurt him, to wrong him the way I was convinced he had wronged me. When I finished violating the woman, she passed out from the pain. I left her there on the ground next to him and walked away. The next day my penance began. I was pursued by Dover authorities, who caught up to me in the forest. I scaled the tallest tree, but they had me surrounded. Rather than giving Lionel the satisfaction of seeing me hung, I decided to take my own life and avoid punishment for my crimes. At least I would die having fulfilled my vow of revenge. I jumped from the treetop, the impact shattering every bone in my body. Once the life had completely drained from my physical form, I awoke a night sender."

When he finished, he looked at Rose but could not discern her reaction.

"Do you remember how it happened?" Her voice was cool but calm.

"Not exactly. I remember my soul lifting upwards, out of my body. But a red energy field with tornado-like force sucked me down, immersing me in a whirlwind of inconceivable pain, my body ripping apart and growing new limbs, hooves bursting through my skin. I think my mind must have blocked out most of it."

Rose shuddered. The thought of Roosha experiencing so much pain was crippling.

"Are you destined to be this way forever?"

"No." So she knew of the punishment, but not the sentencing, he mused. "The length of our sentence depends on the severity of our crimes."

"And what is your sentence?"

"Seventy-five years, of which I've already served ten." He looked at Rose, perplexed, waiting for her to burst out in tears or lash out in anger, but she didn't. She sat, still holding his hand, looking at him as if he were the same person she had always known.

"How can you look at me the same after what I've just told you?"

"Because you're not Daniel, you're Roosha. And I love you, Roosha." Rose paused, thoughtful. "None of us can change the past, we can only learn from it. You certainly have. I saw the pained expression on your face as you described what happened, what you did. That was a different life, one entirely devoid of love. Had you known the love of anyone, a parent, a woman, a friend, or even an animal, I imagine you would have chosen differently, the way you have now."

Roosha gazed deep into her eyes, an unfamiliar warmth spreading through him. She was right. From the day he was born, he had not known love, and after experiencing it with her, he could not live without it.

"I love you, Rose. More than my own existence."

38

That night Roosha stayed, cradling Rose in his arms until she fell asleep. He wasn't sure how she could fall asleep after a bedtime story like that, but she seemed to drift off fairly peacefully.

When he leapt from the balcony, he felt lighter, as though a great burden had been lifted from his chest, one he hadn't realized he carried. He'd spent the last ten years as a night sender judging himself for a past he cannot change. No matter how much good he had done, he never considered it enough to make amends. He was unable to forgive himself.

Avidan was the only one he had personally shared his story with until now, but it wasn't the same. All of the night senders had similar horror stories to share. Avidan's was one of the worst. He was facing a three hundred year sentence for his crimes. When they shared their histories, it was more of an initiation into the realm, an understanding that they all deserved to be there for what they had done. There was no fear of rejection or judgment when everyone was guilty of the same or very similar sins. None of them were innocent or had any justification for their previous behavior. They had all acted with deliberate malice. After all, that's the reason they had been punished beyond death.

Roosha had now faced his greatest fear, telling the woman he loved about his past, without sparing any of the details of his maliciousness. He had been terrified that she would judge him in the same way that he continued to judge himself. But instead, Rose had shown him exactly what he needed, unconditional love. Her love for him, for Roosha, made him realize that he isn't Daniel anymore. Daniel was not worthy of love from a woman of her caliber, but he, Roosha, was.

Time had given them all plenty of opportunities to examine and reflect on their pasts. Avidan, who had the longest sentence of the current generation, had become the wisest of them. And while he gave Avidan credit where it was due, Roosha had never been able to do the same with himself. But no more. He swore he would let go of his past to love Rose even better. He would embrace the man, or creature, he now was, and find the strength to give her everything and anything she needed, no matter what it cost him.

39

That evening Rose sat at the table, awaiting her mother for dinner. It wasn't like Anne to be tardy, but Rose was too lost in her own contemplation to be concerned. She had been so absorbed by Roosha's story that she had forgotten to address the more pressing matter at hand.

In the diary, it stated that the night senders derived pain from another's pleasure. She cringed. Had Roosha suffered every time they were together? Every time she moaned in ecstasy, did he fall further into agony? The thought made her tremble. How could she continue to be intimate with him knowing the harm it inflicted? She despised the idea that their relationship was part of his punishment. Why should he continue to endure pain when she loved him? When she chose him?

"Good evening, Rose."

Rose gasped. "Mother! You startled me. Good evening. Is everything all right?"

"Yes, child. I do apologize for being late." Anne sat down, her face uneasy. "I have some news to discuss with you, but first I'd like to talk to you."

Rose's guard immediately triggered. "What about?"

"Well ..." Anne stuttered, which was unlike her. Rose was intrigued. What had Anne Elizabeth Woodburn grasping for words?

"Did something happen yesterday, with Charles?"

Rose's eyes narrowed. Why was her mother asking that? Had Savannah already spread lies that she seduced him throughout the court? Rose took a deep breath, willing herself to gather more information before reacting.

"Why do you ask, mother?"

Anne lowered her gaze, nervously tapping her fingers on the table. "On my way out of the bathroom last night, I saw your dress in less than perfect condition ..." She trailed off.

Rose stared at her blankly. Was her mother asking because she thought Rose the victim or the assailant? It seemed more likely Charles would be extended the benefit of the doubt.

Anne's eyes grew more concerned. She tapped faster.

"Rose, did he hurt you?" Her voice was grim.

Rose loudly exhaled the breath she had been holding for too long. She was grateful that her mother's preoccupation was related to her well-being, not that scoundrel's.

Rose thought carefully. The way she chose to answer this question could have severe consequences. In Dover, women were never the ones to terminate a courtship. It wasn't by law, but by strict societal standards. If she were to tell her mother the truth, would Anne have the gall to end the courtship? It would be deemed the height of impropriety.

The more crucial question was whether Rose wanted the courtship ended. It would make her and her mother the center of salacious gossip among the entire court. The Devano family, considered the most powerful family in Dover, might retaliate. Rose's head was spinning.

She considered the two most important relationships in her life. She and Vivianna were finally uncovering answers to their questions surrounding the night senders, an operation that needed to remain confidential. And more importantly, she was in love with Roosha. She would not risk his safety by bringing undue attention to herself. She needed the courtship to continue. Besides, Charles had been rude, but he hadn't forced himself on her. Maybe if she were more assertive, he would be more respectful.

Rose sighed. "No, mother. He didn't hurt me."

Anne looked dubious. "Then how did your dress come into its current condition?"

"Well, after our stroll, I was running late for the library event, so I took a shortcut through the trees down by the stream. The dress caught on branches as I ran."

"The corset was ripped. Surely that did not catch on a tree."

Rose pursed her lips. "That was my fault. I wanted to take the dress off by myself, and in my struggle with the string, I pulled too hard ..."

"You were despondent in the bath."

Rose admired her mother's thorough inquisition. Perhaps her concern was genuine.

"I was exhausted from all the events of the day. The children were quite rowdy."

"So, Charles was not the source of your sour mood?"

Rose bit her lip. She disdained the idea of exonerating him entirely. "He was a bit forward ... I think he just loved the dress you picked. Nothing I couldn't handle. You've no reason to worry, mother."

Anne sighed, relieved. "Thank you, child." Anne felt a burden lift. She had not put Rose in harm's way.

"Thank you?" Rose's inflection implied more explanation was necessary.

Anne reached over the table, placing her hand on top of Rose's.

"I'm so relieved that nothing happened. It makes it much easier for me to share this timely news with you." Anne smiled weakly. "I was at a meeting with some of the ladies of the court earlier today, and Charles' mother was there."

Rose already didn't like where this was going. Anne paused as the maid emerged from the kitchen and placed two salads in front of them. Rose picked up her fork and started pushing the lettuce around to ease the tension in her mind. Once the maid went back into the kitchen, Anne continued.

"Mrs. Devano came over to me and told me how positively smitten Charles is with you!" Anne smiled proudly. Rose wondered why her mother was so pleased that a boy liked her, but not that Rose helped break in a wild horse at such a young age. Why did it seem that in Anne's eyes, her most impressive accomplishment had to involve a boy?

"Rose? Rose, did you hear what I just said?" Anne was smiling expectantly. Rose hadn't realized she stopped listening.

"I'm terribly sorry, mother. I was so struck by your previous news I must have missed the last bit." Was this why her mother was so relieved that Charles hadn't assaulted her? So she could spare herself the guilt of conspiring with his mother? Rose blinked back the tears she didn't want her mother to see.

"It's all right, dear girl, it is a wondrous moment to take in! Charles wants to introduce you to his mother. She told me so herself, and she cannot wait to meet you! You'll be having tea with them tomorrow afternoon. Isn't that exciting, Rose?"

Rose dropped her fork. In her mind, Rose was shouting at herself. How was this possible? Hadn't Savannah already tattled to the court about what a harlot she was? That she had seduced poor Charles and was an unfit match.

"Rose dear, are you all right?" Anne tilted her head to the side.

She recovered quickly. "Yes, mother. It's just such short notice, I'm wondering what I will wear to such an important affair."

"An excellent question indeed, love. After supper, we'll go straight up to your room and find a suitable frock."

Rose barely ate her dinner. Anne chattered on about all the good things Mrs. Devano had said about Rose, but she didn't hear any of them. Her mother's voice sounded like a faraway echo, the way it would if Rose's head were underwater.

Rose tried to suppress the panic she felt. She had only allowed the courtship with Charles to placate her mother. She never expected him to like her, and now here she was meeting his exalted mother. Could a proposal be imminent? The thought made her nauseous.

She couldn't possibly marry Charles. She found the man vile and based on the first diary, it seemed to be a trait in the Devano bloodline.

She considered whether her mother knew that, whether she had read the diary, but that was not a subject she could broach. Most importantly, she was in love with Roosha. She would never marry another.

If she refused his proposal, what would her mother do? Rose didn't even want to entertain that circumstance, which meant she had to find a way to prevent it. She had to make herself unsuitable, at least in Mrs. Devano's eyes. If his mother disapproved, that would make the courtship untenable. Rose was resolute. Despite whatever embarrassment it may cause Anne, she had to be the epitome of impropriety.

AFTER DINNER, they headed upstairs to Rose's dressing quarters. Anne went through two rows of dresses but did not pull any garments from the rack.

She shook her head. "None of these will do for tomorrow."

"Perhaps we should reschedule then, mother? That would give us a chance to visit Mrs. Taddy again." And see if I can collect any new information, Rose thought to herself.

"My dear Rose, I've told you before that you don't reschedule social events with one of the most influential families in the city. Besides, Mrs. Taddy's store is temporarily closed."

The blood drained from Rose's face. "What do you mean, closed?"

"The other day I went to the florist and decided to stop by her shop. There was a sign on the door that read, *Gone on Holiday*. It was in the window of her husband's tailor shop as well. I assume they've taken some time off together."

Tears pricked Rose's eyes. She turned away so her mother wouldn't notice. Rose's chest felt heavy with guilt. She never should have mentioned Mrs. Taddy at all in her conversation with Charles. She prayed the woman and her husband were okay, though it seemed unlikely.

"Mother, could we do this later?" Rose's head was spinning. She desperately wanted to lie down.

Anne looked at her disbelievingly. " Of course not, Rose. There's no time. Tea is tomorrow! Now come!"

Anne exited Rose's room and charged down the hallway. Rose sighed, her shoulders slumping forward. She trudged after her mother.

"Where are we going?"

"You'll see."

Anne stopped at the door at the end of the hallway. She produced a key from her pocket and unlocked it.

"I thought you said this was just storage space, mother?"

"It is. I put most of your father's cherished items in here after he passed away, but it also has some of my old dresses from when I was around your age, and not quite as thin as I've become."

Rose decided not to take that last remark as an insult. She wouldn't want to be as thin as her mother, the edges of her bones visible beneath her skin.

The room smelled as if no one had entered in years, a heavy must permeating the air. Anne opened the window, neutralizing the odor. In the corner of the room was a long row of dresses. Rose's face dropped when she saw in the candlelight that they were all beige or cream-colored. None of the garments seemed to possess any personality. Rose couldn't fathom why a svelte young woman with beautiful blue eyes and fiery red hair would want to wear such drab clothing.

As her mother went through them, Rose took her candelabra and inspected the rest of the room. On the opposite side was her father's writing desk, its massive size covering half the room. The cherry-wood surface was buried beneath old books that he would read to Rose at bedtime, his spectacles resting on top.

Her father died when she was only four years old. She didn't remember him well but knew his voice from the magical tales he recited nightly. She ran her fingers along the book spines.

"Mother?"

"Yes, dear?" She called from the other side of the room.

"Did you love my father?"

"What kind of question is that?" Anne's tone was defensive.

Rose sighed. "I mean you no offense. I'm asking if you were in love with my father when you married him."

Anne hesitated. "My parents arranged my courtship with Harold. He was handsome, with the same warm, brown eyes he graced you with," she recalled affectionately. "I did love him, more so after we wed. Sometimes love takes time, you know."

Internally, Rose breathed a sigh of relief. Her mother's sentimental tone indicated a genuine fondness for Rose's father, making her theory that Anne and Renata had an abusive relationship in common unfounded. He was the doting father she remembered, the one who transported her to fantastical faraway lands through his bedtime stories.

Rose continued to the other side of the room, where she found something quite intriguing.

"Mother, what's this?"

"What is what, Rose? Surely you realize I cannot see what you're talking about from all the way over here."

"I've found a beautiful dress. Was it yours?"

Rose was standing next to a mannequin adorned with a stunning ice blue silk dress. It had a corseted bodice with long sleeves, and a flowing skirt with white lace touches down the sides that looked like snowflakes. The fabric glittered in the candlelight. Rose noticed it was the only item in the room without a spec of dust on it.

Anne made her way over to Rose. She looked at the dress forlornly. "Yes, that was mine."

Rose was shocked. She couldn't imagine her mother in such a vibrant dress. It was a standout piece, one Rose would love to have in her collection.

"When did you wear this, mother?" Rose caressed the delicate fabric.

"When I was your age. This is the dress I wore to my eighteenth birthday celebration."

"It's perfect, mother. May I please wear it tomorrow?" Rose was so enchanted by the dress, knowing her mother once wore it, that she momentarily forgot about her quest to appear unappealing.

Anne hesitated. "I don't know, Rose. It may not be appropriate …"

"How can you say that of your own dress, mother? If it was worthy of your coming of age celebration, surely it is fit for tea with Mrs. Devano." Rose smiled. "Besides, it's the most beautiful dress. I wish I could have seen you in it."

Anne looked from Rose's hopeful face to the dress and back again. It brought back so many vivid memories that she had choked down long ago. Now they came back up and burned like flames in her throat. Seeing Rose in the dress would be beyond painful, but the notion of letting her daughter down yet again was still worse.

"All right, dear, you may wear the dress." Anne breathed.

"Oh, thank you, mother!" Rose wrapped her arms around Anne, finally feeling some connection to her distant mother. She skipped back to her room, cradling the gown in her arms.

40

Roosha arrived exactly at midnight.

Rose was standing by the balcony doors in the beautiful red corseted dress she had worn to her eighteenth birthday gathering. When Roosha saw her, he stopped, his eyes entranced. They were filled with longing and trepidation. Rose was pleased by the effect her ensemble seemed to be having on him.

"Good evening, Roosha." Rose sashayed over and kissed him tenderly on the lips.

"Forgive me, my sweet Rose. I'm afraid your radiance rendered me speechless."

Rose blushed a deep crimson. His reaction was more than she had hoped for.

"I take it, my dress pleases you?"

"It does, though, it would be nothing more than fancy fabric without the stunning creature beneath it."

"This dress holds special meaning for me. It's the dress I was wearing the eve of my eighteenth birthday, the night my world was forever changed by you." She clasped her arms around his waist.

Roosha stroked her hair. "That night altered my entire existence, Rose." He kissed her forehead. "I appreciate you sharing your special dress with me. It's so well suited to you."

Rose smiled. Roosha knew her well. He seemed to be the only one who did. She thought back to that night, how her mother had likened her appearance to that of a harlot and was grateful that she now had someone in her life who appreciated her for who she was.

"Roosha, tonight, I would like to show you my appreciation for who you are and what you mean to me."

"My sweet Rose," he caressed her cheek. "You show me that every night."

"Yes, but tonight I'd like to try showing you in a certain manner." Rose looked at him with wanton eyes. She hoped she was suggestive, though this was her first attempt at seduction.

Roosha looked at her curiously. "How do you mean?"

Rose positioned herself directly in front of Roosha. She placed her right hand on his chest and brought her lips to his. As their kiss grew more impassioned, she slowly slid her hand down his torso until it rested on his long shaft. Roosha abruptly jumped back, physically removing her hand.

"Rose, what on earth are you thinking?"

Rose was a bit startled by his reaction. "What am I thinking? I love you, and I want to show you the same pleasure that you always show me."

"Absolutely not. That is wrong." His tone was stern.

"How is that wrong?"

"It's part of our punishment as night senders, Rose. We are built to deliver pleasure, not to experience it."

"That's not necessarily true, though, is it? You experience pain when another experiences pleasure. But who's to say you'd experience any pain if I were only focused on your pleasure?"

Roosha looked at her suspiciously. "How do you know that I experience pain when another experiences pleasure?"

Rose bit her lip. She wasn't sure she should tell him about the diaries. "I heard it from the ladies of the court. It is true, isn't it?"

Roosha sighed. He didn't want Rose to know about the pain because he wanted to spare her any guilt. But he refused to lie to her.

"Yes, it's true. It is our punishment for the unconscionable choices we made in our previous lives."

"I don't like that I cause you pain, Roosha. It's not fair! You shouldn't be punished for my loving you. That's why I was hoping there was a way for me to please you without hurting you."

He took her hands in his. "Rose, I love pleasing you. It fulfills so many different parts of me beyond the physical. The love I've grown to know because of you far outweighs any of the physical pain I'm forced to experience."

Rose's eyes pricked with tears. "But I still want to show you how much I love you, how much I respect you, and how much you mean to me. Please, you have to let me try. I can't keep enjoying all of my own pleasure while you suffer. At least let me try to do something for you that won't cause you pain."

Roosha stared deep into her desperate eyes. He didn't have the heart to say no. He loosened his grip on her hands, which Rose interpreted as acquiescence to her desire. She knelt down in front of him, moving his loincloth to the side. Her eyes filled with lust at the enormity of him. Heat flushed between her legs, her body yearning to know what he would feel like inside of her.

She licked the length of Roosha's long shaft with her tongue, indulging in his smooth skin. She kissed his sensitive tip, slowly enveloping it. His sweet flavor spread to her taste buds, making her mouth water.

Rose initially thought this was an act designed only to please a man, that she would not derive any physical satisfaction from it. But as her mouth settled in, and she took him deeper into her throat, an immense pleasure radiated all the way down to her lower region. Her mind went blank, her senses overpowering her, just as they did when she devoured one of her imported chocolates.

41

Roosha was lying under a tree reeling in pain. He never made it back to the cave.

As soon as Rose had fallen asleep, his peaceful facade wore off. He crumpled quietly to the floor, his shaft feeling like it had recently been severed from his body with an unsharpened sword. His head was throbbing, and he was in no condition to fly.

When it was almost sunrise, Roosha knew he had no choice but to take to the sky. He crawled to the balcony and slowly pulled himself up, holding onto the metal railing for support. He looked out over the city and could see more of it than normal as the darkness was already disappearing. Roosha steeled himself. He knew he had to make it beyond the city limits to be safe. It was probably only a mile flight, but it seemed an arduous task in his present state, not that he had a choice.

Roosha stumbled over the side of the balcony, falling before flying. With each flap of his wings, an excruciating wave of pain crashed over him, like trying to walk on broken legs. He didn't know if he would make it to the city limits, so he changed direction. He flew the course towards the stables, as he had the day he flew Rose there. It was a much shorter distance, and he knew there was a forest of trees where he could hide.

He flapped his wings as hard as he could to gain enough height to glide the rest of the way over. As he reached the clearing by the barn, he was out of energy, the adrenaline in his system wearing off. He crashed into the bushes and crawled on his elbows and stomach until he was under the cover of the forest. There he now laid, unmoving and numb from his bodily torment.

42

Rose stared at herself in the mirror, in her mother's ice blue dress. She looked stunning. The dress was beautiful, feminine, yet still fierce, a perfect reflection of how Rose wished to be. She placed her hair atop her head, leaving a few tendrils by her neck and on her face. As she admired her appearance, she suddenly felt foolish.

"What am I doing?" Her expression changed from one of delight to incredulity. "Why have I made myself look decent today? I don't want this awful man, or his mother, to like me!"

She was about to rip the neat bun from her head when a knock on the door interrupted her.

"Rose?" It was her mother. "May I come in?"

Rose smoothed out her hair and then dropped her hands to her sides. "Yes, of course, mother."

Anne opened the door but paused in the entryway. She was transfixed by Rose's reflection in the great mirror. Rose waited in anticipation of her mother's ordinarily forceful opinion, hoping that she would approve. Moments passed, and Anne was silent, seemingly frozen in place.

"Mother? Are you all right?" Rose asked diffidently.

"Yes, child, of course." Her voice was barely more than a whisper. "You look impeccable, my dear. My dress suits you well."

Rose didn't understand her mother's reaction. Her tone was soft and laced with emotion, as opposed to her typical detached criticism.

"Mother," Rose proceeded cautiously. "Did you keep any of your other dresses from when you were younger?"

"Yes, I kept a few others."

"Which ones, if I may?"

Anne sighed. "I still have my wedding dress, and the dress I wore to celebrate your first birthday." Rose had seen both of them in the room. They were both dull, white frocks similar in style to her mother's current wardrobe, confirming this dress an anomaly.

"And what made you keep this one?"

"I already told you, child. That is the dress I wore to my coming of age celebration." There was a finality to Anne's tone, which Rose took as defensiveness.

While her words made sense, something seemed off to Rose. Her demeanor today, and from the previous night suggested this dress held great significance for her that made seeing Rose in it difficult. It was unlike her mother to allow such an emotional reaction in front of her. It fueled Rose's interest.

"Best hurry, dear, you don't want to be late for tea with the Devanos." Her guarded manner was back.

"Of course not, mother. I'll be on my way then." Rose kissed her mother quickly on the cheek and left. Anne did not follow.

43

Rose sipped her jasmine tea and waited.

When she arrived, one of the maids had escorted her out onto a cylindrical patio encased with glass. Sunshine flooded the warm room, which was encircled by flowers and plants foreign to Rose. She felt like she was sitting in the middle of a rainforest. The maid informed her that Charles was waiting for his mother, who hadn't finished making herself presentable. Rose reclined into an unladylike position in a white wicker chair, soaking up the room's peacefulness before it was to be interrupted by the impending arrival of her hosts.

Moments later, Rose heard voices approaching and automatically stood to greet them. Realizing she was off to a horrible start, she considered sitting back down as that would have been quite rude, but couldn't bring herself to sit. Silently she cursed both her mother and the court for ingraining politeness so profoundly in her core. She wasn't sure how she would appear unsuitable if she couldn't deviate from her court like habits.

"Why, Rose, don't you look enchanting!" Charles' eyes lit up as he gazed upon her, though today, he seemed to appraise her more respectfully, as opposed to his lustful leering in the garden.

"Thank you, Charles." Rose was polite but cautious. She was glad they would have a chaperone this time.

"Might I introduce you to my lovely mother, Lavandra Devano." Charles smiled proudly. He seemed to have a genuine affection for his mother, though he may just have a propensity for showmanship, like his great grandfather.

Mrs. Devano was a slight woman with curly blonde hair that matched her son's. She had a round face and small brown eyes. She was pretty, but not striking.

"It's a pleasure to meet you, Mrs. Devano." Rose curtseyed, again failing to deviate from her gentility.

"Ah, the magnificent Rose I've heard so much about!" She clapped her hands together in delight. "The pleasure of our encounter is all mine. Please, let us sit."

The three of them sat around the small oval table that matched the white wicker chairs. The maid poured tea for both Charles and his mother and placed a freshly baked plate of cookies in the center.

"Charles tells me you have a sweet tooth." She grinned affably, a warmth emanating from her eyes.

Rose was surprised that Charles had remembered any personal details about her beyond her appearance.

"That I do." Rose concentrated on her goal to be deemed unsuitable, though Lavandra's personable demeanor evoked her cordialness. "I've always been told my manner of enjoying them is quite distasteful, even vulgar if you will. Just ask Savannah."

"There's one girl's opinion I would not trust." Mrs. Devano waved her hand dismissively. "Besides, the court ladies are known for having strong opinions on manners that do not concern them." She leaned in close to Rose as if she were confiding in a friend.

Rose blanked. She was not expecting that reaction from the woman, especially regarding Savannah.

"Are you sure? Perhaps you would like a demonstration before condemning Savannah's opinion?"

Mrs. Devano laughed jubilantly. "That's quite all right, dear. But do help yourself to the cookies. They are delicious." Mrs. Devano selected a lemon cookie from the tray and nibbled it. Rose leaned forward and loaded her small plate with five cookies.

"Mother is an excellent judge of character. I trust no one more." Charles kissed Lavandra's cheek. Rose didn't know what to make of him. He seemed so different today in front of his mother.

"Charles tells me you had to cut your garden walk short the other day to make it to a charity event. I do appreciate a woman dedicated to helping those less fortunate."

"Yes," Charles interjected. "It was quite admirable of Rose to volunteer her time with the children."

Rose decided to seize another opportunity to ruffle Mrs. Devano's feathers. "Unfortunately, it is a requirement of our position. I find children to be quite repulsive." Rose was pleased with herself. The Devanos would surely not marry their eldest son to a woman who despised children. She'd be a terrible choice for continuing the bloodline.

Again, Mrs. Devano chuckled. "I'm sure I felt the same way at your age, but the minute you have one growing inside you, all of that changes. You'll see, dear."

Rose gulped. How could she make this woman understand that she wasn't joking? She didn't know what to say to get Charles' mother to dislike her, or at least glare at her in a manner that indicated disapproval.

"Charles, my dear boy, would you leave us for a bit? I'd like some time just us ladies."

"Of course, mother, as you wish. Enjoy your afternoon, ladies." Charles kissed Rose politely on the hand and then took his leave.

"Rose, your mother told me some wonderful things about you."

Rose felt the urge to roll her eyes. She was sure her mother wouldn't have portrayed Rose accurately, but instead only covered the attributes that would make her a fitting bride.

"Don't let her fool you. My talents and interests far exceed those expected of a court lady, which is why I have little interest in my courtly obligations." Rose hoped she sounded as disdainful of the court as she intended.

Lavandra nodded. "So I've heard. She told me that you managed to train your own horse when you were but a child. That's an impressive accomplishment."

Rose's eyes widened. "She told you about that?"

"Why, yes, dear. She seemed quite proud of you for it too."

Rose didn't know what to say. Her eyes glistened. All of this time, she thought her mother was ashamed of her in some way, that she thought Rose an oddity, and wished she had a more normal daughter. Now, here Mrs. Devano was telling her that Anne had boasted about an achievement that actually mattered to Rose, one that was an integral part of the woman she had become. Could it be that Rose was wrong about her mother?

"Would you tell me what else she told you about me?"

"Of course, dear." Mrs. Devano smiled encouragingly.

ON THE WALK HOME, Rose was conflicted. For years, the desire to understand her mother had gnawed at her. And in a critical moment when she should have stuck with her plan, she let emotions sway her better judgment. It was unacceptable that she allowed her eagerness for her mother's approval to deter her from her mission. Her resolve had given way to compliments, and by the end of tea, she was sure Mrs. Devano had grown fond of her. She felt like a foolish girl, as opposed to an awakened woman. Though technically, she wasn't a fully awakened woman. Perhaps if she were, she wouldn't make such foolish mistakes. It was time to take her relationship with Roosha to the next level. Her body flushed with heat as she imagined his manhood pressed deep inside her.

44

Roosha remained under the tree the entire day. He could barely move throughout the morning, so he surrendered to sleep. He nestled himself beneath fallen leaves and branches, hoping he would remain undiscovered while his body healed. On the outside, he appeared unscathed, but internally his body felt bruised and broken. It was an anguish unlike any he had experienced throughout his tenure as a night sender, worse than when he had tasted Rose's essence.

It wasn't until sunset that he could move his limbs. He managed to sit up slowly, leaning his back against the trunk of the tree. As he watched the sun descend, and the very beginnings of nighttime emerge, he thought of Rose. Were he already in the cave, he would not have ventured out to Rose's that night. Even now, though the distance was short, it seemed an impossible journey.

But he didn't want to risk staying in the forest so close to the city limits for another day, which meant he would have to fly. He would give himself a few more hours to rest, remaining as still as possible until it was close to midnight.

45

Rose knew exactly what she wanted that night, and she was ready to be very direct. She wore her deep blue silk nightgown, the same one she had worn the first night Roosha came to visit her, leaving one strap off her shoulder. She turned her head upside down, shaking out her tendrils, the long waves free to go in any direction. She felt fiery, a woman emboldened by her own carnal craving. Rose awaited his arrival perched on her stomach, her breasts forming an inviting cleavage.

Roosha landed quietly on the balcony and stepped cautiously into her room. To her, his movements seemed effortless, but for Roosha, they were torturous.

"I've been waiting for you, lover," Rose cooed.

Roosha stopped by the side of the bed. "My beautiful Rose, you look ..." Roosha didn't have words, but he felt a strong sense of arousal that worsened the pain. "I remember that dress."

Rose smiled coyly. She lifted her body onto her knees and threw her arms around his neck. "Do you now?"

Roosha fought back a wince. "Yes. It's the nightgown you were wearing the first night I visited you."

"Why, yes, it is. I chose this ensemble for a reason." Roosha looked at her, awaiting further explanation. "This is the dress I was wearing the first night you awakened my sensuality, and I want it to be what I wear for another first of ours."

Roosha gulped. "And what first is that?"

"The time you awaken my full womanhood; the first time you make love to me."

Panic overcame him. Roosha had summoned all of his energy to make the flight to her room that night. The amount of pain that would be inflicted upon him by making love to her was unfathomable in his current state. He also didn't even know if it was possible. It was forbidden, an act against the night senders' sacred laws, one that had been in place since their inception.

He withdrew from her arms. "Rose, I cannot. You don't know what you're asking of me." Roosha's voice was low and strained.

"What do you mean you cannot?" She felt spurned by his sudden reproach.

Roosha carefully weighed his options. He shunned the notion of admitting to Rose how incapacitated he was from the previous night. He would not instill an awful sense of guilt within her. If she knew the severity of his pain, it would deter her from ever enjoying her own pleasure again, and Roosha refused to take that away from her. But how then could he deny her without devastating her?

"It's not allowed. I don't even know if it's possible," he breathed.

"Well then, let us try, and we will see if it is possible. I bet that it is." Rose threw her arms around his neck and brought her lips to his.

Even her kiss acutely wounded him in his weakened state. He had to find a way to unnerve her.

"It's not natural, Rose." His voice was harsher than he intended.

She dropped her hands from his neck. "Not natural?" Rose choked. She could feel the turmoil building within her. Asking him to make love to her had taken more courage than she was willing to admit, and now she was ripe with embarrassment at his rejection. "I love you, and you love me. How could this not be natural?"

Roosha put his hand on his forehead, frustrated. He was too exhausted to be having this conversation, and his brashness was only hurting her.

"Because we are two different creatures. It's not right for us to make love. We don't know what the consequences might be."

Hot tears streamed down Rose's face. She could not bear to hear the words coming from Roosha's lips, lips that felt completely natural when pressed against hers. Her mind stopped listening to his words, as she had taken them so personally, like a sword through the heart.

"You don't want me," she whispered. Her voice was thick with grief, her mind clouded by rejection.

"Rose, my love, that's not what I'm saying at all." Roosha tried to place his arms around her, but Rose recoiled at his touch.

"Get out! Get out! Leave! I would never want to force you to be with me!" She shrieked, too loudly. Roosha had no choice but to flee.

Rose regretted the words as she said them, but it was too late. Roosha was already soaring through the sky away from her. Rose dropped to her knees, cursing her short temper. She was angry and hurt, but she didn't want him to leave, especially not under those circumstances. And she couldn't go after him, couldn't scream for him from the balcony without revealing their affair.

Roosha flew straight back to the cave, barely making it before his wings gave way. He loathed himself for not being entirely honest with Rose and giving her the impression that he did not want her. He wondered how she could even jump to that conclusion. He loved her, coveted her, and wanted more than anything to make love to her. But there was no way he could have withstood whatever pain that would have meant, at least not that night. He needed to rest, to recharge his energy levels. Rather than engaging in more self-deprecation, he promised himself he would heal and make things right with Rose. He had until midnight to regain enough strength.

Slowly, Roosha made his way around the back of the waterfall. What he didn't know was that there were two eyes in the distance watching him.

46

Rose sat at the table, wrapped in her silk robe. She was an hour late for breakfast and had dark circles beneath her eyes. Her appearance stood in stark contrast to that of Anne, who was gleaming.

"Good morning, my dear!" Anne's voice matched her bright expression. Rose knew from her lack of comment on Rose's tardiness that she was in an unshakably good mood.

"Good morning, mother." Rose's voice sounded melancholy in comparison.

"Something wrong, dear?" Before Rose could even think of offering a response, her mother continued, as if acknowledging Rose's tone had been but a formality. "No matter! I've got the most riveting news that is sure to brighten your day, or better yet, your lifetime!"

The giddier her mother sounded, the more guarded Rose became. Anne looked expectantly at Rose as if she were waiting for her to inquire as to what news Anne had to share. But Rose didn't want to know.

"Child, you realize this is the part where you say, why, mother, what is this wonderful news?"

Rose stared at her blankly. "Let us dispense with the formalities, mother. If you intend to tell me about this so-called wonderful news, then certainly, you don't need my prompting."

Anne faltered, her face contorting briefly before recovering its congenial smile. "You always were a precocious one, dear. But today, not even your attitude will sour this memorable occasion. I received word this morning from the Devano family that Charles has issued an official proposal. He wants to marry you!" Anne's grin lit up her entire face.

Rose froze. She felt fury rising within her. How could she have been so stupid yesterday? She should have followed through with her plan and mortified Anne with impropriety. It was clear from her mother's excitement that she didn't know Rose at all. Her skin moistened with perspiration from the blood boiling through her veins. She could feel any semblance of logic slowly draining from her mind. Adrenaline pumped through her hard and fast. She felt like a lion backed into a corner, crouched, and ready to spring on her mother. Before she reached the point of attack, which would cause irreparable damage, she knew she had to leave.

Rose abruptly rose from the table, flinging her chair back in a very unladylike manner. The wood toppled onto the floor. Her mother looked appalled.

"I have to go, mother, I'm late."

"Late? What could you possibly be late for this morning?" Anne's tone was reproachful.

"Nothing that concerns you, mother."

Rose stormed out of the dining room, heading quickly up the stairs to her room. Her mother pursued.

"Excuse me, young lady, but exactly what do you think you are doing? I certainly did not give you permission to leave the table, let alone the house. Whatever it is that you have to do can wait. There's nothing as important as a lady's marriage proposal!"

"I didn't ask your permission." Rose's tone was indignant. She quickly changed into her riding ensemble while her mother stood, flabbergasted at her behavior. It felt satisfying to see her mother speechless. When she finished dressing, Rose marched straight by her mother, who grabbed her elbow.

"Just where do you think you are going, child?"

"I am not a child, mother. Now kindly let go of my elbow." Rose stared into Anne's eyes with an intensity that seemed to startle her mother. Without saying a word, Anne slowly released her grip, finger by finger. When her arm was finally free, Rose raced down the stairs and out the door.

As she headed for the stables, Rose tried to take her mind off both last night and this morning. Spurned by her lover, and then issued a marriage proposal by a detestable man. Worse, her mother presented the proposal like it was the most significant accomplishment Rose would ever know. Between her pain and her wrath, Rose felt like a wild animal ready to maul anything in its way. She walked with her head down, focused only on the ground she needed to cover to get to the barn. She didn't even notice the people around her.

"My my if it isn't the future, Mrs. Devano." Savannah's tone was dripping with disdain. She planted herself right in front of Rose, forcing her to make an abrupt stop.

"Get out of my way, Savannah." Rose's tone was calm, a silent fury brewing beneath its surface.

Savannah ignored her command. "When I heard the news this morning, I was absolutely shocked. He must be a charitable man that Charles for being willing to marry such a sorry excuse for a court lady."

Rose stepped around Savannah without saying a word, but Savannah repositioned herself, again blocking Rose's path. Rose looked Savannah directly in the eye with evident ferocity as she breathed fire.

"If you don't get the hell out of my way, what Vivianna did to you in the backyard after you threatened Tomtom will seem like a kiss on the cheek compared to what I'm prepared to do."

Savannah gaped at her, terror in her eyes. Rose was proud. Never before had she silenced that wretched girl. Instead, she had always allowed Savannah's derision to get under her skin. Savannah slowly stepped out of Rose's way. Without another word, Rose continued her rapid pace towards the stables.

47

Carmera galloped at top speed through the countryside, and still, Rose pushed on, willing her faster to the point where she felt like they were flying. She wanted to get as far away from the city as possible, leave everything behind, and ease her searing pain. Hot tears streamed from her eyes and blew off her face, the wind whipping against her skin.

When she reached the stream where she and Vivianna had stopped only days before, she slowed Carmera to a halt and decided to give the animal a rest. Rose slid out of the saddle and onto the ground. She led the horse to the rocky edge, its tongue lapping up the crisp water. Rose leaned down and splashed a few handfuls on her face. The cold water felt refreshing against her flushed skin.

Rose tied Carmera to the branch of a tree and then collapsed on the grass to rest. Her head was pounding from the thoughts running through her mind when she heard another sound added to the mixture, the sound of hooves hitting the ground. She considered jumping back on Carmera, but Rose didn't have the energy to flee. Besides, she could only think of one person who would have followed her all the way out into the forest.

A few moments later, Vivianna broke through the clearing and slowed her steed to a walk. She dismounted and sat beside Rose.

"Hello, Rose. How are you holding up?"

"I love how fast personal affairs are disseminated amongst members of the court." Rose regretted her sarcasm. Vivianna did not deserve to be subjected to her frustration.

"Hmm, yes. A man never proposes to a lady, but to the entire court."

"A cowardly move."

"Indeed. And strategic. It's practically impossible for a woman to say no when the pressure of society is mounted firmly on her shoulders."

"Nobility is a nightmare," Rose sputtered.

Vivianna clasped her hands together. "How did you respond?"

"I didn't. I ran away. I told my mother I had somewhere else to be, left the house as quickly as possible, and came here. Though from my mother's delivery of the news, she seems ready to place a bow on my head and send me straight to Charles like an overdue holiday present."

"I'm sorry, Rose." Vivianna pulled Rose's shoulders to her chest, rocking her gently. "I have something to tell you."

"Mm?" Rose muttered.

"I made it back to the library basement."

Instantly, Rose sat up. "When? How?"

"After our ride the other day, I went to check on my ill mother, and she was only half lucid, in and out of sleep. The library keys were on her night table, taunting me. I made sure she was unconscious, then snatched them and returned to the library in secret."

Rose was glad that Vivianna took advantage of the opportunity, but she couldn't help feeling a bit cheated. "Why didn't you take me with you?"

Vivianna looked at her sincerely. "It wouldn't have been a good idea, Rose. What would your mother have said if you left after dinner and didn't return until very late?"

Rose flinched. She hated that Vivianna was right and that her mother still had control over her schedule as if she were a child. And if she married Charles, he would then be the one to control it. Rose rued the fact that in Dover, she would never have autonomy over her own life.

"Well, what did Edmund say when you were out late?"

"Nothing. Edmund already had plans that night. He was at the club playing poker and smoking cigars with some of the other noblemen. He does it once or twice a week, and he never gets home before ten o'clock at the earliest, so I made sure I was home by half-past nine to be safe."

"Oh." Rose couldn't hide the disappointment in her face. "I understand." It was more a formality when she said it. Still, when she imagined herself in Vivianna's position, she understood her decision. "So … tell me what happened."

"When I arrived at the library, all was quiet. It was a bit eerie. The shadows make it difficult to tell if you're actually alone."

Rose sighed, puzzled. Vivianna switched gears, deciding to be straightforward.

"Someone else had been there before me, Rose."

Rose's skin turned pale. "What do you mean?"

"I mean, I went downstairs and found the trunk already unlocked. And the second diary was missing." Her voice was strained.

Rose jumped to her feet, pacing. "How is that possible?"

"I don't know." Vivianna shrugged.

"I thought your mother was the only person with a copy of the keys." Rose was frantic.

"That was my impression, but I don't know for sure."

"Your impression?" Rose choked. "We went off of your impression?"

"Calm down, Rose. This is not the time to get worked up or point fingers. This is a time for thinking things through."

Rose didn't have the capacity to handle another catastrophe. Between Roosha's rejection, Charles' proposal, and her confounding mother, she was drained.

"Maybe we should tell your mother. Mrs. Weston will know what to do."

Vivianna startled. "We most certainly should not tell my mother! Do you have any idea how much trouble we'd be in?"

"We might already be in serious trouble! What if someone is on to us?"

"Then, hopefully, I threw her … or him … off our trail … at least temporarily."

"How?" Rose retorted, skeptically.

"I made it look like I hadn't returned. I left things exactly as I found them. I did not return the original diary and left without taking the third book. I made sure to leave the trunk unlocked. I was thorough."

"What do we do, Vivianna? I can't take all of this mounting pressure." Rose crumpled back to the ground.

Vivianna stroked her back. "We wait it out. In the meantime, I hid the first diary in a safe place."

"Did you read part of the third book while you were down there?"

Vivianna bit her lip. She had spent the past couple of days debating whether to tell Rose about the contents of the third diary. Vivianna knew Rose already had a strenuous relationship with her mother and that she was desperate to understand her, but Vivianna doubted what she read would improve their rapport. If anything, it may further deteriorate it. Still, Vivianna hated to lie to Rose, even to protect her. She tossed and turned the whole night, agonizing over whether she had made the right decision.

Exhausted from arguing with herself, by morning, she was desperate for someone else's opinion, so much so, that she asked Edmund, indirectly, of course. His insight proved to be valuable.

She had asked, "Edmund, if you knew something about one of your friend's fathers that was very important, would you tell him?"

He put down the coffee he had been sipping and looked at her intently, his soulful brown eyes perplexed. "What do you mean if I knew something? What sort of something are you referring to?"

"Something meaning a secret."

Edmund ran his hand through his thick black curls. "So, you're asking if I would disclose the father's secret to his son?"

"Yes, bearing in mind that his son is your closest friend, maybe your only one."

"It depends. Is this a secret that, if not revealed, is likely to cause my friend some immediate harm?" His tone was matter-of-fact, not surprising from the man who came from a legacy of barristers.

"No, I don't think so. But it would help him understand his father more, maybe bring significant clarity and compassion to the relationship."

The bridge between his eyebrows creased, as it always did when he was deep in contemplation. Vivianna appreciated that he took her seriously, that he did not dismiss her questions as frivolous.

"Then I think it's not my place to tell him. I would not want to interfere with the sacred bond between father and son."

Now, as she gazed into Rose's eyes, she recognized the reason in Edmund's words. No good could come from Rose knowing about the third diary, not when they were missing so much vital information. And it was Anne's story to tell, not hers. Still, she abhorred lying to Rose.

"No. I was too afraid to stay and read. I fled as fast as I could in case the person was still in the library." Vivianna stood and walked over to her horse. "We'd better head back in." Vivianna readjusted the girth on her saddle. "So how was tea with Mrs. Devano yesterday?"

Rose sighed. "It was fine. She seemed perfectly nice, in a genuine way, not in a Devano public persona way."

"Well, she's not really a Devano, is she?"

Rose grinned. "Only by marriage, which I'm sure was not her decision."

Vivianna returned her grin. "Not likely."

Rose pulled down her stirrups. "I'll tell you what I did like—the woman definitely has a bead on Savannah. Mrs. Devano made it crystal clear she does not like her or trust her."

"Speaking of Savannah … Rose, I'm so sorry!" Her words were stricken with regret. "I meant to talk … well, more threaten Savannah to refrain from circulating any rumors about your date with Charles. I even had leverage to use!" Vivianna smacked her forehead, disappointed in herself. "But I got distracted by what happened at the library. It unnerved me."

"Calm down, Vivianna. It's all right." Rose spoke to her in the same tone she used with Carmera, soft and reassuring. "Strangely enough, it would appear that Savannah hasn't said anything." Rose mounted her horse.

Vivianna stared at her blankly. "What do you mean she hasn't said anything? That's not like her."

"Well, the other day, my mother attended an impromptu court meeting with Mrs. Devano in attendance. I thought for certain it had something to do with Savannah. But when my mother returned home, she told me Mrs. Devano had invited me to tea. And now Charles has proposed."

Vivianna's face was twisted in confusion. "What about the other girls? Have they said anything to you?" Vivianna threw her leg over her mare, easing herself into the saddle. The horses charged forward, keeping pace with each other.

"No, they haven't. Not one of them has even uttered the words, Scarlet Rose."

"That is befuddling. Maybe Amelia was telling the truth after all?"

Rose cocked her head to the side. "Amelia?"

"On my walk to the library the other night, I overheard a conversation between Amelia and Genevieve. Amelia claimed to know what really happened on Savannah's date with Charles, and said she would reveal it at the right time."

Rose shook her head. "Some friend she is, the conniving kind."

"This could explain Savannah's silence."

"You think she's afraid of Amelia? The girl she refers to as piglet." Rose's tone was incredulous.

"No, but she might be afraid of the Devanos."

"That I could understand." Mrs. Taddy's face flitted across Rose's mind.

"Was Charles present at tea?"

"Yes. He was surprisingly polite … He didn't leer at me the way he did in the garden."

Vivianna scoffed. "Did you really expect anything different? He was with his mother, of course, he was well behaved. Don't let that fool you. I'd venture to say you saw much more of the real Charles that day in the garden."

"I suppose." Rose knew intuitively that Vivianna was right. A person's actions were a much more significant indicator of who they are than their words.

"So, what are you going to do about the proposal?" Vivianna's tone was softer.

Rose squeezed her eyes shut as the waterworks began all over again. "I can't marry him."

"It might not be that awful, Rose. With someone like him, it's about learning how to manage their personality to your advantage. Find out what makes him angry, what makes him happy, what puts him to sleep, then use that knowledge to make your life as un-miserable as possible."

Rose couldn't believe what Vivianna was saying. She felt like she was talking to a different person. Could she really be suggesting that she go through with this marriage?

"Why are you talking as if I should accept his proposal?" Her voice was low but laced with anger.

"Realistically, what other choice do you have? How are you going to turn down a marriage proposal from Charles Devano and still remain in Dover?"

"I told you I had no intention of marrying him! I was only seeing him to placate my mother!" Rose's cheeks were hot, blood raging beneath her skin.

"But, Rose, didn't you realize that courtship could always lead to a proposal, whether you wanted it to or not?"

"Yes, but ..."

"But what? Name one court girl who has turned down a marriage proposal. It simply isn't done. You knew that going into this."

Rose's cheeks flushed a deeper crimson. Now she was furious, more at herself than at Vivianna. She knew Vivianna wasn't chastising her, but only pointing out a hard truth. Charles wasn't just a nobleman; he was the premiere bachelor of the group, his family name a legacy. It would be social suicide to turn down his proposal, something her mother would never allow.

"But I can't marry him, Vivianna." Rose's voice was small, pleading, her brown eyes rimmed with tears.

"Why not?" There was a hint of suspicion in Vivianna's voice.

"Because I'm in love with someone else." The words poured from her lips.

Vivianna looked taken aback. "That's what you've been hiding? An affair with another nobleman?" Vivianna shook her head. "No, that wouldn't make sense." She pondered a moment. "Ah-ha, you're having an affair with a commoner!"

Rose chewed her lip. "Not exactly."

"With who then? A woman?"

"No, though that might be simpler," she added wryly.

"Then, with who?" Vivianna looked flummoxed.

Rose hesitated. Internally, her protective instincts cautioned her to keep Roosha a secret still. But her heart begged for consolation, for a trustworthy outlet. She was tired of facing her struggles alone, especially ones of this magnitude.

Every moment that Rose remained quiet infuriated Vivianna. After all they had been through together, still Rose questioned her loyalty? She had done nothing to betray Rose's trust. Her hands shook from the anger brewing inside her.

"Rose, have I done something, anything to make you distrust me?" She struggled to keep her tone measured.

"No!" Rose's voice was defensive, tears spilling onto her cheeks.

"Then why don't you trust me?" Rose had not seen Vivianna on the verge of tears since the Tomtom incident. "The day I entrusted you with the diaries' existence, I put my full faith in you, Rose. And still, you refuse to reciprocate!" Vivianna's voice cracked on her last few words. She squeezed her horse and trotted ahead.

Rose trembled. She couldn't bear the thought of Vivianna walking away from her, of losing her only friend. She trotted to catch up, screaming the answer as the horse picked up speed.

"With my night sender!" The words erupted out from the emotional storm swirling violently within Rose. "I'm having an affair with my night sender." Relief washed over her. Strangely, it felt good to finally share her secret, her burden, her albatross, with someone else.

Vivianna slowed her horse to a walk, closing her eyes.

"Rose, no! Please tell me you haven't told anyone else." There was a sharp edge to her tone.

Rose looked at Vivianna like a child desperate for its mother's embrace. "That's your reaction?"

"Of course, that's my reaction!" Vivianna was yelling, which was well out of character for her customarily composed nature. "You do realize the magnitude of what you are doing?"

Rose's lips quivered. Her eyes had become small waterfalls. "But I love him," she sobbed.

There was a wild look in Vivianna's eyes as if she had just heard the unimaginable. "Rose, you have to stop this at once!"

Rose looked at Vivianna, heartbroken. "I thought you'd understand."

Vivianna's heart wrenched in her chest. "Rose, it's you who doesn't understand."

"What don't I understand?" Rose's voice was desperate, her eyes pleading for an answer.

Vivianna looked like she wanted to say something more, but closed her mouth.

"I'm sorry, Rose," she whispered. "End it now, before it's too late." With a firm kick, her horse was off at a canter that soon transitioned to a gallop.

Rose remained paralyzed in place atop Carmera. There was a sense of fear bubbling up inside of her that she was missing something, something important.

48

Roosha still felt downcast over the way things had ended with Rose the night before. He was worried that he had unintentionally hurt her feelings and, worse, made her believe that he didn't want to be intimate with her.

The only good that had come from the previous night's events was Roosha's opportunity to rest. He spent the entire day sleeping and had finally regained most of his strength.

He now sat by the lake outside the cave, waiting in anticipation of midnight so he could profess his desire to Rose, hold her in his arms, and reassure her of his devotion. If she wanted him to make love to her, he would. There was nothing he would deny her.

Roosha looked up at the night sky and knew it was time. He stood and readied himself to fly.

"Have an assignment tonight?" A familiar voice called.

Roosha cringed. "Greetings, Avidan. No, not tonight."

Avidan stood not five feet away, looking at him expectantly.

"Just felt like taking a flight," Roosha added nonchalantly.

"In that case, may I join you?"

Roosha reckoned that Avidan was testing him. "You're not usually one to want company, old friend."

"Tonight, I'm feeling somewhat social." Avidan smiled wryly.

Roosha didn't know what to do. If he refused Avidan, it would confirm his suspicions, which could be dangerous, especially if Avidan followed him. But if he flew with Avidan, it would mean he may not see Rose, and worse, that she would be wondering where he was, her pain augmented by the way they had left things. When he weighed the risk of Avidan uncovering their affair, his protective instincts overpowered his desire.

"Well then, friend, let us fly."

ROSE STOOD ON THE BALCONY staring into the darkness. It was already half-past midnight and still no sign of Roosha. It was the first time he had not shown up, and she was perturbed. Despite her injured ego from the night before, she knew in her heart that he wouldn't have abandoned her, and was afraid he had been injured or worse, compromised. What would the night senders do if they learned of their relationship? Her heart thudded erratically at the thought.

As the minutes passed, possibilities clouded her mind, making her more fearful for his safety. If something happened to him, she would have no way of knowing. She didn't know the location of the cave, nor how to contact him. Involving the court would mean admitting her affair, which could put them both in danger, especially given Vivianna's ferocious reaction. She felt powerless, which she was loath to accept. But as there was currently no other choice, she did the only thing she could do; she stood on the balcony, praying that at some point, he would come to her alive and unharmed.

49

Roosha and Avidan flew for miles, mostly in silence. The only time Avidan spoke was to suggest flying even farther out. Roosha fought to conceal his impatience, accepting Avidan's suggestions with as much fake enthusiasm as he could muster.

It was two hours later when Avidan finally announced that he would return to the cave.

"Have a good rest of the night, friend."

"You as well, Roosha." He cocked his head to the side and gave him one last hard glance before taking off.

Roosha waited until Avidan was no longer visible and then leapt into the air, soaring as fast as he could to get to Rose.

ROSE STARED AT THE CLOCK TOWER, which had just struck half-past two. She was wide awake, trying to suppress the panic within her. She considered going to bed but knew that sleep would evade her. Her brain shuffled through all of the things she could do in the confines of her room to take her mind off of Roosha's absence, ultimately deciding to write.

Writing had always been a healthy outlet for her in the past. Rose went back into her room and retrieved a pen and parchment paper from her night-table drawer. She sat on the edge of her bed and penned a letter to Roosha.

Roosha My Love,

The hour is late, and I am beside myself in your absence. I don't know where you are; I only hope you are alive and well.

If you deliberately chose not to return, I would not blame you. My words and my actions were reprehensible. Desperate to become a full-blooded woman, I blindsided you with my lust rather than discussing my desires. When you expressed concern for the laws of your realm, I took it as a personal affront, selfishly focused on my needs and my ego. Even worse, I failed to hear your reason, knowing that my pleasure causes you pain. Though I deeply regret my actions, I cannot change them. I can only beg your forgiveness.

I love you, Roosha. I will always choose you, no matter how "unnatural" that may be.

Eternally Yours,

Rose

Tears splattered on the paper, making the ink run.

"I hope it's not I who have once again put tears in your eyes, my sweet Rose."

Rose closed her eyes. His voice penetrated her entire being, restoring peace and sanity. She stood and quickly found herself in his embrace, her head nestled against his right shoulder.

"My Roosha," she whispered.

"I'm sorry I was delayed. I didn't mean to frighten you or cause you any concern."

"It doesn't matter," she croaked. "All that matters is that you are here now, unharmed."

Her eyes met his, and their lips quickly followed.

Their kiss was intimate, yet infused with a ferocious passion. As her tongue found his, she held his body, willing him closer to her. She longed to connect with him every possible way, his skin pressed against hers, his manhood deep inside of her.

Roosha's head was already throbbing, but he didn't care. If it killed him, he would make love to this woman who he cherished more than his own existence.

Roosha picked Rose up and laid her gently on the bed. He climbed on top of her, his lips still locked onto hers. He ran his hand down her body, gently cupping her supple breasts as he made his way beneath her silk nightgown. He slid his hand between her thighs, his fingers feeling her readiness. She was warm and wet, and he was tortured with desire and pain.

Roosha met Rose's eyes as he slowly eased himself inside of her.

Rose moaned in a pleasure that far exceeded any of the other wondrous ways he had previously aroused her. Roosha spread his wings outward, wrapping them tightly around Rose, until they were inside a feathered cocoon, hopefully muffling her moans. Roosha thrust himself further inside her, biting into her neck the way he had the first night. Rose panted as her body writhed. Her pleasure center was swelled, its walls contracting, sucking Roosha deeper. He thrust faster, sensing she was on the verge of a harmonious release.

50

Rose's feral scream roared through the silent night. As her life juices dripped from her, Roosha felt a searing pain rip through his body as if someone had taken a dull blade and skinned him alive. He toppled onto the floor, destroyed, while Rose arched back in ecstasy on the bed, barely conscious.

The sound of quickening footsteps brought Roosha back to reality. He knew Rose's mother was fast approaching. But Roosha could not move. His body was still reeling with an agony that incapacitated him. He tried to flip over, onto his stomach to crawl, but his body defied his commands. A different kind of suffering now plagued him—failure. Roosha's weakness was about to get them both caught. He had failed Rose, and for that, he would never forgive himself.

Suddenly, the balcony doors flung open. Midnight blue arms grabbed him, yanking Roosha out of the room and over the side of the balcony only seconds before the entrance to Rose's room burst open.

"Rose, what's wrong?" Anne's voice was frantic as she ran towards the bed.

Rose was lying there limp with a look of innate bliss on her face. Anne took her shoulders in her hands and shook Rose, rousing her from her rapture.

"Child, what's wrong? Tell me."

"Absolutely nothing." Rose's voice was smooth and satisfied, like that of a woman who just had her most intense orgasm. She rested her right arm gently across her eyes.

Anne stood up abruptly and surveyed Rose. Her expression changed from concerned to enraged. Now she really looked at her daughter. Rose's hair was tousled, her nightgown straps hanging off her shoulders, her body flushed with heat.

Anne turned towards the French doors leading to the balcony. They were open. In his rapid departure, Roosha had failed to close the doors behind him. Anne put the pieces together in her mind, and as this last one fell into place, she grew beyond furious.

Her vehement voice came out in a threatening whisper.

"Child, you've gone too far this time. Do you have any idea the consequences of what you are doing? You must cease this foolishness immediately."

Rose snapped back to life at her words.

"Don't be ridiculous, mother! Just because you want to live a boring life devoid of any real pleasure, don't condemn me to the same fate!"

Anne slapped Rose hard, straight across her flawless face. Rose's head snapped to the side. Her hand reflexively covered her cheek, which was red and already starting to swell. Rose stared at her mother, stunned. Anne had never before laid a hand on her. Hot tears began streaming down her cheeks. Rose's voice was shaky as she spoke.

"How could you do that, mother? You've never hit me before. Why? Why would you do that?"

Her mother's eyes softened, her face tormented.

"Rose, please. I'm sorry, but you don't understand," she whispered.

"Then help me understand!" She bade her mother would cease this baffling behavior.

Anne's face was torn. She didn't know if she had the strength to let Rose see this side of her, the side that had suffered in silence for so many years now. The side that so long ago vowed to only do what was proper to spare those she loved from any of her anguish. Worst of all, she didn't know if she should let Rose see how she had extinguished her own fiery nature long ago, the very same one that coursed through her daughter.

"Do you love him?" Anne breathed.

Rose searched her eyes, wondering how much she knew.

"Answer me, child, do you love him, your night sender?"

Rose gasped. She didn't understand how Anne could possibly know about Roosha. But she reasoned that she might learn more if she were honest with her mother.

"Yes."

Anne sighed. "Then, you must end it right now."

Rose's face twisted in devastation. The thought of ending her relationship with Roosha was unimaginable. Losing him would be unbearable. It could destroy her. And worse, she didn't know why Anne was forcing her hand.

"But why, mother, why?" Rose pounded her fists on the bed in frustration. "For once in your life, tell me why!" She hated that her mother was speaking in riddles. She also hated that at this very moment, she was questioning whether she knew her mother at all.

"Because he could die!" Anne screeched. It was a shrill sound tinged with despair, the loudest noise Rose had ever heard come out of her mother's mouth.

Rose sat back, dumbfounded. Roosha hadn't told her that he could die from being with her. He only told her that it caused him physical pain. But something else was eating at Rose. She needed to know exactly how her mother knew of the consequences.

"Mother, how do you know that?" Rose enunciated each word slowly, afraid of what Anne was about to tell her.

Anne took a deep breath. "Because you and I are not as different as you like to think."

Rose stared at her mother blankly. Was this the same woman sitting before her who spent years ingraining in Rose the importance of propriety, of never painting outside the lines, of not wearing too bright a color so as not to stand out? Was her mother, Anne Elizabeth Woodburn, now telling her that she had an affair with a night sender? That at one point in her youth, she was infused with the same passion and desire for life and love and pleasure as Rose herself?

"When?" Rose whispered.

"Nineteen and a half years ago, when I was eighteen."

51

Avidan dropped Roosha hard next to the tree on the hilltop. Roosha could barely move but still managed to pull himself half upright, his back against the side of the tree, legs sprawled out in front of him.

"This has gone far enough, Roosha!" His words were spoken with anger and authority.

Not knowing the full extent of Avidan's knowledge, Roosha asked, "What has, Avidan?"

Roosha's head knocked straight back, landing hard against the trunk. Avidan had delivered a forceful blow that Roosha hadn't seen coming and now had one hand wrapped tightly around Roosha's neck. He was taken aback. In all his years, Roosha had never seen this side of Avidan.

"Don't test me again, boy. I warned you multiple times, but you failed to heed my advice. You have no idea the consequences of the path you have chosen."

"Then enlighten me, friend," Roosha choked.

Avidan's grip gradually loosened until Roosha was finally able to breathe. The fury in his eyes dissipated. There was now a sadness reflecting out of them.

"His name was Thanoine, and he was a dear friend of mine."

52

Anne sat on the side of the bed, the way she had after Rose's father died, and she began regaling her with stories in his place. Only this time, Anne was overwhelmed with consternation, her face pale, hands jittery.

"When I was your age, I was just like you, Rose. I was different from the other girls my age. I had long fiery red hair that ran all the way down to the small of my back. It was wavy and wild, and I refused to ever wear it tied back. My mother couldn't stand it. While all the other girls were sitting around having tea and gossiping, I was off riding bareback on my white mare, Iponella. The last thing I cared about was being proper, which I'm sure is unimaginable to you. My eyes were always pale blue, but back then, there was light and life to them. For the past nineteen years, I have suppressed the girl I used to be. I buried her deep inside me, where her passion could no longer harm me. My eyes have gotten duller each year that she's been locked away." Anne paused, looking at Rose. "If it weren't for your presence in my life, she would have been snuffed out completely." She placed her hand over Rose's.

"A broken heart can break a person's spirit. My heart wasn't just broken, Rose. It was shattered into thousands of sharp, tiny fragments that scraped against my insides until the pain was so unbearable that I had to find a way to disconnect my heart from the rest of me. The only way I could manage it was through indifference."

Tears trickled down Rose's cheek. She sat there frozen, her eyes fixated on her mother. Rose had never seen Anne so open, so vulnerable. The smooth exterior of her face had crumpled like paper, exposing all of the creases of stress and sadness she must have accumulated over the years. She was far from the stern, unbending woman Rose had always known; she was human. Rose wondered if she had always borne this burden alone, or if Anne ever confided her pain in anyone. Did her father know?

"His name was Thanoine, and he was my night sender. Back when I was eighteen, we were told the same thing as you, that under no circumstances were we to enjoy our visit, only we weren't blindfolded." She looked meaningfully at Rose. "Apparently, the court hadn't anticipated the difference in our hot-blooded line. The other girls scared so easily that their eyes were sealed shut throughout the experience."

"The court also didn't tell us anything about the night senders themselves. We knew that we had a duty as court ladies to endure a visit by these strange creatures, and we weren't supposed to enjoy it. So naturally, I was reeling with excitement the night of my eighteenth birthday. Like you, I didn't put any faith in the opinion of the court. I found allure in the forbidden and was determined to decide for myself whether I should take pleasure in the experience."

Anne moved her gaze towards the balcony doors.

"That night changed my world. It opened up so many new avenues of passion in my body and spirit that I didn't know were there. We had certainly never been encouraged to explore them. The pleasure empowered me and made me more rebellious. I did exactly what you did. I fell in love with my night sender. I looked down on the idea of marriage and all the bland noblemen who came along with it. I gave in to passion and pleasure. Thanoine visited me every night, each time bringing me a single white rose."

Rose gasped, to which Anne nodded. So that was why she was named Rose, the reason her mother visited the florist every week. Since she was old enough to remember, there had always been fresh-cut white roses in their home.

Anne continued. "Sometimes he even took me flying with him. We soared through the night, free from duties and obligations and rules until the unfathomable day it was all taken from us in an instant. That was the night I died, Rose."

Her mother paused. Rose could see the gleam of moisture in Anne's eyes. Her normally erect shoulders sunk down towards her chest, and her voice was thick with grief when she spoke again.

"We were found out by my mother in the exact way I walked in on you tonight, only Thanoine was still in the room. My scream was even louder. As soon as he saw my mother, Thanoine leapt out the window. My mother grabbed me tightly by the shoulders and shook me hard. Her nails left indentations in my skin. She screamed at me, called me a harlot, and slapped me across the face."

Anne flinched, her head turning away from Rose. "My eye felt like it was exploding with the impact of her hand. Once the tirade ended, she stormed out of the room and left me there crying."

Her mother collapsed in a sobbing heap, her chest heaving erratically. Rose was afraid of what was coming next.

"I must have fallen asleep because, later that night, I was abruptly awoken to a black sack being tied over my head, and strong arms restraining me. They weren't human arms. I was carried out the window and flown somewhere. All I know is that when the sack was finally removed, I was in a great stone room that looked like the inside of a cave. Above me, Thanoine was chained to a wooden pyre. There were other night senders in the room, maybe fifteen of them. Standing on a small platform just a few feet away from the pyre was a crazed looking woman. I don't remember what she looked like because I couldn't take my eyes from Thanoine's. He looked distressed but hopeless. My heart was pounding so hard I thought it was going to break through my rib cage. I knew at that moment he wasn't coming out of this alive. I screamed, pleading for mercy, but they acted as if I weren't there. No one said a word to me. When the crazed woman spoke, she only addressed Thanoine. I remember what she said, word for word. Thanoine, you have violated the laws of the realm of the night senders. You visited a girl more than once. You derived pleasure from your relations with another even though you were sworn to a life of servitude. And worse, you broke our most sacred law. You laid with a human. There is only one sentence for these crimes, and that is death."

Anne paused, closing her eyes. Rose squeezed her hand. "Then she killed us both. She threw a lit torch onto the pyre. I was made to watch as the creature I loved was engulfed in flames and burned alive. I held his final gaze until I could take no more. My body gave in, and I passed out from the pain. The next day, I awoke back in my bed, wondering if it was some horrible nightmare until midnight came and Thanoine didn't come. He never came again."

Her mother was sobbing hard, her breathing erratic. Rose moved closer until she could finally plant her arms around her mother. For the first time, Anne didn't pull away. She threw her arms back around Rose, and together they both cried until they fell asleep in each other's arms.

53

Roosha sat at the base of the tree, intent on listening to Avidan's every word. Avidan kneeled beside him, but looked up into the night sky as he spoke.

"Thanoine had been a night sender for only ten years at the time, which wasn't much considering the double sentence he was serving. He was good in every sense of the word. He had complete empathy for the girls. It's as if his sentence had turned him into the decent man he should have been when he was one. So when he was assigned to the one court girl who refused to deny her own sensual nature, he was a goner. He went back night after night despite the agonizing pain it caused him because he knew how much she enjoyed it. Eventually, he fell in love with the girl. When the two of them got caught ..."

Roosha watched Avidan's expression closely. His face kept changing slightly as if he was reliving the experience in his mind. Finally, his eyes opened wide, and he looked like he saw a ghost.

"What's wrong, Avidan?" Roosha was genuinely concerned for his friend.

"It was awful, Roosha." Avidan's eyes closed, and his shoulders dropped until he was slightly hunched over. "Madeira burned him alive in front of us all, and the girl was made to watch."

Roosha felt as though he had been kicked in the gut, all of the air knocked violently from his body. He couldn't imagine being forced to watch Avidan burn. But then a more pressing thought crossed his mind.

"Do you know what became of the girl?"

"I do not." Avidan took a deep breath. "Her life was spared. She fainted as the flames rose and was flown back to her room at the end. But one can only imagine the effect the ordeal must have had on her. I doubt she came away unscarred."

Despite the weight of Avidan's words, Roosha still felt slightly relieved. At least the life-ending punishment was reserved for their kind. If Avidan had told him that the girl had been executed as well, he would never see Rose again.

"Roosha, death is not always the worst punishment. At least death has a finality to it. That poor girl has had to wake up every day for the past nineteen and a half years with that horrific event emblazoned in her mind, as have I."

Roosha looked down at the ground. He knew Avidan was right, but he couldn't imagine existing without Rose in his life. Death seemed like a fair trade for all of the moments he was able to spend with her.

"I must go now, Roosha. I am spent. My words are a warning, not a threat. Your choices are your own. I wanted to make sure you had all of the necessary information to do what is best … for everyone." Avidan's emphasis was on his final two words.

Roosha knew what Avidan meant, but at the same time, he was unconvinced.

"Thank you, friend, for both your words and your wisdom."

Avidan nodded at Roosha and then leapt back into the air.

Roosha remained on the hilltop, contemplating. Part of him wondered if Rose's mom had discovered their relationship, in which case there were probably night senders already out looking for him. That seemed unlikely as Avidan probably would have warned him if that were the case. Also, unlike Thanoine, Roosha knew he had made it off the balcony before Rose's mother entered the room, so there was still a chance they were safe.

Assuming they were, Roosha had a more pressing decision to make regarding his relationship with Rose. Could he, in good conscience, continue the relationship knowing the potential fate they both faced? For his part, he didn't fear death, but he also didn't want to condemn Rose to stand witness to it. Though selfishly, he couldn't fathom the thought of existing without her in his world, no matter the cost.

Roosha sat motionless by the tree staring out into the abyss until dawn approached. Under the last remaining cover of darkness, he intended to fly back to the cave, but his body was still incapable. Thankfully, Avidan had left him in safe surroundings where humans didn't venture. His body may have been immobilized, but his mind and heart were working overtime, at odds with each other. Logic urged him to consider his wellbeing. How could he continue his physical relationship with Rose when it was killing him? Love assured him he could overcome his body. No matter how that battle ended, one thing was for sure; as long as he was still alive the next night, he would go see Rose.

54

Rose awoke from a sound sleep feeling groggy but rested. She rolled onto her back and stretched her arms and legs wide, across the entire bed. She knew something was wrong the instant she felt the cool sheets on either side of her. She sat up abruptly, realizing her mother was not there.

Panic immediately spread throughout Rose's entire body. Her heart thudded loudly, and cold sweat licked at her temples. She replayed every detail from the previous night over in her mind. Her mother had finally opened up to her and exposed her own vulnerability. For the first time, Rose had been able to relate to the stoic Anne Elizabeth Woodburn. But Rose was unsure whether that had been a momentary glimpse into the woman her mother once was, or if their relationship had been permanently altered. Perhaps those options weren't mutually exclusive.

All Rose knew at that moment were two crucial facts; her mother was not with her, nor did Rose know her whereabouts, and her mother knew she was in love with a night sender. Rose desperately wanted to believe that, after what her mother had been through, she wouldn't expose Rose's relationship to the court. But Rose didn't know if she had awoken this morning as the proper, rule-abiding Anne or Rose's mother, the endearing, tortured woman who was human.

A quiet knock drew Rose's attention to the door. Her heart raced faster. She dared not open it for fear that she would be forced against her will to witness the death of the man she loved, a fate Rose knew she was not strong enough to endure.

Another louder knock sent Rose beneath her bed covers. She felt like a petrified child as opposed to the full-blooded woman she thought she had become.

The door slowly opened. A soft voice called to her.

"Rose? Rose, are you awake?"

Recognizing her mother's voice, Rose gingerly pulled back the sheets enough so that she could see her mother.

"There you are, my dear. I brought you some breakfast."

From her mother's tone, it seemed to Rose that she had not reverted back to the stoic Anne overnight. She removed the covers to see that her mother was carrying a tray with a small pot of tea and a bowl of porridge. Rose pulled herself upright, resting her back against the headboard. Anne sat down next to her, placing the tray across Rose's lap. She leaned over and gave her a good morning kiss on the forehead.

"Did you sleep well?"

"Yes, did you?" Rose was genuinely curious. Even as a child, she couldn't remember ever sleeping in bed next to her mother.

"I slept more soundly than I've slept in years." Anne looked wistful as she spoke. "And I woke up feeling a bit lighter."

"Did you really carry that secret alone for all those years?" Rose placed a spoonful of warm porridge in her mouth. It tasted of milk and cinnamon.

"Yes."

"But why, mother?"

"Because I had no one in my world who would ever understand. Surely you know what that's like, my dear Rose." Anne gave her a wry smile.

Rose felt a lump rise in her throat as she swallowed the porridge, understanding how much she and her mother had in common. She was sure Anne hadn't alerted the court to her relationship with Roosha.

"Thank you for finally telling me, mother."

"Rose, after that … day … I swore to myself that if I ever had a daughter, I would never allow her to be like me, for her own protection. Clearly, I was unable to keep that vow. You are even more free-spirited and rebellious than I was. You're beautiful, fierce, and strong-willed, which I have always admired."

Rose's eyes glistened. Her mother had always focused so much on trying to change her that Rose never knew Anne liked anything about her, let alone admired these qualities.

"But with this independent nature comes difficult choices. I will not make any decisions for you, as I would never have wanted anyone to make mine. I didn't know the consequences of my actions, but you do. If you love him as you say you do, would you condemn him to death for your own pleasure?"

Rose stared into her porridge. She felt overwhelmed by the magnitude of the decision her mother was putting entirely in her hands. It made her sorry for all the times she mouthed off about how she was now a woman. She felt more like a child who wanted to hide in the closet than face this daunting reality.

"No matter what you decide, you have my word that the court will hear absolutely nothing from me."

Anne stood up to leave.

"Mother?"

"Yes, dear?"

"If you could do it all over again, knowing the consequences, would you have still had the relationship?"

Anne closed her eyes. "No." Without another word, she quietly left the room, closing the door behind her.

Rose moved the tray to her side and slid off the bed. She opened the doors to the balcony and stared out at the quaint town of Dover. Her mother's words echoed in her mind. *If you love him as you say you do, would you condemn him to death for your own pleasure?* As the question sank in deeper, and the consequences permeated her heart's core, she knew the answer.

She also knew that what she had to do next would be a series of the most challenging decisions she'd ever had to make.

55

"Rose, you don't have to do this. It hasn't even been a full day." Anne watched as her daughter put on one of her old beige dresses.

"Yes, mother, I do." Rose's voice was soft but still firm. "It's the only way."

"Are you sure, dear? It may not be the only way."

Rose still found it hard to believe that those words were coming out of her mother's mouth, the same woman who would never rage against even the tiniest of societal conditions while Rose was growing up.

"Why would you say that, mother?" Please don't put false hope where there is none."

Anne sighed. "Thanoine and I never had a chance. We were discovered and found out the hard way what the consequences of our relationship were. You know them before they've happened. Perhaps you can find another way. You have time…"

"Please, mother." Rose closed her eyes. She sounded exasperated. "This morning, you asked me if I would condemn him to death for my own pleasure, and I will not do that. Why are you so concerned with my decision to accept Charles' proposal? You were thrilled about it yesterday."

"I was only thrilled because I thought a normal life would protect you. But you chose differently. And I don't want to see you condemned to my fate either."

"Which fate is that?"

"A loveless marriage." Anne lowered her head.

"But when I asked, you told me you loved my father."

"Yes. I loved him as one would love a brother or a friend. There was no fire, no passion. We were a smart match by court standards, and my mother was eager to marry me off after what happened. It wasn't until I had you that I remembered what fervent love and passion felt like again, which was bittersweet. I adored you, and your life gave me purpose. But it also reminded me of all that I had given up after that horrible night."

Rose enveloped her mother in a tight embrace. Anne's warm tears streamed onto her bare shoulder. "It's the only way, mother. Roosha will never leave me otherwise. And I cannot watch him die."

Anne tightened her grip around her daughter. Despite their mutual horror and grief, both women found solace and gratitude in how similar they were, and how close they were becoming. Understanding each other had created an unbreakable bond for which both women had always yearned. Finally, Anne no longer felt like Rose's mother, but instead, a kindred spirit and a faithful friend.

A gentle knocking on the door drew their attention. "Mrs. Woodburn, Miss Woodburn. Mr. Charles Devano has arrived," the maid informed them.

Rose took the handkerchief from her vanity and dabbed her mother's eyes until the tears were no longer visible.

Anne put her hand on Rose's cheek. "My dear, I do believe you are a stronger woman at eighteen than I could have hoped to be."

Rose wiped the tear from her eye. "Shall we?"

56

Rose steeled herself. It was almost midnight, and she knew Roosha would soon arrive. She hated herself for what she was about to do but knew it was the only way to send him away, and she didn't even know if it would be enough.

Rose looked down at her left hand, adorned with the brilliant sapphire and diamond ring Charles had put on her finger. The stone was so large it covered a small portion of both her pinky and middle fingers. Slowly, she slid the jewel off, not wanting it to be the first thing Roosha saw. She needed to tell him herself; he deserved that much.

Rose took a deep breath, willing herself to have courage. "Courage is what you do in the face of fear, not in the absence of it," she repeated quietly to herself. She knew her imminent fear of Roosha dying was real. It was imperative that she summon the courage to send him away for his own protection, a thought that already had her eyes watering.

For a brief moment, she wished she could be more normal, like one of the other court girls. She wondered how much simpler life would have been if her primary concerns were etiquette and a suitable marriage. But that wasn't her, and it never would be. She still loved going down her own path, which had led to a magical destination. Even though the journey was now ending, she would never regret the experience. At least she had known how much more to life there was, if only for a brief time. And at least she had learned more about herself, and the depth of her capacity for love. No one could take that away from her, not Charles, or the court, or Madeira.

"My sweet Rose, may I come in?"

"Of course, Roosha. You know you needn't ask." She greeted him with a brief kiss on the lips, not knowing if that would be their last.

"I do know. But after what happened last night, I wanted to make sure I wouldn't be putting you in harm's way."

"It's not my safety that concerns me."

"Rose, before you continue, please let me speak." Roosha took her hand in his. She looked at him and remained silent.

"Before you, my life, or my existence rather, held no meaning. I understood that I was brought back into this world as a means of penance for my previous crimes, and I accepted that. I've spent years obeying the rules of my realm and carrying out my duties as a night sender. But my punishment only made me punish myself more. Every day, I replayed the horrible things I did over in my mind, cursing myself for the vile person I once was. It wasn't until you found it in your heart to listen to me and love me without judgment that I realized I was worthy of forgiveness, and that I needed to forgive myself. You showed me that I wasn't some horrible creature, but a decent man who had learned from his grave mistakes. You are my light in this realm of darkness to which I am bound for many more years to come. There is nothing in your world or mine that would ever keep me from you. I choose you now, and always."

Rose felt her resolve weakening. There were already tears rolling down her cheeks. She was so moved by his words and how deeply she had touched his life that she questioned whether her decision to make Roosha leave her was one based on strength or weakness. Her mind felt like a forest covered in dense clouds, obscuring the free flow of reason.

In her emotional haze, she blurted, "I'm engaged, Roosha." The words came out sharper than she intended, and even Rose winced at their impact.

Roosha was silent. Shock slowly registered across his normally calm exterior.

"It's not true," he whispered. "You're just saying that to make me leave you."

Rose walked over to her vanity and slid the sapphire ring back on her finger. "It is true." She held up her hand. "We're to be married soon."

Roosha stepped back, a look of reproach on his face. "You don't love him!" He bellowed.

"What does that matter? I'm a lady of the court. You've known that all along. Did you never expect me to wed?"

"You're no court lady, Rose. We both know that. You're different. That's why I fell in love with you, and you me." His tone was indignant.

She hated to inflict any more pain on him after all he had already suffered. "Yes, Roosha. I do love you. More than my own life. Does knowing that make this any easier? I should think not."

Roosha stared at her in desperation. "Don't give up, Rose. We can find a way out of this."

"I will not bet your life on it!" She threw her hands up in exasperation.

Roosha looked at her, surprised. He wondered how she knew.

"How…"

"My mother."

Immediately, Roosha understood. The poor girl in Avidan's story was Rose's mother. It appeared they had both learned a bit of history last night.

Roosha shook his head. "That was different, Rose."

She felt the blood boiling beneath her skin. She demanded to know how he could possibly stand there and tell her that was different. The fact that they hadn't been dragged to the pyre last night was a stroke of luck, not an invitation to take a greater risk.

"I will not condemn you to death!"

"My fate's my own."

"Maybe so, but the part I choose to play in influencing that fate is mine. You cannot expect me to watch you burn and come out of that alive. I now know what it did to my mother, and I'm sure it would do far worse to me." Rose was struggling to see through her tears.

"Life is uncertain, Rose. The wrong people may never find out about us. Please, Rose." Roosha was on his knees.

"Maybe you're right. But if the situation were reversed, would you be willing to risk my life?"

Roosha's breath caught in his throat. He felt like a lump of hot coal had just been shoved into his esophagus. He inherently knew that if it was Rose's life at stake, he would end their relationship no matter the cost. He would endure the anguish and torment without complaint as long as he knew she was alive and safe. And here he was selfishly asking her not to do the same.

"I couldn't … I would do anything in my power to keep you alive." His chest was shaking as he realized what was happening. His body slowly staggered towards the balcony doors. His heart was heavy, and his shoulders sunken. He looked up to meet her eyes one last time. "I love you, Rose. I will love you forever, and then we'll be together where we belong. Until then." He leapt from the balcony into the night.

"No!" Rose screamed. She was sobbing heavily, her breathing labored. "Roosha, wait!"

But her tortured scream was too late. He was already gone. In his absence, her chest shook violently, as if an earthquake had just ripped through her core and split her heart into fragmented pieces.

57

Rose stayed in bed the next day. Anne brought her warm porridge, but Rose barely ate. She was numb, the pain of loss having not yet set in. Rose remained that way the entire day, cradled against her pillows, which still held some of Roosha's musky scent.

Anne came in twice throughout the day to check on her, but she was the same. It wasn't until the sun went down, and the dark shroud of night set in that Rose felt a persistent aching in her chest. As the hour grew later, so did the paroxysm of grief within her. Anne heard her panting from the hallway and rushed into her room.

"Rose, Rose dear, it's okay, I'm here." Anne pulled Rose against her chest, willing her to breathe deeply.

"Mother, what time is it?" Her voice was laced with panic.

"It's only half-past eight, dear."

"I have to go." Rose was already out of her mother's arms and moving the sheets aside frantically.

"Go? Go where?"

"I cannot stay here tonight. I cannot be here when the clock strikes midnight, and he doesn't come." Rose's hands were shaking.

"Where will you go?" Anne's voice was soft.

Rose knew she needed to go to the one place where she was always able to find peace. The place where just being there would infuse some calmness into her shaken state, hopefully returning her to numbness.

"To the stables."

"I'll go with you," Anne offered.

"No, mother. I need to be alone right now."

Anne looked at her with empathy. "I understand."

"Thank you, mother." Rose changed quickly and left.

When she arrived at the stables, she was grateful it was nighttime. No one else was there aside from the twenty-seven beautiful horses. Rose inhaled deeply, the smell of the hay and manure soothing to her spirit. She went into Carmera's stall and placed her hand on the mare's neck. Carmera nuzzled her head against Rose's shoulder, sensing her despair. As Rose stroked her forehead, sobs welled in her chest, the pent up sense of loss releasing. Time slowly drifted away.

"Hello, Rose," a familiar voice greeted tentatively.

"Vivianna? What are you doing here?" Rose turned, letting go of Carmera.

"I called for you at your house. When your mother said you weren't home, I thought I might find you here. I hope I haven't overstepped my bounds. After learning of your engagement yesterday evening, I wasn't sure you'd be in the mood for company."

"I'm not," Rose snapped.

Vivianna winced, knowing she deserved her reproach. "Then I will respect your wishes. But before I go, I would like to offer a sincere apology for my behavior on our ride the other day."

Rose looked at her blankly.

"I didn't mean for that to sound so formal." Vivianna was flustered. She didn't know how to express how terrible she felt. "Your confession the other day caught me by surprise, to say the least. You see, the other night, when I went back to the library, I did read the third diary." She bit her lip, hesitant to continue.

"It was about your mother." She paused, rocking awkwardly. "It was tough to digest, and it ended so horribly ... I didn't have the heart to tell you." Vivianna's voice was shaking, and her eyes were full of tears. It was the first time Rose had seen her in such a raw state. She walked over and embraced the girl.

"It's all right, Vivianna." Rose sighed.

"No, it's not. I lied to you, Rose! After accusing you of not trusting me! How could I do that?" She sniffled. "And when you finally had the courage to tell me the truth, I was so cold, and I said awful things meant to scare you without offering any explanation. It must have put you in such a terrible state. Terrible enough to ... to ..."

"To get engaged?" Rose held Vivianna at arm's length, an incredulous expression on her face. "You think you are the reason I accepted Charles' proposal?"

Vivianna wiped her eyes with her sleeve. "I thought that maybe..."

Rose cut her off. "No, I'm afraid not."

Vivianna looked at her, confused. "Then, why?"

Rose peered into Vivianna's eyes. They were full of concern and a sincerity that moved Rose.

"My mother told me what happened to her, all of the horrible things you probably read in the diary."

Vivianna was terror-stricken. "Did she ...?"

"Yes," Rose sighed. "She discovered my affair with a night sender."

A rustling of hay drew the girls' attention, followed by neighing from one of the horses. Vivianna stiffened.

"It's just the horses," Rose sighed, resigned.

Vivianna glanced around the dark barn, unconvinced.

She knelt down into the hay. "Please tell me you haven't been subjected to what I read in that book," Vivianna whispered, her eyes squeezed shut.

"I have not, and I will not. That is the reason for the engagement."

"You poor thing." Vivianna enveloped Rose in a tight hug. "I'm so sorry, Rose. I don't even know what to say. You always tell me you admire how strong I am, but here I am in complete awe of your strength."

"What strength?" Rose sniveled. "I sent my lover away because I fear watching him being tortured. I would not allow him to make any choices regarding his own fate. I knew I could not survive seeing him die, so I selfishly ended our relationship. Tell me, where is the strength in that?"

253

Vivianna pulled back, keeping her hands on each of Rose's shoulders. She looked her directly in the eye.

"You released the person you love the most because you refused to sacrifice his life for your desires. You did what was in his best interest, not yours. That takes more courage, strength, and selflessness than most people can muster in the span of three lifetimes, and yet, you did it after only eighteen years on this planet. So yes, Rose Woodburn, today I am in awe of you."

58

The week seemed to pass by in a crawling blur. Each day, Rose had gotten up and gone through the motions of life, barely present. She went with her mother again to Mrs. Taddy's shop to choose a dress for the engagement party her mother was obliged to host.

When they walked through the door, Mrs. Taddy greeted them like long lost friends. "Why, if it isn't the Woodburn family! Lovely to see you again!" Her enthusiasm seemed forced, as was Rose's tight smile.

Normally, Rose would have been flooded with relief that the woman was alive and well, but in her current state, she felt nothing.

"I assume you're here for a dress for your engagement party." She looked at Rose, her gaze flitting to the sapphire ring. "I believe congratulations are in order." Mrs. Taddy smiled, but it didn't reach her eyes. Her natural buoyancy was missing.

"Thank you, Mrs. Taddy. That's very kind of you," Anne offered politely. "Yes, we are here for a dress. We were thinking..."

Mrs. Taddy interrupted. "I beg your pardon, my lady." Her tone was nervous. "Master Devano already informed me how the dress should look."

Anne's eyes flickered with anger. They weren't even married yet, and this boy forced his choice of dress on Rose without consideration or consultation? She would not have it, not today.

"Thank you for letting us know." Mrs. Taddy's hands trembled at Anne's steely voice. "But I'm afraid there's been a change of plans. Rose will be ..."

"Don't, mother." Rose's lifeless voice interjected from the corner of the room. "It's not worth it."

Anne's heart ached as she observed her daughter. The fire was already being snuffed out of her. It was the one thing Anne had sworn she would prevent, her daughter's spirit breaking the way hers had. And now, she was watching it happen before her eyes.

"Whatever Charles chose will be fine, Mrs. Taddy," Anne murmured reluctantly.

"Wonderful!" The tension in the woman's jaw eased.

She emerged from the back of the store with a humongous gown. Mrs. Taddy helped Rose into the dress, lacing the corset snugly to the point that she could not fill her lungs. When she finished, she turned Rose to face the mirror. The entire garment was an ostentatious gold. The shiny fabric clung tightly to her body, making it difficult to move. Rose gazed at her reflection, another shred of life draining from her eyes. She was no longer a person, but a prized possession being added to Charles' collection.

"You look ravishing, dear!" Mrs. Taddy encouraged.

Anne glowered at her. Clearly, the woman was not picking up on the energy in the room.

"That will be all, Mrs. Taddy. Help her out of that dress, now." Anne's voice was hard, unrelenting.

"Of course, Mrs. Woodburn," she obliged, expertly untying the silk at a rapid pace. She helped Rose back into her dress with the same precision. "I'll have the final alterations done by noon tomorrow."

Anne nodded as they left the store.

"Well, mother, I suppose we're off to lunch with Mrs. Devano." Rose's monotone voice irked Anne. She abhorred seeing her daughter lost in apathy.

"Rose, I think you should go home."

"But, Mrs. Devano will be expecting me."

"Leave Lavandra to me, dear. I want you to go home and get some rest."

"I can't do that, mother. It would be inappropriate." There wasn't a hint of sarcasm in Rose's dispirited voice.

"Forget about being proper!" Anne exclaimed. Her eyes were frenzied. "I can't stand to see you this way. For days I've watched you exist, not live. I miss my beautiful, impassioned daughter! I cannot bear to see you this way ... like me."

Rose stared into her mother's crazed eyes. They were a brighter blue than she remembered. "I'm sorry, mother. I didn't mean to disappoint you."

Anne wrapped her arms around her daughter. "Child, you could never disappoint me. I'll never be able to apologize enough for all those years you thought you had. I was the one who was wrong, Rose. All those years I spent forcing you to be a proper lady." Anne shook her head. "I saw so much of myself in you, and I thought I was sparing you from my fate, from passion ruining your life. But seeing you now, barely a shadow of your former self, I realize there's a far worse fate. Losing who you are."

She pulled away, shaking her daughter's shoulders. "Rose, I spent the majority of my life acting, suppressing my true nature. I thought I was doing myself a favor by being strong, shielding myself. But now I realize I wasn't strong; I was weak. It was easier to hide behind my protective walls than to face myself and my grief. This past week, watching you gradually disconnect from your true self, each moment shutting down another fragment of who you are, I've come to understand how stupid I was, how utterly mistaken. Losing someone is a tragedy that time can heal. But to lose ourselves is to condemn ourselves to mere existence, not living. I pray you're smarter than I was, Rose. The world needs your passion and your fire."

Rose gazed at her mother, a tear pricking her eye. For the first time in a whole week, she felt something.

59

"Anne! It's wonderful to see you!" Mrs. Devano kissed Anne on both cheeks.

They sat in the same glass-enclosed patio where Rose first met the woman.

"Won't Rose be joining us?"

"I'm afraid not. You see, she's on the rag and feeling faint. I advised her to rest and assured her we could manage the engagement party between the two of us." Anne mustered an encouraging grin, hoping that would suffice.

"Of course! I do hope she feels better."

"She will." Anne's tone was confident, her statement more an assurance to herself. She needed Rose to be all right, and that single tear in her eye was the first sign that she just might be.

"Good. She is a wonderful girl. My Charles is a lucky man." Anne was touched by the sincerity with which Lavandra spoke.

"Thank you." Anne sipped her tea. "You know, Lavandra, my daughter went to great lengths to select a gown worthy of your son."

"How thoughtful of her."

The maid placed a plate of finger sandwiches in front of them. Anne selected a tiny brioche bun with ham, Lavandra, a baguette with cheese.

"Yes. But unfortunately, we arrived at the dress shop to find that Charles—who is also wonderfully thoughtful—had already picked out a dress for Rose."

"That sounds like him," Lavandra spoke adoringly of her son. "He does enjoy the decision-making process."

"Yes, and he is quite gifted at it."

Lavandra nodded. "That he is. Half my wardrobe was selected by that boy."

Anne leaned in close. "Do you think your son would be terribly heartbroken if Rose were to wear the special dress she chose just for him?" Anne placed her hand over Lavandra's. "As a mother, I don't mean to put you in an imposition, but I'd hate to disappoint Rose. She even did some of the embroidery herself."

"Well," Mrs. Devano wavered, ripping tiny pieces off her baguette. "I suppose that would be fine."

"Are you sure? I certainly do not want a disappointed groom-to-be at the party."

Lavandra nodded, her expression cycling from pensive to resolute. "Yes, of course. A lady is best suited to choose her own dress for such an auspicious occasion, especially when she is talented enough to embellish it herself. I'll let Charles know immediately. He doesn't like surprises."

Anne squeezed Lavandra's hand. "Thank you so much. Your willingness is a gift in itself to Rose."

"Well, pretty soon, she'll be my daughter as well. I'd like us to start off on the right foot." Lavandra lifted her teacup. "Shall we begin the party planning?"

"Of course," Anne enthused.

ON THE WAY HOME from lunch, Anne felt slightly relieved. At least she had been able to accomplish one small mercy for her daughter— Rose no longer had to flit around her engagement party looking like Charles' trophy.

She was also pleasantly surprised by Lavandra. The woman had a congenial demeanor and seemed to like and respect Rose. With a mother-in-law like that, maybe there was a chance that marrying into the Devano family wouldn't be as horrible as her daughter presumed.

60

Again, Rose found herself in front of the large wrought iron frame, the mirror that had witnessed many life-changing moments in such a short period. And it was about to observe another. Soon, her mother would knock on her bedroom door, brandishing the obscene gold dress she was to wear tonight to her engagement party. Rose swallowed hard, suppressing her urge to vomit. Though it had only been ten days since she'd said goodbye to Roosha, her life felt drastically different.

For the past ten nights, against her better judgment, Rose left the balcony doors unlocked. But Roosha never came. And why should he? She was the one who sent him away, the one who broke his heart. Madeira condemned him to life as a night sender, and now Rose had sentenced him to a life without her, a necessary cruelty that punished them both.

Rose wiped a teardrop from beneath her eye. Marrying Charles would seal both of their fates. More importantly, it would protect Roosha. He would no longer suffer the pain from pleasing her, nor would his life be in jeopardy. She would live knowing he was safe, and that was all that mattered. Rose prayed that her mother was right, that time would heal her deepest wounds, as long as she retained some semblance of herself. She owed it to both Anne and Roosha to try and be the Rose they knew and loved, even under regrettable circumstances.

"Rose?" Anne called softly, knocking twice.

Rose nodded at her reflection, resolute. "Come in, mother."

Anne entered, quietly closing the door behind her. "I have something special for you," she cooed. Anne held out a stunning chiffon and lace gown. It was a rich mauve that complimented Rose's skin tone.

Rose's eyes glimmered as she caressed the smooth fabric. "Mother, it's beautiful." Her brow creased. "But I don't understand, what happened to the dress Charles selected?"

"I spoke with Lavandra at lunch and convinced her to let you wear a dress of your choosing. Afterward, I went straight back to Mrs. Taddy and had her make this number." Anne bit her lip. "I hope you don't mind. Given there wasn't much time, I took the liberty of designing something for you. I hope this dress is an accurate reflection of my extraordinary daughter." Anne's expression was nervous. This time it was she who wanted Rose's approval.

"Mother, the dress is perfect." Rose reached for the garment and held it against her chest. "I love it. It's something I would have picked for myself." Rose beamed at her. "Thank you, mother, for standing up for me when I was unwilling to stand up for myself." She paused. "It really is a beautiful gown."

Anne's eyes glistened. "I wish it was for a different occasion."

Rose set the garment on her vanity and enveloped her mother in a warm embrace.

"So do I, mother, so do I."

61

Roosha sat on the hilltop where Avidan had dumped him ten days earlier. He had not returned to Rose's room since their parting and tried to spend as little time in the cave as possible for fear of doing something impulsive, like rebelling against Madeira for her unjust rules and cruel punishments.

He didn't know what to do with himself. His love for Rose had become his purpose, and now that he couldn't see her, there was a void inside him that could not be filled. His existence no longer mattered to him.

"Greetings, friend," Avidan landed silently beside him.

"Greetings, Avidan." Roosha didn't even turn his head.

"I came to see how you are. You haven't been around the cave much lately."

Roosha sighed. "I've taken to being alone. And in my aloneness, I've been contemplating something that perhaps you can help me with, friend." Roosha faced Avidan, his eyes burning with curiosity. "Why is it that only physical pleasure causes us pain?"

"What do you mean?" Avidan eyed him suspiciously.

"I mean, why doesn't another's emotional pleasure, like that of love, cause us pain?"

"Are you not in pain now?"

"Yes, but that is a different kind of pain. It is the pain of loss. When I think of Rose, a wonderful, warm feeling comes over me. I never feel any pain, nor did I feel pain when she looked at me with eyes full of love."

Avidan pursed his lips. "In our previous lives, we delivered a lot of physical pain, so it is sexual gratification we are not allowed to enjoy."

"But we must have also inflicted a lot of emotional pain with our actions, so why should we be allowed to enjoy the elated feelings love gifts us?"

Avidan was silent for a moment, reflecting on Roosha's question. "Perhaps because love is healing, which serves a much higher purpose than punishment. Had we known love in our previous lives, we never would have done the things we did, nor some in this life as well."

Roosha nodded. "You're not the first to make that suggestion." He thought of the night he disclosed his past to Rose, how she had offered the same explanation that love would have saved him from the monster he was. "Perhaps you are right, perhaps love is healing. But then why would Madeira punish us for earning the love of the girls, and loving them in return?"

"Madeira would never take the time to assess whether you or any court girl were in love. Her sole concern is that the rules of our realm are obeyed. And when they are not, she imparts a strict punishment, as you are now well aware of."

"But if she took the time to listen ... if she knew ..."

Avidan cut off Roosha's impassioned plea. "If she knew what?" His voice was exasperated. "You think if she knew how much you loved Rose, she would spare your life? Do not be so naive, Roosha. Madeira is a fierce woman who did not create us out of her love for the court girls. No matter what she says, her purpose in creating us was in her hatred for men. Do not expect mercy where you will be shown none."

Roosha shrugged. "Maybe you're wrong."

"Maybe I am. But are you willing to bet your existence on it?"

"What is my existence worth anymore? Have you ever loved, Avidan, and known the true love of another? To know that and then have it taken away from you ... it's ..." Roosha buried his head in his hands. "What do I have left to live for?"

Avidan moved in close, his hands on Roosha's shoulders. "Rose. She's still here. She's still very much alive, and I'm sure she needs your love more than ever, even if it's from afar. Before you throw away your existence for mad passion, remember that you're not the only one suffering in this situation, Roosha." Avidan leapt from the hilltop and flew back towards the cave.

In his heart, Roosha knew that Avidan was right. Rose might still need him, and if she did, he would not let her down. He needed to keep an eye on her to make sure she was safe, even if only from a distance, and he would start by flying by her room that evening.

62

A nne and Rose walked hand-in-hand down the hallway to the top of the stairs. Below them were close to two hundred court members awaiting their arrival. Rose marveled at the lavish affair Anne and Lavandra had organized. The house was adorned with glittering streamers and silk stitched doves that twinkled in the candlelight.

Maids circulated, brandishing trays of decadent hors d'oeuvres, and glasses overflowing with sweet wine and champagne. A talented ensemble—two violinists, a cellist, a harpist, and a pianist—filled the air with jovial melodies. Guests mingled, decked out in their most glamorous formal wear. But what drew Rose's attention were the spectacular bouquets of intertwining red and white roses scattered throughout the party.

Rose squeezed her mother's hand, feeling the solidarity between them, and mouthed, thank you. Anne smiled, her eyes once again glistening with tears.

The music stopped, signaling that it was time for Rose's descent. At the bottom of the staircase, Charles waited for her, a signature charismatic smile on his face. Rose took a deep breath, bracing herself for the barrage of insincere compliments and congratulations from the court. She was about to take her first step when Anne grabbed her arm.

"Dear, if Mrs. Devano asks, you hand-stitched the embroidery on your dress," she whispered.

Rose nodded, her eyes full of gratitude. She was touched that her mother had lied just so she could wear this dress. And it was stunning.

The lace corset hugged her tiny waist flawlessly, emphasizing her hourglass frame. Cascading down the center of the skirt was an intricate rose pattern with a chiffon overlay surrounded on both sides by solid mauve silk. Only a hint of cleavage peeked through the sweetheart neckline, while the capped sleeves highlighted her delicate collarbones. It was elegant without being overtly suggestive, the way her coming of age dress had been. She felt perfectly feminine, the right balance between alluring and refined.

Rose sauntered down the stairs, scanning the crowd to avoid Charles' stare. Hundreds of eyes watched her every movement, some with admiration, others with lust and envy, and one pair with devious intent. Savannah's dark eyes bored into Rose's. She imagined Savannah was willing her to trip. Still, Rose's movements remained graceful until the end, where she accepted Charles' outstretched hand.

"Ah, my lovely wife-to-be has finally graced us with her presence!" The scent of whiskey was strong on his breath.

"Good evening, Charles." Rose smiled tightly. She couldn't deny he looked dapper in his black suit.

As they made their way through the crowd, they were greeted with handshakes and air kisses from the court members. Rose also noticed plenty of glares from her fellow ladies of the court.

Rose plucked a glass of sweet wine from the tray of one of the passing servers. The reality of the situation was beginning to overwhelm her. Charles kept referring to her as his bride, a term that made Rose nauseous. Her heart rate accelerated, and her head throbbed as throngs of people approached them.

"Would you excuse me for a moment, Charles?" Rose desperately needed some air.

"Is everything alright, dear? People are expecting to greet us." His grip on her tightened.

"Of course. I just need a moment with the ladies. They haven't even seen my ring yet."

Charles smiled widely, relaxing his hand. "Well, go show it off then, Rose! Let them know how much you are loved. Don't go far, though, my dear. You look absolutely ravishing tonight, even in that frock. I dare not let you out of my sight for long." He kissed her shoulder before letting go of her arm.

Rose retreated to the corner of the sitting room, hoping to find a moment of peace.

"Well, well, if it isn't the bride to be!" The unmistakable piercing voice came from behind her. Again, Rose startled at the word, bride.

"Good evening, Savannah."

"I'd say congratulations, but we both know I wouldn't mean it in the slightest, so I'll spare you the formality."

Rose turned to face her. "You seem quite smug this evening. Remember what happened the last time you were smug with me?" Rose shot her a threatening glance, but Savannah stared back at her, unmoved.

"You are in no position to take that tone with me, Rose Woodburn." Savannah tipped her champagne glass up in salute.

There was something about her overconfident tone that made Rose uncomfortable. She looked up to see if anyone else, preferably Vivianna, was around them. She didn't want to be alone with Savannah. Rose spotted Vivianna across the room, but she was engaged in a conversation with her husband and his parents.

"I should really get back to Charles. I'm sure he's missing me." Rose moved to the side, but Savannah placed her hand against the wall, blocking Rose.

Her smirk had an evil edge to it. "But he's not the one you're missing, is he?"

The air Rose had sucked in caught in her throat, her mouth slightly agape. She knew she needed to remain composed, but was too blindsided to concentrate. Was it possible that Savannah knew about Roosha?

"Did you know that my husband plays poker with Vivianna's husband, Edmund, on certain nights? And when that happens, I do find myself bored with sitting at home. So sometimes I like to go for a walk."

The gears in Rose's mind slowly shifted into place. That's why Vivianna was able to call on her that night at the barn. Edmund must have been off playing cards, the same way he was when she returned to the library. Rose's skin grew pale until it was almost translucent.

"The noise in the barn …" Rose's voice was barely audible.

"Why, yes, dear. It was quite a pleasure eavesdropping on you girls. And that secret of yours, I must say, quite a leap from that time I found your erotic book." Savannah moved in until her face was inches from Rose's. "I knew all along you were a debauched whore, but one with beastly fantasies? Why that's an entirely different level of perversion! Perhaps it's time other people knew the truth about you as well."

Rose ducked under her skeletal arm and sped towards the stairs. She wasn't thinking; her body merely reacting from its terror-stricken state. She felt like a helpless child. Roosha was the only thing on her mind, the only thing that mattered. What if Savannah told the court? Could Roosha already be dead? Rose's entire body was in tremors as she made her way up the stairs.

As soon as she reached the top, Rose bolted, running as fast as she could to her room and shutting the door hard, desperately wishing she had a lock. She paced back and forth, not knowing what to do. She still had no way of contacting Roosha to see if he was safe. Rose opened the doors to the balcony and looked over the side in every direction. There was no sign of him anywhere, though he had stopped coming days ago, after the night she informed him of her engagement.

VIVIANNA BLINKED TWICE, attempting to make sense of the scene unfolding in front of her. From the corner of her eye, she watched as Rose darted across the room, away from Savannah, and up the stairs. Vivianna's brow furrowed. That night in the barn, Rose was resolute; she would marry Charles to protect Roosha. What could Savannah have said that would provoke Rose to this degree? To have made her flee her own engagement party, jeopardizing everything? Vivianna's body tensed. She felt the urge to go after Rose, but hesitated, not wanting to draw attention to the situation without more information.

"Vivianna? Vivianna, are you alright?" Edmund rubbed her shoulder lightly.

"Yes, dear. I just …" Vivianna's eyes narrowed. Charles was headed towards the stairs. "Edmund, I'm afraid I must go and check on the bride to be. If you'll excuse me."

Edmund opened his mouth to speak, but Vivianna was already moving, hastily making her way to the staircase. She refused to allow that lecherous lout to corner Rose in her bedroom.

"Where do you think you are going, Vivianna?" Anne stood at the bottom of the stairs, blocking Vivianna's path.

"Excuse me, Mrs. Woodburn. I must go upstairs at once. Rose is distraught."

"It would appear so. And that is exactly why we will respect her privacy at this time."

"Trust me, Mrs. Woodburn. Now is not the right time," Vivianna sputtered. "Something is wrong. Charles followed her up there." She pointed to the top of the stairs, where Charles was turning towards Rose's room.

"They are to be married soon." Anne sighed. "I'm sure he means to coax her back to the party."

"But it's not safe!" Vivianna urged.

Anne tilted her head to the side, eyeing Vivianna carefully. "What do you mean, it's not safe?"

"Mrs. Woodburn, please! We are wasting precious time!" She tried to push past her, but Anne blocked Vivianna with her right arm, grabbing her by the elbow.

"Either tell me exactly why my daughter is in danger, or I will escort you back to your husband," she admonished.

Vivianna's bewildered eyes flitted from the top of the staircase back to Anne's unrelenting stare. Sweat licked her temples. Every second she spent arguing with this woman put Rose in further peril. "I know about everything!" Vivianna blurted. "I know what really happened in the garden with Charles, how lascivious his behavior was, why Rose's dress was torn." Vivianna's green eyes bore into Anne's as she whispered,

"I know about her affair with a night sender ... and yours for that matter." Anne paled, her expression on tenterhooks. "Mrs. Woodburn, I am her only friend, and I am telling you that she is in danger as we speak. So let go of my arm and stop questioning me! Rose needs our help."

Anne abruptly released her grip. She stood still as a statue, overwhelmed with shock from Vivianna's confession. Without another word, Vivianna grabbed Anne by the forearm and hurried her up the stairs.

"ROSE, WHERE ARE YOU, Rose?"

Rose's ears perked up. The voice sounded like Charles', only slurred.

"There you are, my beautiful bride to be. Why are you up here in your room?" His brow creased. "Did you want me to follow you here? I bet you did!" An arrogant grin spread across his face.

"I most certainly did not!" Rose stormed off of the balcony and towards the door. She wanted to get out of her room as quickly as possible, but Charles intercepted her.

He grabbed her arm forcefully and turned her towards him. "Where do you think you are going, Rose Woodburn?"

"Back ... back to the party, of course. Everyone will be missing us." The back of her neck beaded with sweat.

"Everyone can wait." He wrenched her arm, throwing her forcibly onto the end of the bed. Charles climbed on top of her, pinning her down.

"What ... what are you doing?" Rose's heart was palpitating.

"What am I doing? Giving you what you want. Come now, Rose, you always have this glow about you that screams fuck me! I've done my part; I've courted you properly, resisting all those temptations you threw in my face. Now that I put a ring on your finger, I'm entitled to taste the sweet nectar of such a rare flower." Charles ripped at the bodice on her dress.

Rose screamed for help, but the ensemble was in the middle of a crescendo downstairs, so she knew no one would hear. Rose pushed as hard as she could against Charles, but he was too strong, and the position she was in gave her no leverage. Though she didn't stop fighting, Rose mentally prepared for what was to come, reasoning that this could just as well have been her wedding night. At the very least, she was grateful she was not a virgin. Perhaps that would spare her some of the impending pain. She closed her eyes and squeezed her legs shut as tightly as her muscles could muster, thankful for all those years of riding instruction. She felt bruises forming under the pressure of Charles' hands prying her thighs apart.

As her strength began to fail, Charles' weight was suddenly lifted from her. Rose opened her eyes to see Roosha. He had pulled her body from beneath Charles' and now had her cradled in his arms. He quickly put her down in the corner behind him and stood protectively in front of her.

Charles shrunk back, clearly afraid of Roosha. "What the hell is this?" He looked Roosha up and down, bewildered by his massive form.

Roosha glared at him with menacing eyes. "Go now. You will never hurt her again," he growled. Roosha crouched as if he were about to spring. Charles put his hands up in submission and began backing away.

When Charles' hand was on the doorknob, Roosha turned to tend to Rose. With his back turned, Charles seized the opportunity, opening and shutting the door to make Roosha believe he had left.

Charles knelt down, creeping quietly towards the fireplace and grabbing a metal poker. Abruptly he stood, lunging towards Roosha and attacking from behind. Charles struck him across the middle of his back, knocking him onto his knees. Roosha winced, not knowing what to do. He knew he could not fight back, but would die before leaving Rose with this monster.

Again, Charles swung the poker, this time hitting Roosha across the chest. He flinched, raising his arms to shield his head. Charles wasted no time. His eyes were alight with madness now that he saw it was to be a one-sided fight. He drew the poker back and brought it down hard on Roosha's side, knocking him over. He laid in a fetal position, his hands still cradling his head, as Charles beat him repeatedly.

Rose looked on in horror, paralyzed. The scenario confounded her. Roosha was twice Charles' size, with chiseled muscles. Surely he had the strength to vanquish Charles, so why hadn't he? Why did he cower instead of fighting back? Not once had Roosha tried to defend himself.

Rose screamed, pleading for Charles to stop, but he ignored her. He was immersed in his cowardly assault.

"Come on, you dumb beast, fight back! Give me a challenge!" Charles taunted.

At that moment, Rose snapped. Roosha might not want to harm Charles, but she sure as hell did. She charged from the corner, scrambling to the fireplace and grabbing the other poker. Rose swung it back over her head and brought it down as hard as she could against Charles' lower back.

He crumpled to his knees from the impact.

"Rose?" Charles groaned.

Wasting no time, she swung the iron poker again, landing a forceful blow to his head. Charles slumped over slowly until he was unconscious on the floor. Rose was about to take another swing when Roosha stopped her.

"Rose, don't. You'll kill him," he warned.

"I might sleep better tonight if I did," she panted.

"You say that now, but you don't know what it is to take someone's life."

"And you don't know what it means to lose your life to someone like him while you're still alive. When we marry, I'm to be his, as if I'm property." Her grip tightened around the weapon.

"Please, Rose, he's not worth it. Let us leave this foul place instead," he implored. "As innocents, not murderers," he added wistfully.

Rose's crazed stare moved from Charles to Roosha. His amber eyes were wide and pleading. Even after the merciless assault he received, Roosha would not condemn this monster to death. And she knew that having Charles murder on his conscience would be too much for Roosha to bear. Having already caused him enough pain, Rose slowly released the poker. It clanked loudly as the metal frame collided with the floor. Rose threw her arms around Roosha. He winced, sore from the beating.

"Where would we go?" she sobbed. "I can't stay here and marry that ... that vile monster!"

"As far away from Dover as possible, where we are not subject to laws or obligations. Where we can be together." Roosha caressed her cheek.

"I don't think a place like that exists," she whispered. "Besides, they'll follow us," she cautioned.

"Who will, my sweet Rose?"

"Charles will. He's a vengeful man." She shivered. "And won't the night senders?"

"I do not know. No one has ever abandoned the realm before."

"And you would be the first?" she challenged, unsure how serious he was about leaving with her.

"For you, I would." He placed his finger on her quivering lips.

Rose stared into his soulful eyes, once again mesmerized by their subtle glow. Could she really leave with him? Abandon her life in Dover and begin anew, not as a lady of the court, but simply as Rose Woodburn, a common woman? Would her mother have done the same if she had had the chance? Rose felt a tinge of pain at the thought of leaving her mother behind. She was all Anne had left, and they finally understood each other and were growing closer. What if Anne went with them? Would it be too painful for her mother to see her with Roosha? To see her living the life Anne could not? Rose was torn, and there was no time to debate any of her concerns.

"Roosha, I ..."

Abruptly, the balcony doors burst open, followed immediately by the door to her room. A chill permeated the air, one unrelated to the frigid wind blowing in the doors.

Anne and Vivianna entered together and were immediately astounded by the scene in front of them. Three night senders barged into the room bearing black sacks. With rapid precision, they restrained Rose and

Roosha, covered their heads with the rough burlap, and flew into the night with them within seconds.

Anne fell to her knees, horrible flashbacks flooding her mind. "No!" Anne's tortured scream pierced the silence. "No. Not the pyre, not the pyre!" Her chest heaved, her breathing heavy. She stared blankly at the balcony, repeatedly murmuring, "no."

Vivianna positioned herself in front of Anne, grabbing a firm hold of her shoulders. "Mrs. Woodburn, where are they taking her?"

Anne's eyes were far away.

"Mrs. Woodburn, look at me," Vivianna pleaded. "Where are they taking Rose?"

Anne blinked several times. "To … to … to the … cave," she stuttered.

Vivianna nodded. "Where is this cave? Do you remember?"

Anne was paralyzed. The memory of Thanoine surrounded by rising flames consumed her.

Vivianna shook her shoulders hard. "Mrs. Woodburn, please! Stay with me. We need to help Rose!"

Anne winced. "I don't know where the cave is!" She broke down, sobbing violently. Anne felt completely useless, incapable of saving her daughter in the same way she had been unable to save herself, or Thanoine.

Vivianna let go of her shoulders. She paced around the room, racking her brain for any conceivable way to help Rose. As she grew more flustered, her pace quickened. Rose relied on Vivianna for her acuity. She always managed to form a plan, even in daunting circumstances, but now, when Rose needed her most, she was devoid of ideas. Vivianna had no connection to the night senders, no way of contacting them.

Abruptly, she stopped pacing. Her mother might. Mrs. Weston had access to the diaries and had arranged Vivianna's second visit. It was possible she knew some way to prevent this catastrophe, or at least postpone it. Vivianna cringed as she envisioned explaining the situation to her mother, along with her involvement. Her punishment would be severe, but it paled in comparison to the horror befalling her friend.

If she had any chance of aiding Rose, she must take it, no matter the personal consequence.

"Mrs. Woodburn, I …"

"Greetings, Anne," a familiar, foreboding voice greeted her.

Both Anne and Vivianna turned to face the balcony.

"You!" Anne's eyes filled with resentment.

Avidan ignored her reproach.

"Let us dispense with the reminiscing, Anne. We have to go now." His emphasis on the word now was unmistakable, but his urgency was no match for the vivid memories clouding Anne's mind.

"You expect me to go anywhere with you?" Her fury willed her body off the floor. "Give me one reason not to kill you, the sniveling bastard who informed Madeira about Thanoine and me!"

Vivianna gasped, shocked that another night sender had given them away, and not the court.

"Rose," Avidan uttered.

Anne stopped short. "What did you say?"

Avidan sighed. "You said to give you one reason not to kill me."

Enraged, Anne rushed toward Avidan pounding her fists against his muscular chest. "You son of a bitch! You informed on my daughter!"

"I did no such thing." Avidan remained calm until Anne had exhausted herself and dropped to her knees, breathless.

"If not you, then who?" She demanded.

"That, I do not know. But it wasn't one of us." His words were sincere.

Vivianna gasped.

"How can you expect me to believe a word you say?" Anne sneered.

"I don't. I'm not asking you to believe me, and I'm certainly not expecting you to forgive me for my unspeakable actions. I thought I was doing the right thing, but clearly, I had no understanding of the consequences of my decision. You weren't the only one who lost someone that day." Avidan sighed, his eyes wistful. "I cannot change the past, or right my wrong. But I can try and help you prevent your daughter from suffering the same fate. You know what Madeira will do to them."

"Mrs. Woodburn, you must go with him. Rose needs you. You're our best chance of helping her. You have to go now!" Vivianna exhorted.

Anne turned to Vivianna.

"What about Charles? We can't just leave him here! Who knows what he'll do when he comes to?" Anne's voice was frantic.

"Leave him to me." Vivianna was resolved.

"But what will you do?"

"Don't worry, I can handle Charles. You have a much more critical situation at hand, and time is of the essence. Please, go take care of Rose."

Anne squeezed Vivianna's arm. "Thank you, child."

Vivianna nodded.

Avidan scooped Anne up in his arms and leapt from the balcony.

"They're taking her to the same location they took you all those years ago."

Anne shuddered. The cave was the last place on earth she wanted to see again. It was the place that haunted her for nineteen and a half years, the setting of her every nightmare, and the source of her interminable despair. It was the place where Madeira stole her love and her future from her, the place where Madeira now meant to subject her daughter to the same horrible fate. Anne's fear turned to fury. For once in her life, she needed to be strong, if not for herself, then for Rose. Anne prayed she wasn't too late, that she could still stop Madeira before she crushed her daughter's spirit entirely. There had to be a way.

63

Vivianna surveyed Rose's room, still struggling to process what she had just witnessed. It all happened so fast; it didn't seem real. One minute, Rose and Roosha were on the floor, and the next, they were gone; taken against their will. If only Anne hadn't stopped her at the base of the stairs, maybe they would have arrived in time to prevent their capture.

Vivianna circled Charles. Blood trickled down the side of his face, from a gash on the back of his head. She was grateful Rose's night sender had been there. He must have protected her from that louse. Vivianna kicked Charles' unconscious body. One swift kick in the ass for good measure. It was the kick Rose should have given him in the garden, only he was lying on his stomach, saving his groin from her pointed shoe.

Vivianna walked onto the balcony, resting her hands on the railing. The night senders disappeared with her best friend before she and Anne had a chance to react. She didn't know where Rose was—only that she was inside a horrid cave—most likely suffering the same consequences as her mother. Tears poured from Vivianna's eyes, her black eyeliner smudging onto her cheeks. She thought of the harrowing account she read about in the diary and came close to regurgitating the fancy hors d'oeuvres.

And to think, Rose had summoned every ounce of courage she had to avoid this tragedy. She let her night sender go. She even agreed to marry Charles to ensure he would stay away. So then how had it come to this? The only people who knew about their affair were herself and Anne. And, according to Avidan, it was not a night sender who reported them. As she gazed over the sleepy city, her eyes narrowed to slits.

Vivianna's grip tightened around the top rail. Rage churned within her. She knew the answer, knew who had condemned her friend to this grisly fate.

It wasn't just the horses in the barn the other night. There was a rat in there as well, one far more contemptible than she imagined—a rat whose husband played poker with Edmund that night. A rat with the insolence to confront, and probably threaten Rose at her own engagement party. Vivianna's nostrils flared. This time, the rat would not get away with it. She would pay for her turpitude, in spades.

A low groan came from behind Vivianna. She turned to see that Charles was beginning to stir.

64

Rose stood in the great hall waiting for Madeira. The room was cold and dark, the cave lit sparsely. When they arrived at the cave, she and Roosha were immediately separated. She didn't know where they were taking him and was terrified that the next time she saw him, he would be facing death. Grasping for any chance of saving Roosha, Rose demanded a private audience with Madeira. Thankfully, Madeira agreed to the meeting. At the very least, it might buy her some time, though for what she did not know. She had no plan or any ideas on how to get Roosha out of the cave alive.

When a thick boulder at the top of the cave slid open, Rose was surprised to see a woman standing before her. From the first diary, she expected a figure made of smoke. Madeira looked nothing like the creatures she had created, except for her midnight blue skin. She had long, wild hair, the color of burning embers, and intense red eyes. Her features were beautiful, but there was a coldness about her. She wore what looked like a feminine suit of armor, almost the same color as her skin.

"Greetings, child. You dare call for an audience with me after what you've done?" She seethed.

Rose took a deep breath and clenched her muscles together. She had to be brave if she had any chance of changing their fates.

"Yes, Madeira. Thank you for agreeing to speak with me." Rose remained polite, though she had a particular distaste for this woman.

"And why is it that you have come, aside from the reason you were brought here? Do you plan on pleading for mercy?" Her tone was scornful.

"I plan to plead with you for Roosha's life." She spoke fervently. "But I also came to ask you a question."

Madeira shifted. "What is it that you want to know?"

"I want to know why you created the night senders."

Madeira peered at her as if Rose were laying a trap. "I'm sure the court has told you why."

"The court has told me a number of things, though the court often prefers tall tales to the truth. I've found the most accurate answers come directly from the source." Rose stood tall, her hands clasped together behind her.

Madeira glowered. "I did not come here to entertain your questions, Rose Woodburn. I only came to hear your final words on behalf of Roosha."

Rose floundered. She didn't understand why Madeira declined to answer, nor why she deferred to the court. In the first diary, Madeira was in control of both the visits and the flow of information. She explained in detail the reason behind her creation, including the horrific personal account that inspired the night senders. It was her mandate that each of the ladies of the court receive a visit. The court was not offered a say in the matter. She even had an amicable relationship with the girls coming of age, sending them letters and gifts beforehand. But now, as Rose stood in front of her, she refused to explain anything?

It seemed that, for some reason, the power had shifted to the ladies of the court. Unfortunately, Rose was missing a significant piece of the puzzle. Whatever happened to alter the course of events so drastically must be contained in the second diary, which mysteriously went missing right after the girls read the first.

Rose clenched her hands tighter, the bones cracking. She pondered what to say to Madeira now, how much was safe to reveal. By court standards, Rose would not know anything other than fear, which would do nothing to further her conversation with Madeira. But if she exposed the depth of her knowledge, what would the consequences be? Could they be worse than Roosha dying before her eyes?

"I've heard the night senders were created to awaken our sensuality. Is that not true?" Rose observed Madeira's eyes, reading her reaction. Her eyes narrowed, jaw tightening.

"Only to spare you the inevitable pain you would face on your wedding night," Madeira spit.

"Is it not cruel to awaken this sensuality within us, and subsequently condemn us to the same fate we would have faced anyway? An arranged marriage where our newfound passion must be squashed to conform to Dover's societal expectations?"

"In case you haven't noticed, you seem to be the only court girl unable to quell this passion that you speak of."

"Only because now we are taught to fear the night senders. But many years ago, it seems the girls were more like me."

Madeira shifted uncomfortably. "Felonius! Arrange the pyre and prepare Roosha for sentencing!" Her tone was menacing.

Rose faltered, dropping to her knees. "Please, don't do this. Do not make me watch the man I love burn to death," Rose entreated.

Madeira laughed viciously. "Man? This is no man, and even farther from it in his previous life. He is a servant of women paying penance for the pain he caused so many others."

"He saved me from being raped by a nobleman, from suffering a fate quite similar to yours," Rose blurted. "Does that mean nothing to you?"

Madeira swooped down closer to Rose, her voice threatening. "What do you know of my life, child?" Her red eyes bore into Rose's, unwavering. Rose sensed she had divulged too much. "Make with your plea, or I will execute Roosha this instant!"

Rose spoke softly, willing Madeira to listen. "I know that you suffered horribly at the hands of an evil man ... if he can even be considered a man, and that unfortunately, no one helped you. You were alone, as I would have been without Roosha. The creature you created saved me from undergoing the awful experience that caused you to create him in the first place. Can you not spare his life for the good he has done here?" Rose stammered as tears streaked down her face.

Madeira looked at her, conflicted. When she spoke, her voice was more strained than angry.

"He broke all of the cardinal rules!"

"He was serving! I am the one who asked, implored him to come back, begged him for more pleasure. You, most of all, know how much pain he endured for the sole purpose of pleasing me. He is selfless and kind."

"You may have begged and pleaded, but he knew he was forbidden," she shouted. "His heroic actions in helping save you do not exonerate him from his crimes. He is to be executed, and you will watch."

Rose's body shook. Violent sobs heaved from her body, but she barely felt them. Madeira's words had sent Rose into a dark place far from herself.

Anne, who had been standing in the central passageway with Avidan, in awe of her daughter's courage, rushed over to hold Rose.

"Rose, Rose, speak to me. I'm so sorry, child."

She held Rose's face in her hands and saw her daughter slipping away from her. Rose's stare was blank, and Anne knew all too well what that meant. Anger pulsated through her veins, her blood boiling. All of the pain she had suppressed for so many years came flooding through the self-created dams that contained it. Anne was enraged, furious. She had lost herself at eighteen years of age because of Madeira's cruelty, and she refused to lose her daughter. Anne may have failed herself, but she would not fail Rose. She stood up and stepped in front of Rose like a lioness, ready to rip Madeira apart.

"Madeira, you will end this foolishness now." Her voice was a low, fierce growl.

Madeira looked Anne over carefully, recognition registering on her face. "I remember you. Like mother like daughter, I see. I would have thought you of all people would have warned your daughter against breaking the rules, having witnessed the consequences firsthand." There was a mocking edge to her tone.

Anne winced. "I see you've only grown crueler in the years since I last saw you. I will not allow you to destroy my daughter the way you did me. You claim you created the night senders to help the ladies of the court after befalling your own misfortune. But instead, you condemned me to a lifetime of torment. There is no justice in that."

Anne turned back to her daughter. She cradled Rose in her arms, rocking her limp body back and forth.

"She's right, Madeira," Avidan ventured. "You say you created us to empower women, but here you are ready to destroy another life."

Madeira scowled at Avidan, her expression livid. "You dare question me, Avidan?"

"I will when I think you are making a terrible mistake."

"They broke every single rule of our realm. What would you have me do with them?"

Avidan sighed wearily. "I would have you choose kindness over being right. Look at this child before you. She is already halfway gone at the thought of the punishment awaiting her. Must you destroy what's left of her by making her watch as her lover is burned alive?"

"Her lover? None of you creatures are deserving of love!" Madeira bellowed.

Anne stood. "If you say that, then you don't know your own creatures very well. Thanoine was good and true. Not a day goes by that I don't think of him. Never have I loved another as deeply," Anne choked.

Madeira turned, realizing she was now fighting a battle on multiple fronts. Avidan sensed a moment of weakness.

"Let the girl go, Madeira. Do what you will with Roosha, but allow Rose to go in peace."

Madeira's furious glare moved from Avidan to Anne. "I will spare your daughter on one condition. You must both leave Dover, never to return. Not a word will you breathe to anyone about the existence of the night senders, or what you witnessed here today. As soon as you get home, you are to pack your things and leave straight away before sunrise."

Anne nodded sullenly.

"Should you ever return to Dover, mark my words, I will not be so forgiving. Avidan! Escort them home and then come see me. There is much to discuss, privately." It was a command, not a request.

"Thank you, Madeira," Anne managed.

"Consider it my restitution." Madeira strode out of the cave, back to her abode.

Avidan hurried Rose and Anne through a back tunnel. "Quickly, now."

"Where are we going?" Anne asked.

"Roosha is being held in a cell back here. I thought Rose would want to say goodbye."

65

Vivianna poked Charles' shoulder. His body twitched, not fully awake yet. Blood trickled down the left side of his face, over his ear. Vivianna grabbed Rose's sheet and pressed it against his head to stop the bleeding. When Charles roused, he would demand a thorough explanation. Vivianna had a plan, though she wasn't sure how well she could convince a self-righteous man that he was wrong, that he hadn't fought a blue, mythical looking creature with giant wings.

Charles shook his head, groggy.

"Are you alright?" Vivianna knelt beside him.

"Huh?" Charles was still disoriented. He lifted his hand, bringing it to the side of his head. The blood seeped through the thin sheet and onto his fingers. Charles brought his hand back in front of his face, leaping to his feet without warning. His body wobbled from standing too quickly.

"What in the hell is going on?" he raged. He circled, examining his surroundings. The quick motion made him unsteady, forcing him back onto his knees. His head snapped up, his eyes landing on Vivianna.

"You! What happened? Why am I here? And for heaven's sake, why am I bleeding?" He was vexed, irate.

Vivianna searched his eyes. They looked lost, confused. "You don't remember?"

"If I remembered, why would I be asking such an idiotic question?" Charles growled.

As the magnitude of Charles' admission set in, a new, devious plan formed in Vivianna's mind. It was time Savannah was adequately penalized for the events she set in motion.

"I'm terribly sorry, Charles. I was hoping you'd remember the horrible assault."

"Assault?" He looked again at the blood on his hands. "What cowardly bastard hit me from behind? Tell me which pathetic excuse for a man it was!"

Vivianna bit her lip. "It wasn't a man, Charles. It was a woman."

His eyes grew wide, appalled by her words. "A woman hit me?" He smoldered.

"I'm afraid so. You see, she was in a fit of jealousy."

Charles grabbed Vivianna's arm, wrenching her closer to him. "Tell me everything."

Vivianna shook her arm free. "What's the last thing you remember?"

He paused, thinking. "I was talking to my mother. She was asking where Rose was, and I didn't know. I went to look for her."

Vivianna nodded. "Rose had been cornered by Savannah. I wasn't privy to their entire conversation but witnessed Rose running up the stairs to her room, upset after talking to her. You saw Rose and went after her to see what was wrong."

Vivianna was going to spin this in the direction she needed it. If she accused the man of anything, her opportunity for justice would be terminated. "Once you were upstairs, Savannah pursued you. Thinking Savannah was up to no good, I followed her. But I was too late. From the doorway, I watched, helpless, as Savannah nailed you in the head with the fire poker."

Charles rubbed his head, which had a sizable lump on it. "Why? Why would she do that?"

"You'd be surprised what jealousy will make a woman do. She's given Rose hell since you began courting her. Downstairs at your own engagement party, she was threatening Rose to end her relationship with you. When she walked in on you holding Rose in your arms, she snapped."

"Where is Rose? Is she okay?"

"Yes, she's okay. I escorted her and her mother to safety. Savannah is still roaming free at your party."

"What?" Charles roared. "Stay with Rose and her mother. I'll handle this."

Charles bolted out of the room. Vivianna trailed after him, well out of his view. From the top of the stairs, in front of the entire court, Charles issued a decree to all of the noblemen.

"Ladies and gentlemen, I hate to interrupt a celebratory gathering, especially my own, but there's been a terrible crime committed this evening, one that threatened to tear my fiancé and me apart. She's so disturbed by the experience that she cannot even stand with me to inform you of this atrocity. An attempt was made on my honor and my life." Charles displayed his blood-caked hand.

Shocked gasps murmured through the crowd. Guests turned toward each other, pondering who the culprit might be.

"Gentlemen, for the safety of my family and my future family, I require your aid. I ask that you find and seize the culprit, Savannah Strickland!"

Gasps turned to shrieks. The room was in an uproar, as hundreds of eyes darted around the room, looking for the young brunette they all knew as the epitome of a lady.

Savannah, who was standing next to Amelia, hid her face in the plump girl's bosom.

"What is happening?" Savannah whimpered. The blood drained from her face, leaving her skin bone white.

Amelia put her arm around her. "Not to worry, Savannah, we'll get this sorted out," Amelia assured her. "Keep your head low and head towards the door. I'll meet you there."

Savannah nodded. "Thank you, Amelia."

Savannah crouched down, shielding her face with her shawl. She eased through the crowd as nonchalantly as possible in her petrified state. There were only twenty feet left between her and the exit when an unexpected betrayal shook her world.

"There she is!" Amelia shouted. "She's headed straight for the door."

66

When they reached the stone cell, Avidan warned Rose, "I'm afraid I can only give you a moment. We must get you both safely out of the cave before Madeira changes her mind."

"Thank you." Rose embraced Avidan, who was surprised by the gesture.

He nodded curtly and escorted Anne back into the tunnel to give them some privacy. Rose sank to her knees, her body leaning against the cell.

"Roosha, my love." She slid her slender forearms through the bars.

Roosha took her hands in his. "My sweet Rose, are you alright?"

"How could I possibly be alright?" Rose sobbed uncontrollably. "You're to be executed! The only thing that's changed is that I don't have to watch."

Roosha sighed, relieved. He brought her hand to his lips.

"Roosha...I cannot live in a world where you no longer exist." Rose's voice was shaking. "I love you. What will I do without you? I need you."

"Rose, you never needed me. All of the passion and sensual power was always inside you. I just helped you discover it. And there's so much more waiting for you. Never be afraid to go there, and never let any man make you think he is the key to that power. No man could ever be. It's all inside you." He returned her hand, resting it beneath her naval, the same place from where his amber glow emanated. "Now go, my sweet Rose. Leave this terrible place. I am at peace, knowing that I will die loved by you.

There is no greater feat I could have achieved in this life, or my previous one, than earning the love of such an incredible woman. I accept this sweet release of death, knowing I will live on right here." Roosha reached through the bars and placed his hand on Rose's heart, which was pounding furiously.

Rose's eyes were overflowing with tears to the point that she could barely see. Roosha put his hand around her head and pulled her in close to the bars. Their lips met for a desperate, impassioned final kiss, his tongue caressing hers, his desire reminding her how precious she was to him. Their eyes met with a recognition not of this world.

"Rose, it's time." Her mother was standing with Avidan.

Roosha brushed her trembling lips one final time.

"I love you," she breathed.

"And I, you, my sweet Rose."

Avidan grabbed Rose's arm, briskly guiding her out of the cave to face a world she didn't want to know, one without Roosha.

67

A vidan left Anne and Rose on the balcony. He was about to leave when Anne grabbed his arm.

"Avidan…"

"Yes, Anne?"

She peered at him, her eyes exuding gratitude. "Thank you. You saved her life."

"I only wish I would have saved yours as well. Take care, Anne."

"You as well, my friend."

Avidan nodded, an odd stir of emotions welling up within him. For the first time in years, he felt relieved. When he reported Anne and Thanoine to Madeira, he was a stubborn fool hell-bent on being right, no matter the cost. Because they had broken the rules, he felt justified in reporting them and had ruined many lives in the process. This time, he had chosen kindness and saved a life. Still, he leapt from the balcony with a heavy heart, knowing he would lose another good friend that night.

Anne put Rose's arm around her shoulder, helping her into the room. Vivianna jumped up from the bed when she saw them. "Rose! Mrs. Woodburn!" She ran over and grabbed Rose's other side, supporting her weight. Together they eased her up onto the bed.

"Vivianna, how are you, child?" Anne's voice was concerned. "Are you alright?

"Yes, I'm fine, Mrs. Woodburn. How are you doing? Rose?"

Anne shook her head. "It's been a difficult evening for us all."

Vivianna put her hand on Rose's forehead. "Rose, how are you?"

Rose peered at her through red-rimmed eyes. Unable to speak, she shook her head.

Vivianna turned towards Anne. "Did she …"

Anne turned her head, making sure they were alone. She grabbed Vivianna by the hand, pulling her into Rose's closet. Her voice was a whisper when she spoke.

"What I'm about to say to you, you must never repeat, do you understand me?"

"Yes, of course." Vivianna's voice was hushed.

"We had an audience with Madeira."

Vivianna's eyes widened. "With Madeira? The creator of the night senders?"

"Shh …" Anne cautioned. "She swore us to secrecy, but given how true a friend you've been, there are two things you must know. Rose was spared. Roosha is still being executed, but Rose will not have to watch."

Vivianna breathed a sigh of relief. "Thank you for telling me. I was beside myself with worry that she would be scarred for life."

"She still might be. She really loved him."

Vivianna nodded.

"The other thing is that we must leave Dover. It was the only way Madeira would let Rose go. She warned us never to return."

Vivianna's jaw clenched. The thought of losing her only friend was unbearable. "I understand," she sniffled. "When will you go?"

"She said we were to be gone before sunrise."

"Before sunrise," Vivianna choked.

Anne pulled Vivianna into her arms. "I know it's tough, child. You two have become such good friends." Anne sighed. "What I'm about to ask of you is no easy task."

"Anything you need," Vivianna whimpered.

"Can you be strong, for Rose's sake? She's been through so much tonight, I don't think she can take another tearful goodbye."

"Of course. I'll need a few moments to ... compose myself." Vivianna fanned her eyes with her hands. "Is there anything I can do to help you prepare?"

"Fetch the horses from the barn."

"Right away."

Anne squeezed Vivianna's arm. "You are a lifesaver, dear girl."

Vivianna departed quickly before she lost her composure. It was hard enough to be saying goodbye to her best friend. The profuse gratitude from Anne was too much.

Anne shook Rose. "Rose, dear, we have to get ready to leave. Gather whatever possessions you want to take with you." She helped Rose out of bed and then went to gather her things. As the minutes passed, Rose remained still as a statue in her catatonic state.

"COME CHILD, THE HORSES are outside." Anne grabbed Rose's hand, pulling her towards the door.

Rose paused in the doorway, taking one last long look at her bedroom. It was the sacred place where she met and fell in love with Roosha, where they had spent many nights in each other's embrace. It was where Roosha had made love to her. She blinked back the tears, but still, they blurred her vision. Now, Roosha was gone, and she was forced to leave the only place that connected her to him, the room that held the secrets of their entire relationship.

Abruptly, Rose turned, knowing that if she lingered a moment longer, she would never be able to leave. Thoughts of Roosha would draw her back in. Shutting the door behind her, Rose vowed that she would keep every vivid memory of Roosha alive in her heart. He would never be forgotten.

"THERE ARE GOLD COINS in the saddlebags, and enough food for you to make it far from here, prpobnably all the way to Leeds,"

Vivianna explained to Anne.

"Thank you, child." Anne squeezed her hand. "I meant to ask you ... what of Charles?"

"Not to worry, the identity of the night senders is safe. When Charles roused from his unconscious state, he had no memory of what happened."

"What did you tell him?"

"I explained that in a fit of jealous rage, Savannah had followed him to Rose's room and attacked him with a poker from the fireplace. He immediately had her seized, which caused a huge scene that helped me to usher everyone from your house without any questions as to your whereabouts. Savannah is now sitting in a cell. She is to be questioned tomorrow."

Anne's brow creased. "Why would you blame it on the poor girl?"

"She is the one who reported Rose's affair with a night sender."

"Oh," Anne uttered, surprised.

The thought of Savannah in a cell should have made Rose smile after what she had done, but she was too busy tending to her open wound to care.

"Come. child, it is time to leave this world behind." Anne mounted a dapple-gray horse as she spoke. "We will start fresh somewhere new without all of these horrible memories and expectations."

Rose looked at Vivianna, who was the only part of Dover Rose didn't want to leave behind.

"Come with us, Vivianna," she urged.

Vivianna took Rose's hands in hers. "I can't, Rose. I cannot leave everything behind... my family... and the library, of course. Especially not with the mess we've created. Someone has to stay here and clean it up." Vivianna winked at her the way she had at her birthday celebration.

Rose smiled weakly. "You are a true friend, Vivianna, and the smartest person I know. I love you. I will miss you, dearly," Rose mewled.

Vivianna locked her arms around Rose. "Chin up, Rose. You're young and beautiful, and far better things await you outside the confines of this stifling city." She pulled back, meeting her eyes. "Farewell, my brave friend. I shall write stories of your courage so that future generations have someone worth looking up to in the fourth diary."

"I hope to read it one day."

Rose mounted Carmera. Vivianna waved as mother and daughter ventured off together towards the city limits. When they reached the clearing leading to the forest, the one where Rose and Vivianna shared cherished memories, they launched their horses into a full gallop, in search of a new beginning.

Above them, the night senders, led by Avidan, flew fast against the night sky, watching over the two women.

EPILOGUE

Savannah sat, seething on the cold, hard stone floor of the prison cell Charles' had thrown her in, or better yet, had her thrown. Far be it from him to do his dirty work himself. It had been hours since they'd locked the solid wooden door, eliminating any light from the tiny room. She felt like a caged animal, and with each passing moment, hatred thickened in her blood.

She had been publicly humiliated at a lavish affair before the entire court, including her husband and family, her best friend turning her in like some common criminal. She was sure her reputation had been permanently tarnished, though she was still hell-bent on salvaging as much of it as possible.

She sifted through all of the information she had in her mind, trying to piece together exactly what happened. After his accusatory announcement charging her with attempted murder, Charles had stormed down the stairs, blood trickling down the back of his neck. Her eyes had moved to the top of the stairs, where she glimpsed Vivianna, a smug smile on her face. Rose wasn't in the room, and Savannah hadn't seen her since she disclosed that she knew about her affair with a night sender.

Once Amelia exposed Savannah's whereabouts, some nobleman's hands roughly locked around her elbow and forearm, dragging her towards Charles. Without a single question, he grabbed her, pulling her through the crowd amidst shocked gasps, and announcing to everyone that she had tried to kill him for rejecting her advances. The looks of disapproval towards his behavior quickly turned to looks of reproach, directed solely at Savannah. The last thing she registered before being removed from the party was the contumelious look on her husband Henry's face, which had felt like a cannonball blast to her stomach.

She knew Rose and Vivianna were behind this ordeal.

She had threatened Rose, warning her that she would reveal her secret to Charles. But it was only to ruin her night and her engagement party. Savannah knew she was obligated by the court to keep the night senders a secret from the noblemen. If she were to betray that law, she could never again call herself a proper lady. She would be a traitor, unfit of the title, a devastating notion she refused to face. Surely they had known that, she thought to herself. Surely they couldn't possibly believe she would have ever carried out that threat. Yet, here she sat, in an awful cell, her hair a mess, her dress ripped, her arm bruised from how hard Charles had wrenched it, and her pride slaughtered in front of all the people whose opinions mattered.

It seemed that their girlish games were over. They had now entered into a world where the stakes were higher. There were no more empty threats. Now, there would be consequences. Savannah had not caught on early enough and was the first to suffer. But now that she was aware, she swore she would not be the last.

She knew she owed them revenge.

ACKNOWLEDGEMENTS

One thing I've learned recently is that, while writing can be a lonely process, publishing is a team sport. I would not be where I am today with this book if it weren't for the wonderful people around me.

With love and gratitude, I'd like to thank:

Marvin (aka Merlin) – You are a gifted and special soul who has believed in my potential since I was fifteen years old, and knew I was meant to be a writer before I did. For years, you selflessly dedicated countless hours to nurturing my abilities and helping me become the person I am today, a debt I will never be able to repay. From the bottom of my heart, thank you for loving me.

My Incredible Parents – From the day I was born, you gave me the gift of your time, love, encouragement, travel opportunities, and a solid education. But more importantly, you gave me your unconditional support and trusted my decisions. Thank you for always being there for me, and for accepting who I am with love and understanding.

Julia—My creative and incredible best friend and soul sister. I remember sitting at Starbuck's with you, telling you I had jotted down ideas for a story called *The Night Sender* and then immediately questioned why anyone would want to read it. You believed in those ideas before I did, and made me promise to write this story because you wanted to read it. You inspired both belief and discipline in me, holding me to a strict regimen of writing at least one chapter per week. Without your love, enthusiasm and desire to read the story, *The Night Sender* may never have taken flight.

Lesley—You are as talented as you are beautiful. Thank you for pushing me to take my writing to the next level.

Stefanie, Vivien, and Anne—My original readers, and wonderful friends who helped give me the courage to pursue this project.

Dane—You are an extraordinary artist. Thank you for bringing my vision of the cover to life.

Kitty—You are the greatest cat and muse a girl could ask for! Watching you sleep kept me sane throughout the editing process.

John—Last, but certainly not least. My amazing partner in life, I would not be here without you. Your unconditional love, support, and infectious enthusiasm gave me the courage to spread my wings and take flight. I love you.

Coming Soon:

Book II of this spellbinding new series…

The Night Sender

For more information on
The Night Sender series and upcoming release dates,

visit:

www.christinatsirkas.com